DEATH
of an
IRISH DIVA

The Nuala Anne McGrail Mystery series
by Mollie Cox Bryan

The Cumberland Creek Mystery series
by Mollie Cox Bryan:

SCRAPBOOK OF SECRETS

SCRAPPED

DEATH OF AN IRISH DIVA

DEATH
of an
IRISH DIVA

Mollie Cox Bryan

KENSINGTON PUBLISHING CORP.
http://www.kensingtonbooks.com

KENSINGTON BOOKS are published by

Kensington Publishing Corp.
119 West 40th Street
New York, NY 10018

All Kensington Titles, Imprints, and Distributed Lines are available at special quantity discounts for bulk purchases for sales promotions, premiums, fund-raising, and educational or institutional use. Special book excerpts or customized printings can also be created to fit specific needs. For details, write or phone the office of the Kensington special sales manager: Kensington Publishing Corp., 119 West 40th Street, New York, NY 10018, attn: Special Sales Department, Phone: 1-800-221-2647.

Kensington and the K logo Reg. U.S. Pat & TM Off.

ISBN-13: 978-0-7582-6633-0
ISBN-10: 0-7582-6633-2

First Kensington Mass Market Edition: February 2014

eISBN-13: 978-1-61773-029-0
eISBN-10: 1-61773-029-7

First Kensington Electronic Edition: February 2014

10 9 8 7 6 5 4 3 2 1

Printed in the United States of America

Dedicated to Emily Oleson and Matthew Olwell,
two of the finest dance teachers (and people)
I've ever known.

Acknowledgments

Thanks so much to all of you, the readers of this series. You make the magic happen for me. My husband, Eric, and my daughters, Emma and Tess, deserve a huge amount of gratitude for their support. Also, a huge thanks goes to Jennifer Feller, Christy Majors, Chrissy Lantz, and Leeyanne Moore for reading early versions of this book and giving me much-needed thoughtful feedback. Special thanks to John Craft for hours of talk about police work while our daughters were in dance class. Thanks to attorney John Hill for answering legal questions.

My daughters participated in Irish dancing for many years and were blessed with a fabulous teacher, who went on to marry another fabulous teacher. I am grateful for the time Emily Oleson and Matt Olwell spent in our lives. We are sorry Emily left the area to find her bliss—but we are happy she found it. Thanks to both of them for the inspiration and for answering my questions all those years ago. I feel like I should point out that Emily McGlashen is a character and is *not* based on Emily Oleson. They just share first names.

A huge hug goes to my fabulous agent, Sharon Bowers, for her steadfast belief in my writing. Another big hug goes to Martin Biro, a dream editor, and to all the Kensington team: Alexandra Nicolajsen, Adeola Saul, and all of you who work hard to promote, sell, and edit the Cumberland Creek mysteries.

A very special thanks to the folks and readers at Malice Domestic for the Agatha Award nomination for *Scrapbook of Secrets*.

In Gratitude,
Mollie

Chapter 1

A green velvet dress, the skirt of which was flung over the top of the right hip of the victim, revealed she was naked from the waist down. Her white thigh and buttocks were so muscled, taut, and perfect that she almost looked like a statue, lying twisted, facedown, on the floor. Her long brown ponytail of curls was askew, but the green ribbon was still intact. A pair of tights was crumpled in a corner of the dance studio. Her underwear, if, indeed, she had worn any, was missing. One of her shoes was lying next to the tights, and it was without a lace, of course, because its lace was still wrapped around Emily McGlashen's neck.

"How long has she been here?" Annie asked Detective Adam Bryant after settling her stomach with a deep breath and calming thoughts.

Poor woman. So young. So talented.

And just yesterday Emily astounded Annie with her high leaps, twirls, and fast footwork during the St. Patrick's Day parade and festival. The green velvet dress had swung in off rhythm to the Irish music against Emily's in-sync movements. Bursting with life. Hard to believe that same skirt was now askew across Emily's lifeless body.

He shrugged. "As far as I can tell, maybe all day. We think it happened sometime early this morning. She was supposed to be at a meeting this afternoon, and her friend came looking for her, and this is what she found. You here officially?"

Annie grimaced. She had been working on her book about the New Mountain Order and had taken a leave of absence from her freelancing, and he knew it. But her editor called her to see if she'd cover this. Big news to a certain segment of the population, namely, those who followed Irish dance.

"Maybe," she said.

He went on. "Not much of a story here. Just the murder of a person who maybe was just in the wrong place at the wrong time."

"She was in the public eye. And strangling is a personal act, isn't it?" Annie twisted a curl around her finger. She was wearing her hair down, which was all part of the newer, more relaxed version of her former self. She didn't need to pull it back. She didn't need to control it. It was a relief. Chalk that bit of advice up to her mysterious friend and yoga teacher Cookie Crandall.

"Most of the time, yes," he said, his blue eyes sparkling. "But there was a robbery. Looks like the safe was ransacked. Maybe she surprised the perp. Maybe he didn't have another weapon."

"So he used her shoelaces?" Annie said. "C'mon."

The detective's mouth went crooked.

Still, it probably had nothing to do with the NMO. There were none of the symbols they had used in the past. Maybe it was true. Maybe they had really cleaned up their act.

"But she was a famous Irish dancer," Annie said, almost to herself.

"And?" he said with a crooked smirk. "One of her fancy-dancing competitors offed her?"

Flashes of *Riverdance* played in Annie's mind. There was nothing "fancy" about those dancers. They were in extraordinary physical condition. A hugely successful international dance show consisting of traditional Irish dance, *Riverdance* was spurring Irish dance classes across the country. And Emily McGlashen was in one of those big productions and had made a name for herself, which was one reason the kids in Cumberland Creek loved her. Besides all that, she was young and hip.

Annie crossed her arms and glared at Bryant.

The police photographer entered the studio again, and his camera flashed in the dim room, a large dance studio with beautiful polished wood floors, a mirror along one wall, and bars that ran along the side of it. Posters of Irish dancers, medals, and trophies decorated the facility. You could say what you wanted about Emily—and many townsfolk did—but she knew her Irish dancing. An international champion who came to Cumberland Creek and opened a new studio, Emily had drawn attention to herself right away.

A couple of uniformed officers pulled Bryant away to show him something they had found. Annie stepped out of the way of another officer, now bending over the body. A glint of a flash from the camera reflected in the mirror.

"Damn, it's hard to get good pictures. These mirrors are a problem," the photographer said and looked around for another angle. "Can you run and get some sheets from the van?" he said to the younger person who was assisting him.

"Well, that's an interesting piece of evidence," Bryant said.

Annie turned around to see his gloved hands reach for a red handbag that looked vaguely familiar to her. She was not a handbag kinda woman; she was more a designer shoe devotee turned sneaker aficionado. She didn't really pay much attention to purses, given that she avoided carrying one as often as possible.

But she was certain she'd seen that bag somewhere.

The detective reached in and pulled out a wallet, still there and full of money, credit cards, and a driver's license, which inspired a huge grin to spread across his face.

"Vera Matthews," he said and looked at Annie. "And I think we all know what Vera thought about Emily McGlashen."

"Don't be ridiculous," Annie said, but her heart sank. Vera had made no attempt at hiding her feelings about Emily. She hadn't been herself. But still she was far from being a cold-blooded killer. Vera? Not likely. "Vera Matthews may not have liked Emily, but she didn't kill her."

"But, Ms. Chamovitz, her purse is here. How do you explain it?" Bryant smirked as he placed the handbag in a plastic evidence bag.

"I don't have to explain it. You do," she said.

"You're wrong about that, Annie. She does," he said, slipping off his gloves.

She walked away from him. It took every ounce of restraint she could muster to not run out of the studio and call Vera to warn her that Bryant, or one of his underlings, would be stopping by to question her. As if it mattered, really. She was certain Vera hadn't killed anybody, especially after seeing the compassionate way she'd behaved over the past few years. Still, a little warning would be nice.

Vera's life had changed drastically recently. Her ex-husband, Bill, had moved in with a woman in Charlottesville and was rarely around to help with their daughter, Elizabeth. Her mother, Beatrice, was also living with the new man in her life. Vera was alone and claimed she preferred it. After Emily McGlashen came to town, stealing many of Vera's students by offering cheaper classes and preaching against the "archaic" dance form of ballet, her business income had plummeted. Vera was in such financial trouble that she was renting her house out, hoping to sell it, while she and Elizabeth lived in the apartment above her dance studio.

"Didn't she write a letter to the editor recently about Ms. McGlashen?" Bryant asked, still holding the purse as he approached her. Annie refrained from smiling at the decidedly manly man holding the evidence bag with the purse in it.

"Yes. Wow, you read," she taunted him. "Did you also see the letter she was responding to? The one that Emily wrote? The one that claimed ballet was an archaic dance form and that Vera was ripping kids off?"

"Oh, gee, I must have missed that," he said. "I'm sure I'll be reading it in about an hour, right, Johnson?"

"Yes, sir. Right on it."

Bryant started to walk by her and brushed up against her. "Sir," he said in a low voice. "Just how I like it."

His breath skimmed across her neck as he walked by. Telling him that she was a married woman, again, would do no good. He had been blatantly flirting with her for months, and sometimes right under Mike's nose. If they hadn't shared that one kiss during a moment of drunken weakness, she'd have more solid ground on which to stand. But he knew.

He knew what he was doing to her. And he was enjoying every minute of it.

Chapter 2

When Vera opened her apartment door to Detective Bryant holding her purse in a plastic bag, her first thought was one of relief.

"You found my purse," she said. "Oh, thank heaven. I was looking everywhere for it." When she went to reach for it, she was interrupted by a crashing sound. "Oh, shoot," she said, taking off toward where the noise was coming from. "Come in, Detective," she managed to say, waving him in.

"Oh, Lizzie!" she said to her grinning daughter, who was sitting in the middle of a huge stack of CDs that had been piled nicely in several stacks around the floor. They were just too tempting for an inquisitive three-year-old. At least the silver disks were all still inside the covers. Lizzie hadn't gotten around to that yet.

Vera reached for Lizzie and pulled her up to her hip. She looked at the detective, who stood by awkwardly with her purse. Annie had just walked in behind him.

"Hey," she said.

Lizzie squealed and squirmed down from her mother. "Annie!" She ran to her.

"You want to come and play at my house?" Annie said.

"Yes!"

"Annie, why do you want my daughter? Don't you think you should check with me first?" Vera asked, smiling. She was so glad Annie and Lizzie got along so well. After all, Lizzie's father was mostly never around these days.

"Detective Bryant wants to talk to you. I just thought I'd help out by taking Lizzie home with me for a little while. Do you mind?"

Vera sighed. "Look at this place. No. I don't mind. I'm still trying to unpack."

Lizzie grabbed Annie's hand.

"Her diaper bag is in the hall closet there, just in case," Vera said. Lizzie was mostly potty trained. Mostly. Sometimes Lizzie was indignant at the thought of diaper bags, because she took great pride in using the potty.

After she kissed her daughter good-bye and watched as she and Annie left the room, Vera turned back around to face handsome, but annoying Detective Adam Bryant.

"Well," she said, straightening out the stacks of CDs on the floor, "what can I help you with?"

"How long has your purse been missing?" he asked.

"You know, it's the craziest thing," she replied, stacking up the last group of CDs. "I woke up this morning and thought I should charge my cell. I meant to do that last night, when I got in, but I was exhausted. I just fell into bed. So I looked for my purse this morning and couldn't find it. I thought maybe I left it downstairs. "

"Your cell is usually in your purse?"

"Usually," she replied. "So where did you find it?"

"Before I tell you that, can you tell me where you were last night?"

"After the Saint Patrick's Day parade and show, Lizzie and I went to my mother's house. We had dinner with Jon and Mom. Why?"

"Any reason your purse would be in Emily McGlashen's studio?"

"What? Why? No. That bitch. Did she take my purse? I knew the woman had some screws loose, but to take my bag? As if ruining my business wasn't enough, she had to steal my purse?"

Vera had hoped that Irish dancing was a fad, and that Emily McGlashen would have moved on by now. For God's sake, ballet was so much more important to the development of a dancer. Why would her dancers leave her studio to study with Emily? Okay, the dancing looked like fun, with its jumps and turns and precision footwork. And then there was the fact that Emily made sure her classes were cheaper than Vera's. How did she do it? Vera couldn't discount any more classes and make financial ends meet.

"Sit down, Vera," Bryant said and gestured with his arm.

"Why? What's going on?" she asked but sat down on her secondhand couch. Oh, how she longed for the comfortable, light blue, deep-cushioned couch sitting in her house. This couch was uncomfortable and stiff. Not very pretty, either, with its green plaid cushions. In fact, her apartment was full of mismatched, uncomfortable furniture. She had rented her house out fully furnished, which was what her Realtor had advised. And it went quickly: a visiting University of Virginia professor snapped it up.

He looked deflated momentarily. His eyes scanned the room. "You really do have your hands full, don't you? Big changes, huh?"

"Yes," she replied. "At least we have a roof over our head and food for the table."

He sighed. "Emily McGlashen is dead, Vera."

She gasped, and her hand went to her mouth. "What—what happened to her? So young . . ."

"Twenty-eight, to be exact," he said. "She was strangled. Murdered at her studio late last night or early this morning. Time of death is inconclusive."

Vera felt the room spin as her mind sifted through the recent murders in her small town. Cumberland Creek had always been so safe. Except for the past few years.

"Vera, your purse was found at the scene of the crime. I'm going to have to take you to the station for questioning," he said.

"I don't know anything about this, Detective. Why would you need to question me?"

"Vera, you're the only suspect I have right now."

"Suspect? Me? I just told you that I was with Mom and Jon last night."

"What time did you leave?"

"Around eight," she said. "I had to put Lizzie down."

"What did you do after?"

"Nothing. I mean, I took a bath and went to bed, if you must know."

"And what was your purse doing in the studio?"

"I don't know."

Could he take her to jail? Who would stay with Lizzie? Who would run the few classes that she had left at her studio?

"It's a matter of public record that you two didn't get along," he said. "She wrote an editorial, didn't she? About how ballet is bad for children psychologically, physically. And she claimed that anybody taking parents' money for ballet lessons was a rip-off. And you wrote a scathing editorial back, right?"

"I won't deny that. I didn't like the woman," she replied, with eye contact. "Maybe she took my purse. Maybe that's why you found it there."

"Maybe," he said, looking away for a moment. "I think you better call your lawyer. I'm taking you in for questioning, Vera. Just procedure."

"Well, now my lawyer happens to be in a love nest in Charlottesville. God knows when he'll get back to me. At least our daughter is in good hands. Annie will take care of her."

The detective looked off into the distance; a stiff, pained expression came over his face. Was it the mention of Annie? Was he still brooding over her rejection of him? What made him think that a happily married woman would give it all up for him?

Chapter 3

Beatrice and Jon were sitting on the screened back porch of her home, watching as the contractors dug a huge hole with a backhoe. She had thought for years about getting a pool in her backyard. It was a double lot, meaning it was deep, and there were no neighbors behind her. Ed, her first husband, had the foresight to buy two lots, for which she was grateful.

March in Cumberland Creek made it difficult to plan. They could start the digging and have to stop for weeks if it snowed or rained. Spring weather was tricky business.

Jon got up from his wicker chair when the front doorbell rang. "I'll get it," he said.

Beatrice sat back in her chair. She loved to watch his quick little walk. It was so nice to have him around. Well, for the most part.

She'd gotten so used to being alone that sometimes just having another person around all the time was enough to make her want to scream. She was learning to go off in a room or to go for a walk when she felt as if she couldn't stand to hear him breathe one more minute. If she didn't get away from him, she'd find herself lashing out at him. And that was not good; it wasn't what she wanted. After all, she did love the man, even if he was French. At least he'd learned to stop bringing that up.

"In France, we do it like this. . . ."

"If you were a Frenchwoman, I'd say this. . . ."

"It's better in France. . . ."

She had just about had enough of it and had told him so.

"Look, I love you, Jon, but if you'd like to go back to France, please do. Otherwise, please stop telling me about how wonderful it is and how much better it is than here."

He laughed.

"I'm sorry," he said. "It's so arrogant of me to be in your country and go on and on about France. Perhaps I miss it. Let's visit together this summer, yes?"

"Maybe," she said.

Instead, they decided to build a pool in Beatrice's backyard and spend the summer lounging and swimming together in Cumberland Creek. They might go to France next year. His visa was going to expire, so he had to go back. Whether or not Beatrice was going with him was up for debate.

When Jon came back to the porch, a police officer accompanied him.

"What now?" Beatrice said, viewing a woman who looked like a sixteen-year-old teenager dressed up in her daddy's police uniform. Good Lord, were they taking these kids out of school? Or was she just getting to be so old that everybody looked like children?

"Excuse me?" the woman replied. "I'm Officer Melinda Jacquith. I need to ask you a few questions about you daughter, Vera Matthews."

"Have a seat, please," Jon said, pushing the chair up to her.

"Thanks," she said, sitting down and smiling politely at Jon. "I won't be long."

"Is something wrong with Vera? Has there been an accident?" Beatrice asked, sitting on the edge of her chair.

"Excuse me, ma'am," one of the contractors said as he opened the screen door. "We have a problem."

"Can it wait?" Jon said.

The man shook his head. "She said if there were any problems to come get her immediately."

"I'll take care of it, Bea," Jon said and accompanied the contractor back to his ditch.

"I didn't mean to startle you. Your daughter is fine," the officer said to Beatrice.

She exhaled. "Then what's the problem?"

"She's being questioned at the station right now about the murder of Emily McGlashen."

Beatrice coughed up the iced tea she had started to sip. "What?"

"She was found murdered this afternoon."

"What? Oh, that's awful! She was so young," Beatrice stammered, thinking of seeing her just yesterday, leading a group of green-clad children along the parade route, then later dancing on a makeshift stage in the center of town. Her legs were amazing—fast, strong, and elegant—and her upper body remained perfectly straight, just like those dancers in *Riverdance,* which Beatrice loved, though she'd never tell Vera that.

When Emily first moved to town, Vera was excited that another dance studio was opening and was looking forward to partnering on some projects. Emily didn't want anything to do with her—or with the "archaic," "elitist" form of dance that Vera had made her life. The woman really hated ballet.

"We need you to corroborate Vera's whereabouts last night," the officer said.

"Well," Beatrice said, "we all went to the Saint Patrick's Day festivities and came back here for dinner."

"What time did Vera leave?"

"I think around eight. She mentioned it was past Lizzie's bedtime. Lawd, the child was getting fussy," she said.

"Well, thanks. That's all I need to know." The officer stood.

"Wait a minute. Why would you be asking me about Vera? Why is she being questioned about this?" Beatrice said, standing to accompany the officer out.

"Sorry, ma'am," the officer said and smiled. "I'm not at liberty to discuss that with you. I'll find my own way out. Thank you."

With that, she turned to walk through Beatrice's Victorian home, toward the front door.

Well, now, if that wasn't the damnedest thing she'd ever heard. Vera questioned about a murder. She just never knew what was going to happen in Cumberland Creek these days, or with her newly pronounced independent daughter. She did know that Vera and Emily hadn't gotten along. Hell, everybody knew that.

Beatrice wanted Vera and Lizzie to move in with her and Jon until Vera's financial situation was resolved. But Vera wouldn't hear of it. She'd never stood up to Beatrice like this before. She didn't know what had come over her daughter since her divorce and becoming a mother, but she was stronger than ever. Beatrice hadn't made up her mind whether or not that was a good thing.

"Beatrice." Jon was calling her. "Will you come out here? You've got to see this."

"What's this?" Beatrice said as she walked up to Jon and several men in hard hats, with hands on their hips.

"It looks like a very old foundation," one of the men said.

"Do what you need to do to get rid of it," Beatrice said,

thinking how odd it was that an old foundation was there. Her home was one of the first built in Cumberland Creek proper in 1895. Of course, there had been rumblings about older homes, but she had thought they were closer to the mountains.

"It's not that simple," the man told her. "Look at this." He pointed to a strange-looking root about halfway down the ditch. "You see?"

"Can you get rid of it?"

"I can't get rid of it."

"Why not? What's the big deal about a root? Chop it out of there."

"That's no root. That's bone. Old bone, I'd say. Petrified. I think it's human. And I don't have the authority to mess with it."

"Well, who does?" Beatrice said. "I don't really like the idea of human bones in my backyard."

"We'll call the police, but I think it will be a state matter."

"What? What do you mean?"

The man took off his gloves, wiped his forehead with a handkerchief. "I'm no expert, but I think this may be historical. You may need to excavate this site."

"Well, for heaven's sake," she said almost to herself.

Chapter 4

It had been two weeks since the scrapbookers had gotten together, all of them in one place, to scrapbook. Last weekend the big Saint Patrick's Day parade and festival occupied them. Since Vera's dancers were performing, and Sheila was just getting back in town Saturday evening from a scrapbook conference, the other croppers had called it off. Annie took a long swig of her beer and set the bottle down gingerly next to the scrapbook she was working on for her parents, who were divorced years ago and were now back together, which made her uneasy. But she thought it would be fun to try to record in a scrapbook their lives before the divorce. She had decided on a black-and-white album, and it was turning out to be gorgeous.

"It's really awful what happened to Emily," Sheila said. "I mean, she was a bitch, but who would have wished her dead enough to actually kill her?"

"Well, it wasn't me. And I think I have Bryant convinced of that," Vera said. She sounded more convinced than she looked.

"Bryant," DeeAnn said with disdain.

"Isn't that a lovely photo?" Sheila said, pointing to DeeAnn's picture of a huge rustic pie—crusty and thick, with berry juice spilling over the edges. DeeAnn's project was a scrapbook for her bakery. She had had the bakery in town for about five years and had taken photos all that time, just like a good scrapbooker. "I respect how you are recording and journaling your bakery. You are on top of it."

"Thanks," DeeAnn said. "I wish I'd been better about recording the kid's stuff."

"The way Emily walked around town like she owned it because she was a McGlashen really annoyed me," Paige said after a few moments. "And it annoyed all of us in the historical society. I mean, just because she traced her lineage back here doesn't mean she had any right to behave like that."

"Evidently, all you ladies at the history society were not the only ones annoyed with her," Annie said.

"So are you going to write about this one?" Sheila asked, looking up from her laptop. She was trying to learn all about digital scrapbooking. She'd tried to get this group excited about it, but there were no takers, at least not yet.

Annie shrugged. "I'm keeping my eye on the story to see if it develops into something. I mean, it's getting to the point that murder is almost commonplace around here."

Vera gasped. "Don't say that, Annie. I know it must seem like it to you, because it's been like that for the past several years. But it's just some kind of strange fluke. All these new people moving to town in droves. I'm sure the police will find out who killed Emily, and it will all be resolved soon and we can go back to our safe little lives."

"Humph," said DeeAnn. "The police didn't solve those other murders. It was us, but mostly Annie, remember?"

And Annie wanted to forget all of it. She wanted it all to go away. She and her husband, Mike, had moved here from Bethesda, Maryland, to raise their boys in a safer, quieter place, where they would not be spending all their time stuck in Beltway traffic, shuttling their kids around. The plan was for her to stay at home, give up journalism, and just focus on the boys. But somehow she'd been sucked back into journalism. Mike wasn't too pleased about it. The situation was becoming an issue in their marriage, so she had talked about it with her brother, Joshua, who was a psychiatrist.

"You have an addictive personality," Joshua had said to her during one of his visits. "You're addicted to the adrenaline rush of a good story. The more dangerous, the better. Careful, Annie. You know all about Mom and her addictions."

"Oh, please, Josh," she had said and waved him off.

But she was afraid, and it had nothing to do with her mother's cocaine addiction. She was not in the least attracted to cocaine. Still, there was something that kept gnawing at her, that pulled her into these dangerous situations. Why couldn't she be at peace?

Now her eyes glazed over the silver SHALOM sticker. She was deciding where to place it. Shalom. Peace. She told herself it was really all she wanted in her life.

"My mom always said to leave the past alone," Paige said, then grinned. "Maybe that's why I love history so much."

"But why didn't you get along with Emily, then? I mean, she was all about the past," Sheila said.

"It was the way she was about it. Okay, she traced her family back to the founders of the town. Big deal. Many of us here could say the same thing, I bet. She came in making demands from the society, throwing her money around. Wanting to dig in several areas, no matter whose property it was. And for what? So she could strut around town and make everybody else feel small," Paige replied.

"I hate to speak ill of the dead, but good riddance," Vera said.

Annie shivered, thinking of seeing the young woman's twisted body. She silently thanked the universe that she couldn't see Emily's pretty face. It would have been devastating. Yes, she wasn't well liked by many of the locals. But Annie was curious about her. Why would an international dance champion come to Cumberland Creek to open a studio? It had never made sense to Annie. She was certain there was more to her story. Maybe she would investigate a little further on her own, if she could find the time. But she would have to be quiet about it because Mike had had just about enough of her investigating. At that thought, a hard ball formed in her throat.

She looked around the table at the women she called her friends: Sheila's face slightly blue from the glow of her laptop; DeeAnn's large arms leaning on the table, her brow knitted; Paige pasting a flower sticker onto her scrapbook page, then tucking a piece of her wavy blond hair behind her ear; and Vera, the dancer, who used to dye her hair a different color once a month and used to be perfectly coiffed at all times. But no longer. The past few months had taken a toll. She had bags under her blue eyes and gray hair sprouting everywhere. Annie wondered if Vera even realized it.

"Vera, I didn't get a chance to tell you," Annie said. "I loved watching your dancers at the festival."

"Oh, thanks," Vera said, smiling. "I thought they did very well. Of course, Emily was sneering at me the whole time my dancers were onstage. I tried to ignore it."

"Oh, I saw it," Sheila said. "I also picked up one of these flyers. She was handing them out." She read the flyer out loud. "Do you know? Emily McGlashen, an international Irish dance champion and *Riverdance* sensation, is now taking students in Cumberland Creek, at her new dance studio. Irish dance and performance classes are less than half of what locals have been paying for ballet at the other local studio. Irish dance is better for students' intellectual, physiological, and physical development." Sheila paused.

"According to who? Where did she get this stuff? It's just so unprofessional of her. Of course, issues are debated within the dance community. But to go around making public statements?" Vera said. "I'd never do anything to hurt kids. Ballet is good for them. I know that, even though Cookie used to say kind of the same thing, that it went against natural body alignment. And it's true. But if you develop the strength to support those positions, it's just not a problem for most students."

"Thought we weren't going to mention her again," Annie said more sharply than what she had intended. Cookie Crandall, a past member of their group, was arrested on suspicion of murder and had escaped jail. None of them had heard from her ever again.

"I'm sorry. You're right. I never should have mentioned her," Vera said, then bit her lip.

Silence fell over the Cumberland Creek crop. Annie felt as if her breath had been sapped out of her. Vera sighed.

"It's getting late," Vera said, gathering up her things. "I need to go."

"Sounds like a good idea to me," Annie said and then drank the last bit of beer.

Chapter 5

When Vera woke up, she was standing at the kitchen sink. It was still early enough to be dark, and in her confusion she groped around and cut her finger on a knife left in the sink.

"Damn," she said out loud to nobody. Elizabeth had spent the night with Beatrice and Jon. She flipped on a light switch and was startled by the amount of blood splashed in the sink. She ran cold water over her finger and realized that she must have been sleepwalking, which she hadn't done since she was a child.

She reached for a paper towel. Damn, where were the bandages? She knew there was a package of Sesame Street ones in Elizabeth's room. She tiptoed over the toys in her room and reached for it. She wrapped her finger with an Elmo Band-Aid.

After her first cup of coffee, finger all wrapped up, she sat at her ugly plastic kitchen table and ate a toasted blueberry waffle, reveling in the silence of the apartment without Elizabeth.

She telephoned Sheila.

"What are you doing?" she said into the phone when Sheila answered.

"Just back from my run," Sheila said. "You?"

"Getting ready to go and get Lizzie in a little while."

"Lonely?"

"Well, maybe. I mean, I don't know. I like the quiet. But at the same time . . ."

"It's mother guilt," Sheila told her. "You can't enjoy your time to yourself, because you feel like a good mom should be missing her child. I know."

Vera smiled. "I guess. Four kids. How is Donna?"

"She's doing better this semester," Sheila said. Her oldest daughter, Donna, was in college, studying design, and Vera's had yet to learn the alphabet. "That first year was rough, though."

"I woke up at the kitchen sink this morning," Vera said.

"Sleepwalking?" Sheila said after a minute.

"Yes, and I cut myself," Vera said.

"Well, it's no wonder. You have to be stressed with all the changes. I mean, why don't you admit it? Why do you go along like nothing is wrong?"

"There's no point in bitching and moaning, or feeling sorry for myself," Vera responded.

"I know that. But you're broke. Your ex is living with a woman in Charlottesville. You have a three-year-old that keeps you hopping. And you were hauled down to the police station for questioning. None of that is pleasant. And you are allowed to bitch and moan a bit."

Vera sipped her coffee. "I suppose."

"And now you're sleepwalking. That's just great," Sheila said. They had been friends since they were girls, and she remembered Vera's first bout with sleepwalking.

Soon their conversation was over and Vera was out the door, off to get Elizabeth from her mom's place.

She walked down the steps, glanced over at the still closed inside studio door in the foyer. One of the reasons she had chosen this space for her studio was that she liked the foyer, which meant that people were not walking straight off the street into her office and studio. She opened the outside door in front of her and was almost smacked in the face with a black leather shoe hanging in the doorway. She gasped as she realized what it was—a gillie, an Irish dance shoe, with a note attached to it. Someone had hung the dance shoe in her doorway. Vera walked backward into the stairwell and raced back upstairs to her apartment. Her heart pounded and tears stung at her eyes as she called the police.

Why would someone do this to her?

She sat on her couch and waited for them to come. This would be the second time in two weeks she'd have to deal with Detective Bryant. She dreaded his crooked smirk and shifty eyes. But now, obviously, it had gotten out that she was questioned at the station. Someone else must think she killed Emily McGlashen. Was that Emily's gillie in her doorway? Why hadn't she heard someone hanging the shoe there? Maybe she had. And maybe that made her sleepwalk? Could she tell the police that? Well, she wasn't certain she had heard anything. So maybe she should keep the whole sleepwalking thing to herself, lest they think she killed Emily while she was walking in her sleep.

But had she? Surely not. Surely she'd have awakened if she was struggling to kill someone. Just like with the knife cutting her, if she was touched, she'd wake up. Or at least that was how it had always been when she was a child.

She clasped her hands together, noticing that her knuckles looked white, as she listened to the noise at the door. She was sure it was the police doing whatever it was they did at a crime scene.

"Vera?" She heard Detective Bryant at the door.

"You can come in," she yelled. "The door is unlocked."

"I hope you don't keep your door unlocked," he mumbled as he walked into the room.

"Certainly not," she said. "I was going out and unlocked it when the shoe swung down in my face."

She gestured in the direction of the gillie, a black leather slipper with strings hanging off it. The dancers tied the laces around their feet and ankles, like ballet pointe shoes.

His hands went to his hips, and he looked around the apartment. "Where's Elizabeth?"

"Mom's."

He sat down next to her. "What did you do to your finger?" he asked.

"I cut it with a kitchen knife," she replied.

"Now, Vera, I know this is upsetting—"

"Humph. You're damned right it's upsetting." Her voice shook with anger, fear, and loathing. "First, I'm questioned about the murder of Emily McGlashen, and then this."

"Someone wants us to think you killed her," he said. "And it's probably the killer."

Vera shivered as she thought of the person who had strangled Emily being at her front door, the door to her studio, her apartment, her life.

She noticed a small piece of paper in Bryant's hand and realized he held the note that had been tacked on to the shoe.

"What's it say?" she managed to ask.

"Killer ballerina," he said with a grimace.

Killer ballerina? If she wasn't so frightened, she might laugh.

Chapter 6

When Annie opened the door, Detective Bryant stood there with a six-pack of imported beer and a bouquet of spring flowers. She smiled. "C'mon in. Mike's all set up."

"These are for you," he said sheepishly.

"Thanks," she said, walking into the living room, where Mike was firmly planted in front of the TV. "Look, Mike. Adam brought me flowers."

Mike barely looked up from the pregame basketball show. "That's nice," he said, distracted by the game on the television.

Bryant sat on the other end of the couch.

Annie had fixed trays of lunch meats, bread, and cheese with some veggies and dip. The coffee tables were spilling over with snacks. Mike and Bryant had struck up a Sunday friendship, watching whatever sport was on TV together, commenting, cheering, and so on. It was unlike Mike. When they dated, he had never mentioned football, or any sport, really. Suddenly, he was interested. Well, maybe not so suddenly. Maybe just since they had become parents to boys.

She cracked open a beer for herself and sat on a chair near the couch. Both of the boys had gone to a friend's house for the afternoon, otherwise she wouldn't be drinking a beer. She didn't like drinking in front of them.

"How's the case going?" Annie asked.

"Huh? Oh yeah. Not bad," Detective Bryant said.

"I'm just back from over at Vera's place," he said a few minutes later, when a commercial was on.

"Why?" she said after she took another drink of beer.

"There was an incident."

"Incident?" She sat up on the edge of her chair.

He told her what happened. "Before I left, her mother, Jon, Sheila, and Elizabeth were all there. Someone had called her mother when they saw police cars. Same old story."

He leaned back into the couch and wrapped his lips around the bottle. Annie looked away.

"So everything is okay?" Mike said.

"I think someone is trying to set her up," Bryant told them.

"But who even knew she was being questioned?" Annie asked.

"Maybe nobody. Maybe it's the killer, wanting to keep us occupied. Away from him," the detective said.

Annie thought a moment. "Must not be anybody from around here."

"What makes you say that?" Bryant asked.

"Vera and her family are highly thought of in this community. If the killer really wanted to frame someone, it should be someone like me, an outsider," she said.

"Obviously, the killer isn't that bright," Mike said. "Excuse me. I told my boss I'd give him a call."

He left the room, and Annie's eyes went directly to the TV. But she knew Bryant was looking at her.

"How did you get to be so smart, anyway?" he asked.

She ignored him and continued to watch the game.

"Why are you being like this?"

She looked at him. "Like what?"

"So standoffish."

"I don't want to lead you on," she said with a lowered voice. "There's nothing between us, and you need to stop pushing."

She was hoping he'd sink back even farther into the couch and look crestfallen. Acquiescent.

Instead, he sat on the edge of the couch, leaned toward her. "I wish I could believe that. How do you think this makes me feel?" He glanced toward Annie's bedroom, where Mike was still on the phone. "Do you think I want to be lusting over my friend's wife?"

Annie leaped up out of her chair and slammed her beer bottle down on the table.

"I'm leaving," she said. "You can tell Mike I'm at Vera's place."

"Don't," he said, following her to the door. "Annie, I tell myself it's going to be okay. That as long as I'm in your life, it's going to be okay. I don't need anything else from you. I don't have to touch you. Nothing. But then I think about that kiss. And I know it's not all me. I need you to open up and tell me what you're feeling."

He was less than six inches from her, and she could so easily lean into him and test that theory. That it was more than a kiss. But she held her breath as she felt a tear stinging.

She took it all in: There he was, in her home, which she shared with Mike and their sons. *Their home.* And yet there he was, standing in their entryway, professing his feelings for her, wanting her to do the same.

It was just so wrong on every level she could imagine. Yet, unreasonably, her body responded to him as she remembered the way his lips felt on hers, his breath on her neck, the way their kiss had shot sparks through her.

She turned away from him, and he grabbed her. "Please. At least give me some explanation."

"Adam," she whispered. "I am married."

"Are you . . . happy?"

Damn. She knew it was coming. How dare he stand in the home she shared with her husband and ask her that?

He dared because he was, after all, the arrogant detective Adam Bryant. She had despised him when she was investigating Maggie Rae's death. Then they had worked together again on the New Mountain Order case. It was then that he had become approachable to her. The first time she realized she was seeing him in a different light was when she was sitting on the floor of Cookie Crandall's vacant house. And he had brought her the remnants of Cookie's scrapbook of shadows, which Annie had refused to even look at because she was so angry with her.

"We are fine," she managed to say. "Now, let me go. Oh, damn. Let me get the keys," she said, reaching around him to the key rack, brushing against his shoulder.

"I wish I could believe that," she heard him say as she walked out the door.

Chapter 7

"Now, Vera, you need to settle those nerves," Beatrice said to her. "Maybe you should see a doctor, you know?"

Her forty-three-year-old daughter was pale and shaken. Was someone trying to frame her for murder? And was that person a dangerous killer? Oh, bother. This would wear on Vera. Beatrice knew she was taking it personally, as if this person didn't like her. "What have I ever done to anybody in this town but be friendly and kind?" she had said earlier. It was the worst thing in the world for some people to feel unliked. Beatrice really didn't care if anybody liked her. In fact, it always surprised her when someone actually did.

"I don't know, Mama. I don't like the idea of taking medicine, let alone nerve pills. You know what happened to Flossy," Vera said.

Sheila spoke up. "Well, that's Flossy. You're you. I'm sure you wouldn't get addicted. I'm sure you wouldn't let that happen." She looked at Beatrice. "We couldn't let that happen."

"Besides," Beatrice said, "that was years ago. They've come a long way with antidepressants and things."

Jon came back into the room, carrying a tray with a teapot filled with chamomile tea. It had always worked to soothe Vera, even when she was a teenager. Beatrice couldn't remember if it was Ed or her cousin Rose who had first told her about the calming effects of chamomile. She'd always wondered how much of it was psychological. Whether it was or not, it worked for Vera. Beatrice always grew some chamomile in her herb garden and kept some packaged chamomile tea, just in case. She loved the fresh, sour scent of it.

Beatrice leaned back onto her chair as Jon poured the tea in Vera's beautiful blue willow cups. At least Vera was able to bring most of her dishes with her. The family that had moved into her house didn't need them; they had brought most of their own dishes and pots and pans. But they'd left their furniture behind in North Carolina, at their home. Beatrice was dying to meet the family but hadn't had the opportunity yet to take them a pie or some muffins and introduce herself.

She watched as Vera's still unsteady hand lifted the steaming cup of tea to her lips. She blew on it, the way she always had. Her daughter had very predictable movements. Always had. But these days, Beatrice knew she was troubled, and to witness the old familiar habits of tea held some comfort for her.

"Antidepressants? First, you're talking about antianxiety drugs, and now antidepressants. I don't know," Vera said, looking uncomfortable on her dilapidated couch.

"Well, just talk to a doctor and see what he recommends," Sheila said. "In the meantime, I think you need to break down and get a burglar alarm."

"So expensive," Vera said, waving the subject off with her hand.

"Let me buy it for you," Beatrice said. "Land sakes. Let me help."

Vera smiled and sighed. "Okay." She looked over at Elizabeth, who was stacking up blocks to create a tower.

Beatrice tried to place positive spin on all of it, but she was dismayed to hear that Vera, her only daughter, who was the mother of her only grandchild, was sleepwalking again. She hoped and prayed it wouldn't happen again, let alone while Elizabeth was in her care. God only knew what could happen. Once, when Vera was twelve, they caught her walking down the middle of the street. Betty Hawthorne beeped her horn, woke the poor child up, and she became hysterical.

"Maybe I should have told the police about my sleepwalking incident. I mean, you know how tricky sleep and dreams and all that is. I wonder if I might have heard something and that's what set me off."

"Unless there's a reason to tell them, I'd keep it to yourself," Sheila said. "Next thing you know, they'll have you strangling Emily in your sleep." She laughed and rolled her eyes.

Beatrice glared at her. Honestly. Why would she say that when Vera was so upset? She looked back at her daughter, who looked startled.

"What if I did?" Vera sat up on the edge of her chair. "What if I killed her and don't remember it? I mean, my purse was there. And we all know I despised the woman."

"Vera! C'mon!" Beatrice said, setting her cup down. "That's nonsense. You never hurt anything—not ever—when you sleepwalked before."

"Yes, I can't imagine," Sheila agreed. "It's ridiculous."

But Beatrice saw a faraway, almost haunted look in Vera's eyes. It was exactly what she feared, and Vera would obsess about it and dwell on it, until something else caught her attention. Beatrice needed to change the subject. And fast.

"Did I tell you that the Department of Historic Resources is coming to my place sometime this week?"

"Why?" Vera asked.

"I told you about the contractor finding bones and maybe an old foundation in the backyard. We called the police, and they came by and looked, said if it was a crime site, it was too old for them to do anything about. They called the history folks in Richmond. The Department of Historic Resources. Who knows what they are going to find?"

"Very exciting," Jon said. "I love American history, and to have bit of it in the backyard? Extraordinary!"

Beatrice loved this man. She looked at his dark eyes gleaming and didn't know how it happened, given that she had always just been in love with one man, Ed, her whole life. Suddenly, there was Paris and Jon. And Jon tracking her down in Cumberland Creek. Life was surprising. You just never knew about the human heart and its capacity to love.

"So now, unfortunately, our pool construction has come to a standstill until they see if there really is any historical significance to it."

"I wonder what they will find," Sheila said. "You ought to scrapbook it, Bea. Take pictures as they're doing their thing. And then create a scrapbook about it."

Beatrice took a long sip of her tea as she looked over at the Scrapbook Queen. A long look was exchanged between them. Beatrice didn't have to say a word. She lifted one eyebrow, and Sheila looked away.

Chapter 8

As the week went by, Vera was pleased by the lack of incidents in her daily life. Everything appeared normal, with the same few dance classes, the same issues with Elizabeth, and she appeared to be sleeping the whole night. Just yesterday, she purchased an alarm system and made an appointment to see a doctor, just to be on the safe side. She had visited her mother and photographed the start of the archaeological dig occurring in the backyard of the home where she grew up. The exact spot where they found the human bones was where she had whiled away the hours, aboveground, swinging on a tire swing that hung from the majestic oak tree, listening to music, dreaming of dance routines.

But that tree had been cut down years ago, leaving behind a huge stump and a gnarly root system.

"Here it is," Vera said, holding an old black-and-white snapshot of her younger self on the tire swing. "Here's the old oak tree. And there I am on my swing."

"I remember that," Sheila said. "And to think there was a dead person underneath. . . . Well . . . it makes me feel strange."

"I know, but if you think about it, we are probably

walking around over dead people all the time," Vera said. "The historian explained to Mama that they probably would never know who the bones belong to, even though they will take a DNA sample. They need something to compare it to. What are you working on, Annie?"

"Here's a picture from when my mom and dad were married, the first time. And here's one from the wedding last month," Annie said.

"I love that you're doing that," DeeAnn said.

"Maybe we'll be doing one for Bea at some point," Sheila said.

"Oh, I shouldn't think so," Vera said. "They both seem content with the situation."

"So what's going on with the dig?" Annie asked.

"They were pulling out a lot of things that just looked like pieces of rock to me. But there was this interesting piece of rounded pottery. Who knows if it was a cup or a bowl," Vera said. "It's the only thing I saw that made any sense to me. And it's been raining for two days, so, of course, they stopped. Mom hopes they'll be back soon. Good God, she was right down there in the ditch with them." Vera handed Annie a picture of her mother "supervising" the progress. Annie laughed.

"I'm so excited. I wonder if your mom would let me bring my class by sometime this week," said Paige, the high school history teacher. She was supposed to retire last year, but they asked if she could stay on another year.

"She'll probably charge admission," Sheila said with a grunt.

"She might really like that," Vera said. "She's now on the board at the museum and really seems to be getting into history."

"Speaking of history," DeeAnn interjected. "I heard a rumor about Emily McGlashen's body."

"What?" Paige said.

"They say it's still in the morgue."

"What?" Annie said. "I thought they finally reached her parents."

"We all thought that," DeeAnn said, "but evidently, there was a mix-up with the names. It was the wrong people."

"That's odd in this day and age," Annie said.

Vera's stomach fluttered. "And sad," she said. "I didn't like the woman, but someone should give her a proper burial. I mean, a life is a life, and death should be handled respectfully."

"So," Annie said to DeeAnn, "have they found her real parents?"

"I don't know. Annie, I was hoping you could find out," she said. "My source doesn't know anything else."

"Your source, DeeAnn?" Vera said and smiled. "Everybody knows your favorite customer works in the morgue."

They all laughed. Shorty Swice came into her bakery every day and always ordered six blueberry muffins. *Where does the man put it?* DeeAnn often wondered.

The funny thing was that he had a bit of a crush on DeeAnn. It was harmless, of course. She was a big-boned, happily married woman, and he a tiny man with a big appetite, as henpecked as could be by his wife, Valerie.

Just then, there was a knock on the glass sliding door in the Sheila's basement, which was where she held her crops. She answered the door. "Why, Detective Bryant." Her voice went up a decibel or two.

Vera's eyes shot to Annie, whose face reacted by coloring pink. Annie looked at her, then looked around the table at the other women sitting there. Some were looking her way; others were twisting their necks already to see the handsome detective as he entered the room.

"How do?" he said to the group of women. "How goes the crop this evening?"

They all murmured their separate answers.

Vera's heart felt like it sank into her stomach as she witnessed the discomfort of Annie. Vera was probably the only one at the table who knew about the kiss Bryant and Annie had shared and knew how tempted Annie was by this man. She had opened up to Vera one night, while they were sitting on Beatrice's front porch together. The woman was in some turmoil. Vera wanted to tell her to hang on to her husband, the father of her children, with all her might; that it was only human to be tempted, after all; to be kind and gentle to herself. But it didn't come out that way at all. In fact, she bumbled around the conversation. But she felt for her.

"Annie, we need to talk," the detective said.

Annie's mouth dropped open, and she leaned back.

"It's business, of course," he said quickly. "We've had a break in the Emily McGlashen case."

"And?" Annie said. "I've filed my story about her. I'm not working on it anymore. You know that. And when I wrote about the other murders in Cumberland Creek, you were not forthcoming. So what gives?"

"Well, it turns out that Emily is not who we thought she was. . . . She, um, had these tattoos."

"Tattoos?" Annie said.

"Rune patterns."

Vera's heart leapt to her mouth, DeeAnn dropped her drink on the floor, and Annie gasped. In the rush to clean things up, Vera's mind ran a mile a minute. *The NMO? Again?* They were going to lose Annie, Mike, and their boys. Cumberland Creek was going to lose them. Just like they lost Cookie Crandall.

Chapter 9

Annie stood and gathered up her photos, shoving them into their envelopes, then into her bags.

"Annie," Detective Bryant said. "I need your help."

"I'm the last person whose help you need," she said, trying to stop her voice from shaking.

"I know what this must feel like, but—"

"You know?" Annie said with her voice lifted. "I don't think you do. I don't think any of you could possibly know what it feels like. It's like I've stepped back in time fifty years or something. There's a group of neo-Nazi pagans in the hills nobody wants to talk about. There's my boys in a school system that promotes Bible education. And let's not forget about the weird, hateful symbols painted on barns and houses around town a while back. And then there's Cookie."

Annie felt herself unraveling there in Sheila's basement, surrounded by her friends and the ephemera of scrapbooking, such as the paper, the scissors, the glues, the colored pens and pencils. All of it seemed to mock her right now.

"Now, Annie." Sheila led her to the couch in the corner. "I know you're upset. You've got every right to be. But you need to calm down. Take some deep breaths."

"Yeah, uh, I didn't know it was going to upset you this much," Bryant said, looking to the floor, then back up at her. "It's just that you've got these great investigative skills, and I know you've been working on this book. I don't know if there's a link or not, but I thought you could answer some questions. We are so short of staff right now."

Annie took a deep breath as she watched his discomfort. He was admitting he was in over his head—and he was doing that in front of the Cumberland Creek Scrapbook Club. She smiled. Then laughed.

Sheila shoved a glass of water in her hand. "Drink up, Annie."

As Annie drank the cool water, she began to calm down. She looked up and realized the other women were not looking at her anymore. They had gone back to their projects, or at least they wanted it to look that way. She caught Vera looking at her out of the corner of her eye; then she looked back at the paper in front of her.

Bryant crouched down next to her.

"What do you say, Annie? Can you help me out?"

"I don't know if it's a good idea," she said. "Let me think about it, okay?"

He was too close to her face. She could see the shadow of his whiskers on his face and wanted to reach up and run her hand along his chiseled cheek. No, probably not a good idea.

Because sometimes you wake up in the middle of the night and realize it's been three months since you and your husband have made love. Because sometimes you want to scream from the boredom of it all—the house, the kids. Because sometimes all you want to be is a woman. A woman who is nothing more than that. And you want a man who makes you feel that way.

He stood too close to her. She felt a psychic pull from

him. And knew she couldn't resist this project, was unsure she could continue to resist him. But one thing she knew was if Emily McGlashen was NMO, it would make a hell of a story. A story she wanted. It reached into to her guts, and she felt it forming there.

Was Emily McGlashen an NMO member? She had come to town, reclaiming her roots as a McGlashen, part of the Scotch-Irish founding family of what was then called Miller's Gap, now Cumberland Creek. And she had come as an international Irish step-dancing champion. She had appeared to be on a mission to destroy Vera's business and to take over the historical society. Maybe, just maybe, they had her all wrong. Maybe she had been on a different kind of mission. And now Annie wanted to find out.

Annie took a deep breath and stood, gathered her bags. "Okay, Bryant. Where do we start?"

"We start tonight, if you don't mind," he said. "I know it's Saturday night and all that." He looked at the ladies. "I don't think they will mind if I borrow you for just the night."

"Just one night, Detective," Sheila said.

"Okay, I'll give Mike a call and let him know I might be late," Annie said, following Detective Bryant toward the door. She turned around to find Vera on her heels.

"Annie," she said quietly. "Can't this wait? I mean, I don't think Mike is going to like you digging around again."

"Vera," Annie said, "I think Mike is going to have to get over it."

Vera's hand went to her chest in concern, and her brows knit.

Annie rode in the police car with Bryant to the station, and she called Mike along the way. As predicted, he wasn't happy, but he felt a little better knowing Annie was with his new best friend.

Before they left the car, Annie told Bryant what Mike had said. He looked back at her with a pained expression.

"I know you care about him," she said. "So do I. Believe it or not. Let's keep this arrangement platonic and professional. If you can't do that, I won't help you."

"Annie, I—"

"I mean it. Don't push me," she said, glaring.

He leaned back into his seat, then fumbled with the door. "It's your call, Annie. All of it."

Chapter 10

When Beatrice woke up, she was startled momentarily—
a man snored softly in her bed. *Oh yes. Jon.* He had come
padding into her room last night, wanting to make love.
After, instead of going back to his own room, he had stayed
with her. He preferred to sleep with her. Beatrice didn't feel
the same about sleeping with him. She had grown used to
sleeping alone and liked it. Just because she didn't want
to sleep with him didn't mean she didn't want to have sex
with him. She never told him no, always welcomed his
touch. Sleeping alone after Ed died had been difficult. But
now she liked to spread out and to pass gas and scratch
her ass if she wanted to. Hardly attractive.

She left the room quietly, glancing back at Jon, with his
mouth open, snoring a bit. She smiled to herself. He was
cute. She loved him madly.

Now she had a lot of work to do. She'd invited the business professor and his family to Sunday dinner. Vera and
Elizabeth were coming, and she hoped her no-good ex-
son-in-law would come, as well, sans new girlfriend.

"Now, Bea, she's a part of my life," he had told her when
she issued the invitation over the phone. "You are going to
have to get used to it."

"Like hell," Beatrice had said. "She is not welcome in my house. Your ex-wife and daughter will be here, and you are welcome here. Please don't complicate things by bringing your child bride into my home."

"Beatrice! She is not a child, and we are not married," he'd said.

"Well, you might as well be. The way you've turned your back on your family, you ought to be ashamed."

"I haven't done that, Bea. Times are tough everywhere," he said. "I am still sending Vera money for Elizabeth. It's just that she's not making as much on her own."

"Men. Do you always equate love with money? One of these days Elizabeth isn't even going to know you, Bill. Then how will you feel?"

"I just saw her what? Two, no, three weeks ago."

"*Three* weeks? Humph," Beatrice said.

Silence on the other end of the phone. Then, "I'm sorry, Bea. I've been very busy settling in here. You're right. I need to see Elizabeth."

Beatrice took the roast out of the refrigerator. She'd taken it out of the freezer last night. She placed it in the kitchen sink. Child brides. Ex-wives. Money. Love. When did modern life get to be so mixed up, you couldn't even have a simple Sunday dinner without causing a ruckus?

She scooped coffee out of the can, placed it in her coffeemaker, turned it on, and went to sit on the sunporch, wondering when Jon would get up. The scent of the coffee brewing filled her with comfort.

As she sat down in her wicker rocking chair, it creaked and sighed with age. She should probably get another one, but it suited her.

"Good morning," Jon said as he entered the porch and kissed her on the cheek.

"Morning," she said.

"Ready for your coffee?"

She nodded.

He came back with a cup of coffee for her and had the paper, as well. He sat down and started reading it.

"Well, this is something," he said. "Emily McGlashen's murder gets more mysterious."

"What's going on?" Beatrice asked after taking a drink of her morning elixir.

"Her body still remains unclaimed by her family, though the police say they've found them and they are on the way to Cumberland Creek."

"But that is odd. It's been what? A week? I thought there was a couple here a few days ago. . . ."

"No. There was a mix-up with her name. Her parents have a different last name, from what I've heard."

"Really?" She mentally leafed through the article Annie had written about Emily. No mention of any of this. She remembered Annie had said she had problems getting anything on Emily. It was all the smoke-and-mirrors press release standard stuff. Maybe she should read it again. She thumbed through her stack of newspapers.

"Her parents are living in a commune of a sort."

"Fascinating," Beatrice said, sipping her coffee, gradually feeling her senses come alive.

"I wonder if Annie knows all this," Jon said. "She seems to be in the know most of the time."

Beatrice skimmed the article. "International Irish dance champion . . . from California, lived in London, Madrid, Rome, Galway . . . studied with so-and-so . . . . retired at the age of twenty-seven to teach . . . will be greatly missed." No mention of her parents. No names. Nothing.

"I can't help but think of the NMO. Surely, the NMO would not be so foolish as to murder another young woman, not now, with this book being written about them. All this attention. Even they could not be so stupid," Jon said.

Beatrice loved listening to him speak. With that French accent, even the word _stupid_ didn't offend her.

Beatrice thought for a moment. The paper hadn't mentioned any NMO trademarks being at the scene of the crime. So it seemed unlikely. Besides, strangulation was a personal way to kill someone. Someone really wanted to watch her die and didn't mind watching the life drain out of her. Beatrice shivered.

Sometimes, Beatrice wished this country wasn't so free. People had the right to believe what they wanted, but she just wasn't so sure about acting on those beliefs. She often thought of the innocent lives taken based on nothing more than ignorance. She couldn't dwell on it, or her blood pressure would skyrocket. As if she didn't have enough to worry about. But if the NMO didn't have anything to do with Emily's murder, who did? And was the murderer really trying to frame Vera?

Chapter 11

Vera's mother had seated them next to one another. Was she harboring the hope that she would get back together with Bill? Hard to believe. Beatrice had never really liked Bill. Well, she had for a while, when he stayed with her. But these days, Beatrice was back to not liking him, and her mother never minced words or feelings.

"Pass the potatoes, please," Vera said to him. He did so, avoiding eye contact. He held a smitten Elizabeth on his opposite knee. Beatrice had tried to get her to sit at the table in her own chair, but nothing doing. Elizabeth hadn't seen her father in three weeks and stuck to his lap.

Vera spooned the potatoes on her plate, noticing that Dr. Reilly was watching her. She looked up at him and smiled. "Mama has a way with potatoes," she said.

"Indeed," he said. "With everything. This is a delicious meal."

"Quite," his wife said.

"Thank you kindly," Beatrice said, looking pleased with herself.

"So I understand you are a business professor," Jon said to Dr. Reilly.

He nodded. "Yes. I specialize in marketing. I'm also

consulting for some Irish music groups and researching the influence of Irish music on Appalachian music for them. Great fun."

"Fascinating," Vera said, though she could care less about it. "Did you hear about Emily McGlashen?"

Leola Reilly spoke up, with her mouth half full. "Oh, yes." Vera had never seen the woman wear anything but a long denim skirt. She had been beginning to wonder if she wore anything else. But tonight she wore a black skirt and a white shirt. Very simple and almost in the same style as the denim skirts she wore.

"We knew her work, had run into her at many Irish music and dance festivals. It's a small community," Dr. Reilly explained. "We are waiting on word about her memorial service or something. Nobody seems to know a thing."

Vera squirmed in her chair. She wasn't sure how much Detective Bryant and Annie would appreciate her adding to the conversation.

"It's the oddest thing, really. She was quite the superstar in Irish dance and traditional music circles, but nobody seems to know a thing about her personally. What makes it even stranger is that the nature of the traditional art form is that you see a lot of the same families, you know, for generations in the field. Even if families aren't in the art, they are around in support. I don't think I've ever seen anybody around Emily. She was a loner," the professor said.

"I understand her parents are on their way, but it's taking them a while to get here," Vera said after a few moments.

Leola coughed a bit and reached for her wine. Goodness, her face was red from just a little cough.

"Such a shame. Such a young woman," Beatrice said, then changed the subject. "I do love good bluegrass, and I have quite a collection of local music. You're welcome to check it out anytime."

"That would be lovely," Dr. Reilly said. "How is the apartment, Vera?"

Vera felt Bill's eyes scanning her. "It's fine," she said. "We're doing okay there."

Vera looked back at him and smiled, then glanced over at his wife, whose face was still pink, her eyes bloodshot and red rimmed. Their eyes met, and Leola quickly looked away.

"I've thought about this for a while, but you look so familiar to me, Leola," Vera said. "How do I know you?"

Leola wiped her mouth with her linen napkin and shrugged. "I don't know. We are from North Carolina but have traveled a bit with John's job. This is the first time we've been here for any length of time. A lot of people tell me I look familiar," she said and smiled. "I guess I just have one of those faces."

"And it's a beautiful face, my dear," her husband said.

"Well, now, who's ready for dessert? There's custard pie and apple cake. Who wants what?" Beatrice asked.

Vera stood and gathered the dishes, while everybody else followed Beatrice into her living room, where hammer dulcimer bluegrass music was being played. The conversation turned to music.

Vera was a little uncomfortable sharing a meal with the people who were renting her house, but her mother had insisted. After all, it wasn't their fault that she was next to broke. They were helping her out a good deal. They were going to rent only for a year, during the time of Dr. Reilly's teaching gig, and then he'd be heading back to Carolina.

Handsome couple, Vera thought as she rinsed off the dishes and opened the dishwasher. Laughter came from the next room. There was something odd about them, though.

She didn't like the way he looked at her. Bill seemed to notice. Even though they weren't married anymore, they still had this unspoken communication, a mix of body language and glances. Dr. Reilly couldn't be flirting with her right in front of his wife, could he?

Well, of course he could, she reminded herself. The older she became, the more she saw that most men just weren't to be trusted at all. The situation with Bill was like a veil being lifted from her eyes. She saw the world much more clearly now. It seemed as if everywhere she looked, there were men cheating on their wives. Why hadn't she noticed before? Was she just naive?

Jon entered the kitchen. "Can I help?"

She turned around and smiled at him. "Of course you can."

She handed him a stack of dessert plates and reached into the refrigerator for the pie. Everybody wanted the pie. Fancy that.

"Fascinating couple," Jon said. "Good thing they showed up in Cumberland Creek when they did. Good for you. Good for them. Not much of a commute to the university for him, given that he teaches only two days a week."

"Nice situation," Vera said, slicing the pie, then scooping a piece up and onto the plate Jon held for her.

"Elizabeth is pleased to see her father," he added. "The dinner seems to be a success."

The last slice of pie placed on a plate, Vera reached for the bottle of wine that she carried into the kitchen from the dining room table. Only a sip left in it. She uncorked it and lifted it to her mouth.

Jon gaped as he held the tray of desserts.

"To success," Vera said and smiled, lifting the bottle in a mock toast.

Chapter 12

Annie was chopping onions and crying. She didn't know if it was just the onions or not. Her eyes stung, and once the flow started, she couldn't stop it. Finally, she placed the onions in the frying pan, wet a paper towel with cool water, and held it to her eyes.

"Are you okay?" Mike walked in for a beer, opened the refrigerator door.

"Onions," she said.

He grabbed her and kissed her on the head. "Poor baby," he said. "Whatchya making?"

"An omelet," she said. "I'm using up the eggs and milk before we get our next delivery."

"I wish Adam was coming over today. What a great guy," he said.

Annie rolled her eyes.

"C'mon, Annie. You worked with him last night. You know he's not that bad," he said, leaning against the counter.

"I helped him out a bit last night," she said. "When he found out Emily had those tattoos, he just assumed I could help."

He grimaced. "Yeah. He's kinda like that. He makes assumptions. I don't think he means anything by it. Underneath it all, he's got an open mind."

"I expect his mind is a bit more open than many of the members of the New Mountain Order," she said. "Speaking of which, I really need to get cracking on that."

"How much more do you have to write?"

"I think I'm about halfway there," she said, reaching in the drawer for a spatula, then moving the onions around a bit. She added some peppers to the pan, and the scent of them filled the room.

"Last night must have been kinda intense," Mike said after taking a drink of his beer.

The bowl of eggs almost slipped from Annie's hand.

"Careful," he said.

"My hands are slippery," she mumbled and wiped them.

"Well?" he said. "How did it go?"

"I don't know, Mike. There were no symbols at the scene of the crime, other than on Emily. In the past the NMO has always used symbols. Of course, they could be a little more clever about it now, since two of their henchmen are gone," she said. "The real mystery, other than who killed Emily, is how she was connected to them, if at all."

"Did she really hide the connection, or did none of us know her enough that she would even tell us?"

Annie thought a moment. "Either could be the case. But she seemed to be okay with all the other attention she attracted. In fact, she seemed to want it."

"She was a real bitch," Mike said. "I never met anybody so ambitious, not even—"

"Me?" Annie said, turning to face him.

He grinned sheepishly. "I wasn't going to say that, but now that you mention it."

She threw her towel on the counter. He jumped back.

"Sorry," he said mockingly.

"I'm a failure, Mike," she said after a deep breath, concentrating on keeping her voice level and low so the boys wouldn't hear her. "I can't be the person you want me to be. The wife you want me to be."

"Hey! Whoa! Who said that?"

"You didn't have to say it, Mike. It's all over you," she said.

"Hey, where's this coming from? I was just teasing. You know how much I love you. I adore you," he said.

She took a moment. "I'm sorry, Mike, for jumping on you like that. It's just that sometimes I wonder," she said, whisking the eggs. "It's just, um, it's been a while."

"Hey, you're up late at night, working. And I'm already asleep by the time you get to bed," he said, looking away from her.

The scent of onions and peppers hung in the air. Annie stirred them around and poured the eggs into the pan, It sizzled, and then the sizzling faded out.

"Annie, finish up this book and we'll go away for the weekend. Just us, okay?" His arms went around her. His chin to her shoulder, his breath hot on her neck. "You know I love you. You know I want you. C'mon. Things have just been a little awkward and crazy."

That was true. She knew that. The boys were always in and out of their bedroom, up and down all night long. He worked crazy hours sometimes; so did she.

It was like he had always said, and he said it again in her ear. "We are about more than sex."

She smiled. Her heart melted a little, but it was different now.

Now that there was someone around who was all about the sex. Or at least it was for her.

Chapter 13

Beatrice blinked her eyes. Was there someone in her backyard, or had something blown over from a neighbor's clothesline? A sheet? It was 3:00 a.m. She had fallen asleep early and awakened hungry, had come down into the kitchen, and was distracted by a movement in her backyard.

She stood in the dark. A flimsy whitish thing moved in her backyard. Could it be a ghost? Ed had never looked like that when he visited her. He had looked like himself. Whatever this was, it did not glow, but floated in the wind.

She squinted, wondered if she should turn the light on or wake Jon. If she turned the light on, she surely could see it so much better. And what would Jon do? He didn't even know how to use a gun. She vowed she would teach him one of these days. She tiptoed into the library, where her husband's gun stayed in the top drawer of his desk, which was the same place he'd kept it the whole time they'd lived together as husband and wife.

She heard the creaking noise of someone walking down stairs. Jon!

"Bea, put that gun away, dear," he said quietly.

"Now, hold on, Jon," she said. "There's someone in the

backyard. And when I turn the outside light on them, I want to have this handy. It's not loaded. Okay?"

He grimaced. "You Americans and your guns! Just call the police!"

"Good idea," she whispered back to him as she headed for her kitchen. "You call them, and I'll wait in the kitchen. Watch to see he doesn't get away."

But she took the gun with her, just in case. Who was he to tell her she couldn't have her gun? She had been using them for years and had taken classes in gun safety.

She looked out the window in the dark, listened to Jon dialing the police and explaining while she watched the still form in her backyard. It seemed to be attached to the large stump of the old oak tree that had been cut down. Something about the shape of it reminded her of a crescent moon.

Jon came up behind her. "They will be here any minute." He wrapped his arms around her.

She froze. Suddenly she saw a white foot pointed against the stump. There was something about the foot. Something about the perfect arch of it. Vera!

She shook Jon off of her. "Oh, God, it's Vera!"

She ran outside, then along the edge of the pool ditch, Jon trailing behind her. "What? What?" he was saying.

They both stopped in their tracks as they looked at Vera, clad in a long white nightgown, sleeping against the tree, one foot wrapped around the stump.

Jon looked confused.

"Shh," Beatrice told him. "She is sleeping. Try not to startle her."

She'd done this countless times when Vera was a child. But this time, it scared her. Her granddaughter was at home, in bed, alone. What if she were to wake up and need her mother? What if there was a fire?

Beatrice wrapped her arms carefully around Vera and led her to the door of the house; Jon held it open.

"Jon, can you get dressed and go and stay with Elizabeth?" Beatrice asked.

"Certainly," he said. "The police—"

"I'll deal with them," Beatrice said, sitting her daughter down on the couch, then lying her down.

"No good," Jon said. "This is no good, my love."

Their eyes met in concern.

Vera lay on the couch, as if she'd never been anywhere but there all night. Her feet and hands were covered in mud. Mud smeared across her cheek, but she was still sleeping.

Jon opened the front door for Detective Bryant and then headed for his car.

"I'm sorry, Bryant," Beatrice said, standing up from her crouched-over position next to her daughter. "We didn't need to bother you, after all."

"What's going on?"

"I thought there was someone in my backyard when Jon called you. But it was only Vera."

"Vera?" He looked at the couch and saw her sleeping.

Beatrice motioned for him to go into the kitchen; she followed.

"She's sleepwalking," she whispered. "I sent Jon over to look in on Elizabeth."

"Does she do this often?"

"She used to. When she was a child, it was a big problem," she said after a moment. "It seems the stress has gotten to be a bit much for her. I don't know what to make of it."

The front door opened farther, and a few uniformed police officers walked in, followed by Leola Reilly.

"False alarm," Bryant called from the kitchen. The two officers turned and left. Leola didn't. Dressed in a purple jogging suit, Leola looked as if she planned to stay. Beatrice didn't think she'd been jogging at this hour.

"Is everything okay?" Leola said as she entered the kitchen.

"Yeah. What are you doing hanging out outside at this hour?" Bryant said to her.

"I couldn't sleep, so I went for a walk and saw the police cars. I just wondered if you needed any help," Leola said. But she looked rattled and unkempt.

"Mama?" came a voice from the living room. "What am I doing here?"

Beatrice ran into the living room. Vera was just waking up, the way she always did. You thought she was awake, but then she'd go back to sleep and then be back up. It was maddening.

"Vera?" Leola said loudly.

"Don't—" Beatrice started to say, but Vera's scream brought them all to her side. She watched as Vera glared at Leola.

"Get her out of here!" Vera cried.

"Goodness, Vera, calm down," Beatrice said. But her daughter's face was as pale as her nightgown.

"Let me escort you to the door," Bryant said to Leola.

That Bryant, sometimes you just had to love him. But only sometimes.

Chapter 14

Vera sat at her mother's kitchen table, slumped over it, as she watched the sun come up over Jenkins Mountain in the distance, a view that she had loved and found comfort in for years.

She picked at the plate of eggs Beatrice had put in front of her.

"I don't think I've ever seen you so quiet," Detective Bryant said.

She smiled at him and shrugged but wondered what he meant by that. Was she a chatterbox? Maybe he thought so. But she didn't really care what he thought.

"We are going to get the best doctor we can for you," Beatrice said. "We can't have you traipsing around Cumberland Creek, sleepwalking."

Queasy, confused, Vera didn't know what was happening to her. Was she losing her mind?

"I don't understand the reaction to Leola," Beatrice said.

"Me neither," Vera said. "She seems nice enough. Kinda cold. But nice enough. I must have still been dreaming."

"That must be it," the detective said.

"You've been through a lot over the past year. Maybe you need a vacation?"

"I can't afford a vacation," Vera said. "In fact, I'm going to teach all summer long this year. Not closing the studio. Now that . . . Emily is gone. Maybe I can pick up the business again."

Just then the doorbell rang. It was Annie.

"Are you okay?" Annie said, hugging Vera.

"I am now," she said.

"Well, I better get going," Detective Bryant said, standing. "Thanks for breakfast, Ms. Matthews. How do, Ms. Chamovitz?"

"All is well, Detective," Annie said, barely looking at him.

Vera saw the detective's lingering looks at Annie. But she looked at Vera.

"Do you want me to take Elizabeth today?" Annie asked.

"Jon has her, and we'll spend the day with her," Beatrice said with finality.

Vera was still a mess by the time the Saturday night crop rolled around. The Cumberland Creek Scrapbook Club was all atwitter at the news that Emily McGlashen's mother and father were finally in town to claim her body. The fact that she had those tattoos had not been reported in the papers.

"You're off your game," Sheila said to Annie. "Her parents are obviously very strange hippies, I'd say."

"Obviously," Annie said, grinning. "Yes. Evidently, they only have one phone at the commune they live at, and it was shut off to observe some festival or something. So it took a while to reach them. They don't have a car and didn't know anybody who did, so they took off on foot and hitchhiked all the way from the other side of West Virginia."

"Backpacking hippies parading around town can't be kept a secret for long," Vera said, grinning.

DeeAnn laughed. "I had no idea what they were," she said. "They came into the bakery yesterday, and at first, I thought they were from some cult. It was kind of scary."

"I have an aunt who dresses like that, and she lives outside of Bethesda and doesn't even belong to commune," Annie said and laughed. "That branch of the family has always freaked me out a bit." She stood and walked over to the snack table, surveying the food.

"Speaking of being freaked out," Paige said. "How is the sleepwalking?"

"Well, the doctor gave me some sleeping pills, and I've been sleeping very deeply," Vera replied. "I guess he thinks I may have a sleep disorder. In the meantime, the sleeping pills seem to be working."

"Then what?" Sheila said, clicking on her computer screen. "I mean, you can't stay on sleeping pills forever."

Vera sighed. "I don't know. There will be more tests. But you know as long as the pills work, I don't really know why I should bother."

"You should bother because those pills are just covering your problem up, not getting to the root of it," Annie said.

Vera looked over Sheila's shoulder. "Oh, I love that," she said to Sheila. "You are getting so good with this digital stuff."

"It's so easy," Sheila said. "I wouldn't want all my scrapbooking done this way. But it's so easy to keep up with the school pictures and day-to-day pictures because everything is digital. You don't really even need to get the pictures developed."

"I love that idea," Annie said, "but I'm so sick of being at my computer all the time. I can see it being a great space saver."

"That's what I was thinking. I don't have the space anymore," Vera said. Her heart sank. She missed her home. But she supposed she should be grateful for what she did have.

"You don't have to be at your computer long," Sheila said. "You could sort of do a hybrid scrapbooking. You know it sort of combines the tools and techniques of both. You could, for example, print your photos out on a scrapbook page and then embellish it."

"I've used some fonts I found on the computer," DeeAnn said. "I printed them off on good paper, cut it out, and used it for my pages. I didn't know I was doing hybrid scrapbooking. Humph. I guess I'm ahead of my time."

The women were all quiet as they worked on their individual projects. Annie and Vera hovered over Sheila.

"And look at this. I've actually designed some digital elements," Sheila said. "I met this man at the last conference who said he'd take a look at anything I gave him. . . ."

"What?" Paige squealed. "Oh my, Sheila! You better be careful what you show a strange man!"

Sheila's face turned red, but she joined her friends in laughing.

Annie sat back down in her chair and took a long drink of her beer. "I can't believe my parents are remarried," she said, looking over the scrapbook she was making them. "I think if I got divorced, I'd not want to remarry that same person. Or anybody, really."

"Is that how you feel, Vera?" Paige asked.

"Well," Vera said after a moment. "There was a time I thought the Bill and I might get back together. But too much has happened. For a while, you know, there was Tony. And now Bill is with that woman in Charlottesville. Even though I miss certain parts of my life, like my house, I don't think I'd want to go backward. I sort of like being alone."

As she said it, a kind of lightness filled the mood of the room. She reckoned many of her friends dreaded being alone and had been worried about her. It was a relief for them to think she was fine. And that was what she wanted them to think.

Chapter 15

"Annie, do you think you can talk to them?" Bryant asked her.

"Yeah, sure, but I wonder why they won't talk to you," Annie said, placing the last file back into a box labeled MCGLASHEN.

Annie and Bryant were sitting in his office. It was Monday afternoon, and they had just been through boxes of Emily's papers and had found nothing that linked her to the NMO, yet. But they did find adoption papers. Turned out Emily was adopted. Her adoptive family name was Greenberg. One reason it was so hard for the authorities to track her parents down.

"I don't know. Maybe it's because I'm so cute?" he said and grinned at her.

"Or it's because you've offended them somehow. More likely, wouldn't you think?" she clipped.

He grabbed his chest. "I'm hurt!"

She laughed, loving the sound of his laughter coming up from deep in his chest.

"Okay," she said. "I'll talk to them. At least I can ask about her adoption. It seems odd that Emily would take another name." She paused, looking across the desk at him. "Have we ruled out the NMO?"

"Nothing has been ruled out yet. We've talked to a couple of their members, and they say they don't know Emily. That they were not really representative of the group, but . . . ," he said and grimaced.

"What?" she said, sitting up on the edge of her chair.

"The runes. Not something you see every day, you know. We have to pay attention to this. The NMO uses the same symbols as what is on Emily's ass. And add to that your crazy friend Vera, who has yet to come up with a reason her purse was found at the crime scene."

"Vera is not crazy," she said. "Have you talked to the members of the historical society?"

He nodded. "Not much help, as you can imagine."

"How about the Irish dance community?" Annie asked.

"Yes, we've spoken to several dancers. None of them were even in this area around the time Emily was killed. There was this man, Ian something or other, who obviously didn't like Emily. But he's in Chicago."

"Can you give me his contact info?"

"Sure, but why? We've already talked to him."

"As I told you before, Adam, people react differently to you because you're a cop. And a smart-ass cop, at that."

He rolled his eyes, leaned back in his desk chair, and placed his hands behind his head. Annie tried not to let her eyes drift to his biceps, because that would lead to her wanting him to wrap those arms around her. She didn't look. *Think about Mike.*

"You may be right. There may not be a link with the NMO," he said, letting out a groan as he released his hands from behind his head.

"I mean, I've been looking at the NMO's documents very closely," she said. "They say nothing about killing people. Though they do think that all the strange symbols are sacred. And they think that anybody who doesn't believe that Jesus is the Messiah is going to hell."

Bryant harrumphed.

"The dangerous part of it is that they thought Zeb was a prophet and was getting messages directly from Jesus. So, many of them did what he asked them to do. But now that he's gone . . . at least for now, I'm not sure who would be giving orders to kill Emily. And for what reason."

"Me neither."

"So if we rule out the NMO, who and what is there?" Annie persisted. "No real leads on the Irish dancing . . ."

"I've got to admit, Annie, this Irish dancing thing has me thrown. What is it? I don't think I've ever seen it," he said.

"Have you ever seen *Riverdance?*" she asked.

"What?" he said, with a look of bewilderment.

"Oh, never mind," she said. "It's a form of dance that has its roots in Ireland. Sometimes the dancers wear those soft shoes, gillies, and other times they wear hard shoes that are sort of a cross between a clog and a tap shoe. Either way, it's pretty amazing to watch. Especially the group dances, all of them together, making fancy, complicated formations while performing difficult dance moves."

"I think I'll check into renting *Riverdance,*" he said after a moment.

"You should, but in the meantime, I recorded a bit of Emily dancing the other day on my phone. Check this out," she said and pulled out her phone. "Sam was very interested in hard shoes. The shoes are thick and have taps on the bottom. I'm sure he just likes the noise. I prefer the soft-shoe dances, the ones where they wear—"

"The gillies with all the crisscrossed laces," he said, finishing her sentence.

Annie pressed a button on her iPhone screen. They

heard the *clack-clackety-tap-tap* of Emily's shoes as she danced in sync with fiddle and drum rhythms, jumping and spinning without missing a beat. A huge smile spread across her face, her ponytail bobbing up and town. Her skirt and legs were moving so quickly that they blurred on the iPhone screen.

"Whew," he said after it was over.

"I know. Amazing, right?" Annie said. Then, a few moments later, she added, "Any other leads?"

"Just Vera, unfortunately. And for the record, I can't see her as a killer. But people surprise you."

The look on his face startled Annie. Could he really think that Vera was capable of murder? Well, he still harbored suspicions about Cookie, even though they now knew she wasn't guilty of killing those two young women. They had simply known too much about an illegal operation and were killed because of it. Bryant looked serious.

"Between you and me, the killer probably had to have a lot more upper body strength than what I think Vera has. I mean, Emily was held down, along with being strangled. I'm not sure Vera could manage that physically," he told her. "But if she murdered Emily when she was sleepwalking . . ."

"What? That's a stretch."

"There have been cases like this. It's rare. I mean, where someone kills a person and doesn't remember it, because they were sleepwalking, for lack of a better term. No, wait. There is a term. Homicidal somnambulism. Look, I don't understand it. But there you have it," he said. "Something is troubling Vera. I hope she gets to the bottom of it soon."

"What will happen if you don't? Will you put her in jail, like you did Cookie?" Annie asked, with a note of bitterness in her voice.

Just then a uniformed officer walked in and handed Bryant a file and mumbled something to him.

"Excuse me," Bryant said, getting up from his desk. "I'll be back in a minute."

She glanced at her watch. "Well, I need to go, anyway. It's almost time for the boys' bus to come."

"Call me," he said, standing in the doorway.

Her eyes met his, and one of her brows lifted. She felt a flush of heat move across her, along with jolt of energy. Good God, what was happening to her?

"I mean," he stammered, "I mean if you find something more about the NMO or Emily. And, um, once you've talked to her parents."

He left the room, leaving Annie to gather up her things and rush out of the police station. As she was leaving, she saw Leo Shirley walking through the hallway in handcuffs. That man was always in trouble. Didn't he just get a DUI?

He'd also attacked Robert Dasher when the two of them were sitting at Pamela's Pie Palace a few years ago. The man was a menace. She wondered what he had managed to get into now.

But for now, Annie wanted to chat with Ian Jones, the Irish dancer. After several attempts, she finally reached him.

"Like I told that cop, Emily McGlashen was a bitch, nobody liked her, but she was a highly respected dancer. That's about all I can tell you," he said.

"Did she have any friends?" Annie asked.

He harrumphed. "No. It's strange. The Irish dance community is competitive. But the guy that's my biggest competitor? Well, we are friends. But Emily? She was quiet, kept to herself in rehearsal and competitions. She was so focused that it was, um, kind of scary."

"How so?"

"Well, it was just like, you know, she was oblivious to anybody else. She hated dancing in groups, as part of a team, because that meant she'd have to work with others. It got to the point where nobody wanted to work with her. She was just so difficult. Dancing is really such a team effort. Man, if you messed up, she'd let you have it. Wasn't helpful about it at all."

Annie heard commotion in the background.

"Sorry," he said. "That's my roommate. He's just getting up."

"Now?" Annie looked at her watch. It was two in the afternoon.

"Yes," he said. "We keep odd hours, you know, especially when a show is running. We sleep most of the day. Sort of like vampires," he said and laughed. "Imagine that, if you will. Irish dance vampires."

Chapter 16

The crews from the Virginia Department of Historic Resources were gathered in Beatrice's backyard. They had already carefully unearthed the bones of a man—er, what was left of the bones, which were, scientifically speaking, petrified bones.

"Curious," Beatrice said. "Why wasn't he buried in a box?"

"Well, times might have been hard," the crew leader said. "Or he could have been murdered. Or it could be a Native American, although most of the time, their bones are found in cloth or hide bags. So I don't think that's what our guy is. But ya never know."

He then explained that if the bones were found to be Native American, there would be complications for her.

"There's some kind of law stating that the government has the right to come in and pretty much take over if it's a burial ground. But, as I say, it doesn't look like it. Won't know until we run those tests. In the meantime, we appreciate you letting us look around a bit."

"No chance of finding out who the bones belong to?" Beatrice asked.

"Very unlikely. They will do DNA tests, of course, but

unless we already have DNA belonging to this person in the system, there's nothing to compare it to."

"And since people didn't go around collecting DNA back in the day . . ."

"Precisely," the man said.

Beatrice stood over the ground where other things were being removed. She had no use for them and planned to donate them to the state. Every day they discovered another item. One day they pulled up a hairbrush. Another day a razor. When you grew up in a place like Virginia, history was just a part of everyday life. It was marked by signs, monuments, and museums. But to think that all these years, Beatrice's backyard held historical treasure. Well, it was astounding.

"Ho!" one of the men called out. "I found something here." He pulled out a box, covered in earth. He brushed it off carefully. Everybody stilled. "Tin," he said. "And there's a bigger box under it, or something. Maybe a trunk."

Beatrice heard a sound like a loud train and felt a rumbling beneath her feet. The earth vibrated; she reached out for Jon, who steadied her. Some of the ground caved in just as the last man was pulled out of the ditch.

Cell phones began to sound.

"What the heck was that?" Beatrice said, looking around.

"A confirmed earthquake," the head honcho said.

"Well, imagine that," Beatrice said. "An earthquake in Virginia."

"I think we need to call it a day. There will be aftershocks, and I'm uncertain about any of my group being down there." He pointed to the hole.

"Understandable," Beatrice said. "But what about the box? Can we open it?"

"Sure," the guy said and laughed a little. "If you're sure you want to. Could be a pet buried. You never know."

"I'll take my chances," she said. "Come inside."

He dismissed his crew and followed Beatrice and Jon into the kitchen, where she spread out newspaper on her chrome and turquoise 1950s table.

She watched as he sat the box down. It looked really old to Beatrice, yet oddly familiar. Jon's brown eyes were wide saucers of excitement.

He carefully opened the box. It was partially filled with dirt, but he pulled out some metal piece that had colored thread hanging from them.

"Hmmm," he said.

"Hmmm, what?" Beatrice said impatiently.

"I think these are medals." He held them up to the light. "Perhaps Civil War?"

"Glory be," she said. "There wasn't any fighting in these parts. Maybe a skirmish or two."

"This could belong to our bone guy," he said. "Of course, this could have been where he lived. Or maybe it belonged to someone else."

"How do we find out?" Jon said.

"Well, I don't know, but the guys in Richmond will be able to add something to it, no doubt. They have an extensive collection of Civil War medals and some kind of database. . . . I'm a field guy. Don't know too much about it. But I think this is a gem. A real gem."

Beatrice grinned. In her eighty-three years of living, she'd never been so awestruck. The fact that a Civil War soldier might have been buried in her backyard or lived in the house, here on this property, spun around in her mind. She hadn't felt this excited about anything since she learned about quantum physics and then with Cookie and all her machinations about time travel—or not. She thought about that conversation nearly every day.

"We'll get back to you, Mrs. Matthews," the man said and gently placed the medal back into the box. "Hopefully, we'll see you tomorrow. Sam said there was a bigger box down there. You may have a real treasure here."

"Don't you mean the state of Virginia?" she said.

"Well," he said, "yes, I guess I do, since you've been so gracious. And in the meantime, the medals are in safe hands, I'm sure."

"It's amazing," Jon said after the man left. "First an earthquake, then the medal business. Quite a day."

"Yep, I'm hungry. How about you?" Right now, Beatrice's stomach gnawed at her. She knew she had some corn bread and leftover beans in the fridge, which was one of her favorite lunches. She smacked her lips. After lunch she'd check on Vera and then call Rose, her cousin who still lived on Jenkins Mountain. She was going to love the news. She read anything and everything she could get her hands on about the Civil War. She had actually been thinking of going on a vacation to tour the Civil War battlefields. But she'd have to leave the mountain. And she'd never been off of it.

Chapter 17

Vera had just finished making all the phone calls. She had switched her Thursday night dance class to Wednesday night, and thankfully, all the families could arrange their schedule to accommodate. Keeping the studio open on Thursday nights for one class just didn't make sense.

She turned to the computer and began working on her summer brochure. She would offer several workshops and camps, along with a six-week ballet refresher course.

She heard the bell on her studio door ring. Someone was coming into the studio. She turned to face Leola Reilly.

"Why, Leola, hello," Vera said, turning around in her chair.

"I thought this was your studio," Leola said, looking around. "Oh, look at that poster of Baryshnikov!" she exclaimed. She wore the same denim skirt she'd worn when Vera first met her. Very long, closer to the floor than her knee. There was something odd about it. It fit her snugly, so it was kind of sexy, and it even had a slit going up the center of the back. But yet Vera was certain it was meant to be conservative, because of the length and because of the flat shoes she wore.

"Hmm," Vera said. "Beautiful dancer. Can I help you with something?"

"I wondered if it was too late in the year to sign Elsie, my daughter, up for classes. I know she couldn't be in the recital. It's too late for that. But she'd like to stay in shape, you know, kind of audit some classes." Her well-shaped and plucked eyebrows were lifted in interest.

"Sure," Vera said. "I didn't know that she dances."

"Well . . ." She sat down across from Vera's desk. "She's a talented ballet student, but she sometimes lacks interest. More interested in boys, I'm afraid. At thirteen, she's all hormones."

"I see," said Vera, suddenly feeling a bit uncomfortable. Maybe it was nothing. Maybe mothers of thirteen-year-old girls discussed their daughter's hormones with acquaintances. "Well, as long as she wants to dance, she is welcome here."

Vera gathered a stack of paper together and looked down at it, hoping Leola would leave, but she sat there.

"I was hoping for a schedule," she said, tucking a strand of mousy brown hair behind her ear.

"Oh," Vera said. "Bring her by on Wednesday at seven thirty. I have a group of ballet students about her age at that time. Lovely group of girls."

Just then a hippie couple walked by the studio. Emily's parents. Vera's heart sank. What could she say to them? Anything? It looked like they were heading to the bakery.

She glanced back at Leola, who had also been looking at them.

"So, I hope you don't mind my asking," Leola began as her face softened. "What exactly happened between you and Emily?"

Vera jumped back in her chair. She hardly knew this

woman, and she asked such personal questions. What was her problem?

Her rose-painted lips were smiling, but her eyes seemed cold.

"It was nothing personal," Vera stammered. "I mean, I hardly knew the woman."

"Funny." Leola sat up in her chair. "Rumor has it that you killed her."

Vera's face flushed with embarrassment. She was certain steam would come pouring out of her ears at any minute. Whereas now Leola's face was cold as stone.

"What?" she said, clutching her chest. She felt like she couldn't quite catch her breath.

"You heard me," Leola said.

"I'm sorry, Leola," Vera said, gathering herself. "I don't listen to ugly rumors, and if you are going to get along in Cumberland Creek, you shouldn't, either."

"That's not a typical small town rumor," she said, smirking. Her hands were folded neatly in her lap. Perfectly manicured, with her nail polish matching her lipstick.

"No," Vera managed to say. "People who know me would never say such a thing."

"I don't know you very well, Vera, but I'm an attorney and I'm thinking you might need representation," Leola said.

Oh, so that was it. She was trying to drum up business.

"Well, thanks," Vera said, smiling, relieved. "I have a lawyer. You met Bill?"

"Your ex-husband? Bless his heart," she said with her lilting Carolina accent. "If it comes to pass that they file murder charges, I wouldn't think an ex-husband lawyer would be the way to go. Especially not that one."

Vera knew what that "Bless his heart" really meant, as only a Southerner would. This woman had Bill pegged. He wasn't the brightest bulb in the pack. Right now he was more concerned with his penis than anything else. Honestly, it was hard to believe her ex-husband, the father of her child, was living with a twenty-four-year-old woman.

"What makes you think they'd charge me?" Vera asked.

"Look, I know the pressure on these small towns when there's a murder like this. The DA will want answers. The cops will have to give them something," she said. "You don't want that to be you."

"But I didn't kill her. I didn't like the woman, but I wouldn't kill anybody."

"Do you know how many innocent men and women go to prison every year?" Leola asked.

"Well, I—" Vera started to say, and then she immediately thought of Cookie, innocent, yet kept in jail for weeks, which was something Vera had never understood.

"I'm just saying if you need help, call me. Don't call Bill Ledford, for God's sake," she said, with a knowing look in her eye.

"I don't understand why these rumors are flying. I've never done anything wrong in my life. Okay, everybody knew I didn't like Emily, but I had my reasons. She pushed me," Vera said.

"She pushed everybody," Leola said when the ringing of the studio phone interrupted.

"Excuse me. I really have to get this," Vera said. When the call was over, she intended to turn back around to ask Leola what she meant by that. Just exactly how well did she and her husband know Emily McGlashen?

Chapter 18

When Annie walked into DeeAnn's Bakery, the scent of cinnamon nearly made her swoon. She looked around and saw the Greenbergs sitting in the corner. She waved to them and ordered a coffee and a scone.

They looked incongruous in their dark hippie clothes in DeeAnn's chic, bright pink–walled bakery. It wasn't just their barely clean clothes. It was also their somber appearance. She was beautiful, with deep brown eyes setting off the longest eyelashes Annie had ever seen. A strong jawline and nose. She recognized the look because she'd seen it on many of her Jewish friends and relatives. Her father, even darker complexioned, smiled at Annie, but it looked as if he didn't smile much.

"Hello," Annie said, shaking his hand, then her hand. They exchanged greetings.

"I'm sorry for your loss," Annie said after she sat down.

Emily's mother, Rachel, looked down at her fingers. A tear fell onto her hands. She fussed with the beads that fell carelessly onto her chest.

Good Lord, the woman is not wearing a bra.

"My wife, she's not taking this well."

"Of course not," Annie said. "I'm not sure any mother could."

The woman glanced up and smiled a bit. "Thank you." She looked frail and haunted. A walking ghost.

"The thing about Emily is that she was new in town and a bit of a mystery to us."

"You are working with the cops." He said the word *cops* as if it were the nastiest word he's ever spoken.

"Sort of," Annie said. "I'm a journalist, and I'm helping with the research."

"What research?" he asked. "She was killed. And we need to find her killer. What is there to research?"

"I'm working on a book right now about a local group, a cult, that may have some involvement in your daughter's death."

"What? Why Emily?" Rachel said after a few moments of consideration.

"Well, she had these tattoos that were runes. This group has used runes in the past. Did you know anything about her tattoos?"

He shrugged, and she nodded in the negative.

"Look, the police haven't ruled out the connection, but I don't think that's the case. But nobody here knew much about her, including me. While you're here, you should co-operate with the police," Annie said. "They are trying to find Emily's killer. I'm sure you want that, as well."

Donald Greenberg clicked his tongue on his teeth. "Not Bryant."

"Would you speak with him if I were there?" she asked.

"Maybe. If he maintains a sense of respect. This is our daughter," he said. "She is not a thing. They've done an autopsy, which we didn't approve. Her body is . . . Well, we hardly recognize her."

"I'm sorry about that," Annie said. "It took a while for us to find any family at all."

"I see."

"She was an enigma. On the one hand, she was very public with her life, with the Irish dancing and her history interests. On the other hand, nobody knew much about her. We didn't know what to do. It's almost as if she was trying to throw people off or something. Some documents said she was from Ireland. Others, from California. One said she was from New York. And, of course, you have different names."

Her father bristled. "This is so typical of her. She had this real thing about being Irish. At first, I thought it was because of the dancing. But it became like an obsession with her. But she's an American through and through."

"When she found out she was adopted, she rejected our heritage and changed her last name. It's not like we're practicing Jews, but it still hurt," Rachel said. "She never seemed to get over it. She was loved. Not just by us, but by everybody where we live. Love is love and has nothing to do with blood. But she left us, anyway."

Annie was startled. Was it that easy to walk away from a part of your heritage? Erase a part of your past? Ignore it and it will go away?

"Did she have ties to anybody in Ireland? I mean, the name . . ."

"I don't think she's related to anybody in Ireland," her father said. "She was adopted in California, where we used to live. The agency said her parents lived in the area."

"I've often wondered why she came here, to Cumberland Creek, of all places," Annie said. "It's a small town surrounded by mountains. It seems she was worldly. Why here?"

The Greenbergs looked at one another.

"She traced her lineage back to Cumberland Creek. The

McGlashens have been in California for generations. But she said the first that came here settled in this valley a long time ago," he told her. "It was important to her, and we tried to support it. But, man, I never could wrap my head around that."

Annie, a little distracted by his dreadlocks, wondered when his hair had been washed last.

Focus, Annie.

"From what I hear," Annie said, "the McGlashens who founded this area had very few descendants. Or so the story goes. It's interesting that she claimed heritage here."

"She hired someone to help with the tracing. A scholar. What was his name?" he asked his wife.

"Luther Vandergrift." She spoke succinctly, and Annie felt her throat clutch. That just might be the link she needed.

Chapter 19

"So with the earthquake and everything, they stopped digging," Vera said after swallowing a bite of strawberry pie. "Oh my God, Annie, you've outdone yourself with this pie."

"I just am so inspired by the strawberries around here. I try to get some from the Mennonite Farmer's Market every week. The boys love them, too," Annie said, beaming.

"Who was it that said strawberries are the fruit of the Goddess?" DeeAnn said as she stretched over her scrapbook.

"It was, um, you-know-who," Sheila said after a few moments.

"She who shall remain unnamed," Vera said jokingly.

Annie glared at her, then softened as Vera began cooing over the pie. "Look," Annie said, "I know she was a part of this group, that we all miss her."

The room filled with silence. The cutting of the paper, the click of Sheila's laptop, the sound of Sheila's printer going off, it all stopped as the women looked at Annie.

She was different from them, but they all cared about her. The only other scrapper at the table who wasn't from Cumberland Creek was DeeAnn, who had lived there for thirty years and in some circles was still considered an outsider. But not in this one.

Vera knew that Annie felt out of place, still. She wondered if she would ever feel completely at home here, though she tried. She also knew that she and Cookie were close. It hurt her more than any of the others when Cookie disappeared. Vera's mind sifted through the changes since then. The most glaring one was the lack of Cookie at their crop; the other one was that Annie and Detective Bryant had gotten closer. It was as if something had happened during that case that brought them together. Vera couldn't imagine the specifics. But that friendship skirted along some dangerous turf. That she knew.

Annie went on.

"I miss her, too," she said. "But the fact is, she escaped from jail and disappeared into thin air. She never reached out to one of us. Before that, we welcomed her into our lives, into our hearts. She used us."

"For what?" Vera said. "It's not like she took our money or set us up for murder or—"

"I really think that she didn't mean for any of it to happen," Paige interrupted. "I think it was all a mistake."

"What do you mean?" Vera said.

"Well, she shouldn't have been in jail in the first place," Paige said. "That was mistake number one."

"Well, the real killer is there now," DeeAnn said and sighed. "I'm grateful for it."

"But then . . . I don't know." Paige twisted a blond strand of her hair and looked off, as if she hadn't heard DeeAnn at all. "She was always a bit off. It was almost like she never belonged here."

"Yes!" Sheila said. "That's exactly how I feel when I think about her."

"You are wrong," Annie said. "She was here for a reason.

She was supposed to be here. I'm certain of it." Annie started to pack her things up. "I promised Mike I'd be home early tonight. So, I'm on my way."

Annie had just purchased a new case for her scrapbooking materials. It was a big black bag on wheels. The inside of it offered special slots and pockets specially designed for scrapbooking ephemera, like pens, stickers, paper, adhesives, ribbons, buttons, and other embellishments. Annie fit at least two scrapbooks in the bag. It appeared to be so easy to stay on top of what she was working on: she just slipped her things in the bag, zipped it up, and rolled away with it. Vera needed to get one of those bags—so sleek and contemporary, compared to her bulky bag.

"Oh, before I go . . ." She turned before heading out the door. "I found out from Emily's parents that she was using a researcher who helped trace her roots to Cumberland Creek. It turns out that Luther Vandergrift was freelancing as a genealogist."

"What?" Sheila cried. "You've got to be kidding me."

"So how well did Emily know Luther?" Paige asked, setting down her glass of wine.

"Well, that's what I'm trying to find out. I'm going to see him on Monday. I mean, she definitely hired him, but I don't know that they had much to do with one another once she moved here," Annie told them.

"You're going to see him?" Vera said, aghast. "I can't believe you'd want to be in the same room with him."

"I won't be. He'll be behind glass," Annie said and smiled. "And it's as safe as it could be. After all, he's in jail still."

"But still," Vera said, her stomach twisting. "I don't know how you do it. How you face a man like that."

The others nodded in agreement as they each tended to their own projects in front of them.

"I'd be more worried about who murdered Emily. They are still at large, and the evidence is scant," Annie said and turned to leave.

"Honestly," Sheila said, looking up from her screen, "you don't have to remind us of that. Be careful walking home, Annie."

Vera shuddered. As far as she knew, she was still the only person of interest in the murder case. It felt unreal to her that she would even be suspected of such a hideous crime. *This is how Cookie must have felt.* It was probably worse for her because they actually held her in jail for several days.

After Annie left, Vera looked around the table. It felt empty without her. No, the crop wouldn't be the same without Annie. She'd been in Cumberland Creek three years now, a cropper for two.

But then again, it still felt empty without Cookie, as well. And she'd been with them a little less than a year.

Shortly after Cookie left, Emily had shown up in town. Vera's studio had been starting to show signs of the bad economy—but she at least had been making a profit. But between her ex-husband's shenanigans and Emily's business practices, she no longer made a profit and now was just able to pay the bills. More than anything, it saddened her that her students and their families could be so easily fooled by Emily and her propaganda. Ballet was the foundation of all dance. And more than that, well, hadn't she given these families all that she had for the best years of her life?

Vera decided to think about something else.

She picked up the photo of the young dancer she was making a scrapbook for, and she was lovely. She would be graduating from high school and going to college to study medicine. Vera was so proud of her. She cut the photo in an oval shape and placed it on the page, which had tiny little glittering stars all over it. The photo needed a mat. Hmm. Which one should she use? If she used the blue one, it would pull out the blue of her eyes. If she used the yellow one, it would bring out the yellow flowers on the dress. Decisions, decisions.

Chapter 20

It tugged at Beatrice, this knowing more historical goodies existed in her backyard and it would probably be another week or so before the dig would commence. First the earthquake, then meetings in Richmond. So she decided to get down in the trenches and dig around a bit. After all, it was her backyard. If there were valuable objects of history, she'd happily turn them over to the state. She didn't feel the need to own any of it, but she did feel the hunger for knowledge.

"What are you doing down there?" Jon hissed out the upstairs bathroom window. He'd been taking his morning constitutional, and Beatrice knew if she was going to get into the ditch, she'd have to do it when he was otherwise occupied. Men!

She shrugged. "What does it look like?" She held up her shovel.

"Bea!" he said, leaving the window.

She couldn't help but smile. She certainly was in good enough shape to be trudging round in a hole in her backyard, but at one point in her life, she'd have made an issue out of his concern. Now she was just glad he cared about her, glad to have someone in her life, old fool that she was.

She thrust her shovel in the earth next to the spot where the archeologist had told her there was a bigger box. She felt it with the edge of her shovel. She ran it along the box, which was about two feet wide. Who knew how deep it was?

She lifted small patches of earth from on top of the box. The scent of the ground filled her and moved her, as it always did. She loved the red Virginia earth, the way it smelled, the color of it, the feel of it between her fingers, beneath her feet. By the time Jon got to her, she had shoveled the dirt off the trunk, which was, most assuredly, what it had been and maybe still was.

"Fascinating," Jon said. "Now, let me help you up out of there."

"Wait a minute," she said. "I'd like to at least try to lift the lid, if not get the whole box out of here."

Jon made a ticking noise with his tongue, looked around, and said, "Beatrice, let me see if I can find something." He walked off to the side of the house.

He was as intrigued as she was. Once again, Beatrice found herself smiling.

"Hurry up, would you?" Beatrice called after him.

She crouched over and brushed more dirt off it. She drew in a breath. Amazing. This trunk had probably been here a hundred years or so. What kind of wood was it? Maybe chestnut, which she knew to be one of the strongest, most water-resistant woods. How did it last so long unprotected in the ground?

Jon came barreling around the corner, his dark eyes lit with excitement. "I found something," he said and held up a crowbar.

He stepped down the stepladder into the deep ditch, grunting, his hair blowing a bit in the breeze.

He stuck the crowbar down along the edge of the trunk.

"Ah-ha," he said. "There is the groove I need." He pushed down on it, and the lid came off.

Beatrice leaned farther down and lifted the lid gingerly off to the side and gasped, turning away. Hair, tiny limbs, clothing . . .

"It's a doll!" Jon said, reaching for her.

"Oh!" she said and laughed. "Thank God. I thought it was a child."

She looked closer at it. A doll, all right, and very old, she reckoned. The face was barely there, embedded in a mass of hair and clothing. Maybe its arm was detached.

She reached in and touched it. Damp cloth. Soft hair. Porcelain cool face.

Moved by the innocence of the doll, and that of the girl who had once played with her, Beatrice swore she could almost hear a child's laughter, singing, see a child dressing the doll as she hummed some favorite song.

She ran her hands along the side of the doll and found something sticking out from under her. In fact, there was a good bit of stuff under her, in the deep chest.

"Oh!" Beatrice exclaimed as she lifted a musty book from underneath the doll.

Jon whistled. "A book? A diary?"

"Mama!" Vera's voice rang through the house.

"Oh, bother!" Beatrice said, shoving the book into her jacket pocket as Jon placed the cover back on the trunk.

"Mama?"

"After you," Jon said, waving for Beatrice to go up the ladder first. She did so and hurried through the back door of her screened-in porch.

"There you are!" Vera said as she entered the room. "Mama, you're filthy!"

"Oh," Beatrice said. "Yes, I was just outside, puttering around."

"Oh," Vera said.

"Where's Lizzie?"

"With Bill. He was a little miffed about my having her late to him the other day because of my sleepwalking, so I let him have her a little longer. He's dropping her off here," she responded. "Got any coffee?"

"Yeah, sure. Just made a pot," Beatrice said. "Help yourself." She followed Vera into the kitchen, itching to get her out of the house so that she could look through the book in her pocket. She had no idea what kind of book she'd found. All she knew was that she wanted to look it over in private.

Chapter 21

Annie headed down the stairs to the new visitor room at the jail. It used to be that she sat in the same room with the prisoners, but not anymore. She figured that Cookie's escape had shamed the police force into getting with the twenty-first century and placing a glass barrier in the room, among other things.

Luther was already sitting behind the glass when she entered.

"Luther," she said, making eye contact, then reaching into her bag for her recorder.

"Annie," he said, looking more clear-eyed and alert than the last time she'd seen him. Medication?

"How are you?" she said and clicked on her recorder.

"Fine," he said, then lowered his eyes. "Well, as fine as I can be in jail."

She took a deep breath. *Don't feel sorry for this man. He carved runic patterns into the bodies of young women after they were killed.*

"How can I help you?" he said and smiled. Charm oozed from him now.

"I'm investigating the murder of Emily McGlashen," she said.

He nodded. "Yeah, I read about that. Too bad."

"I spoke with her parents a few days ago, and they mentioned that Emily knew you."

He cackled. "Yeah, but I've been in here. I don't know anything about who killed her."

"I didn't say you did," she snapped at him, with her eyebrow lifted.

He jumped back, startled. "Well . . ."

"I'm trying to find out more about her. That's all."

"And?"

"Exactly how did you know her?"

"She hired me. I do research on the side sometimes. She contacted me a couple of years ago, when I still lived in Pittsburgh. Told her I really couldn't help her then, but that I was thinking of moving here." He stopped. "And might be able to track some stuff down for her."

"And did you?"

He grinned. "Of course I did. I was only too happy to make money for the NMO. Or what I thought the NMO was. At the time."

Annie knew the "story" of how he had a nervous breakdown in Pittsburgh after his family died. How Zeb and the NMO reached out to the brilliant young scientist. How he claimed he was in too deep before he knew what was really happening. And before he knew it, he was a slave to meth and would do anything for Zeb just to have it.

Annie wasn't buying his story, at least not completely. She was no scientist, but she was a writer and knew a walking cliché when she saw one.

"So what did you learn about her?"

"I was able to trace her lineage back to the much-vaunted McGlashen family. She seemed pleased and then began writing to me about feeling the call to come home to

Virginia," he said and smiled. "Very romantic, don't you think?"

Annie couldn't help but smirk. "Misguided, to say the least."

"Humph," he grunted.

She took a good look at him. Blond. Blue-eyed. Not wearing his earrings anymore. The first time she saw him, he had a rune in his ear. She sat back in her chair. His skin and eyes were much clearer, and it looked like he'd gained weight. No drugs. Jail was good for some people, especially addicts who couldn't get ahold of their drug. He looked like a shining example of a healthy male.

"There was also this about her," he said, leaning toward the glass. "She was really smart. I was surprised, you know, little Miss Irish Dancer. I thought she'd be a bit vacuous or something, but she wasn't. She was well read. And she was one of the few people I know that picked up languages very quickly. She spoke like . . . I don't know . . . seven. Let's see. Spanish, French, Greek, Italian . . . hmmm, yes, and she even knew a bit about runes."

"Really?" Annie tried not to appear too interested.

"Yes. She fell in love with the designs, you know, the looks of them. She was thinking about getting a tattoo. I don't know if that ever happened," he told her.

One mystery solved, Annie thought. She may have had nothing to do with the NMO, other than she hired one of its leaders to do research. But then again, Luther could be lying about the whole rune thing.

"Yeah, now that I think about it, Emily said she knew Russian, Arabic, and Hebrew." He emphasized Hebrew.

Annie looked him straight in the eye. "Hebrew?"

"Yes, you know, she grew up in Israel," he said and smirked.

Annie smiled.

"What?" Luther asked.

"Nothing," she said with an even voice, belying her inner turmoil. "She didn't grow up in Israel. I just spoke with her parents."

"What? Her hippie-dippy parents are here? She told me all about them." He sat back and laughed. "Well, well, well . . . I'm just trying to imagine them walking down the streets of Cumberland Creek in commune clothing."

Annie grimaced. "There's nothing funny about that, Luther."

She stood to go, began gathering her things.

"Wait. Why are you going?" he said.

For a moment, Annie could see a different guy sitting there. Was it the way the light played off his skin? He looked younger, more innocent, even though she knew exactly that he was a neo-Nazi who soon enough would be out of jail, wreaking havoc.

"I don't want you to go," he said. "C'mon."

"Let's get one thing straight, Luther," Annie said as she flung her bag over her shoulder. "I really don't care what you want. I just came here to question you about Emily to help solve her murder for her family. So they can have a sense of peace, of closure."

She turned to go.

"You're looking in the wrong places, Annie. Word on the street is that your friend Vera went a little crazy and offed her," he said.

She spun back about and glared at him. "You shouldn't believe everything you hear, Luther."

He looked her straight in the eye and frowned.

Something about the look in his eye unsettled Annie. It went back to the first day she met him, when they were stranded along the road to Jenkins Mountain. Even though he was definitely clean now, he flustered her. She took a deep breath as she closed the door behind her. His trial was next week. He was pleading temporary insanity because of his drug-induced state and the fact that he was addicted at the time.

Annie swallowed hard as she made her way out of the jail, certain Luther Vandergrift would be a free man way too soon.

Chapter 22

After a particularly grueling session with her new therapist, Dr. Long, Vera stopped at Pamela's Pie Palace to treat herself to a slice of chocolate pie. She always felt a twinge of guilt coming here, rather than going to DeeAnn's Bakery. But sometimes only pie would do, and DeeAnn made and sold mostly bread, muffins, and pastries.

She loved the atmosphere of the Pie Palace: black-and-white tile floors, red vinyl booth seats, and jukeboxes on the tables. The waitresses were all dressed in cute little black dresses with white ruffled aprons, darling little hats on their heads. She just loved the theatricality of it, but even better than that, the pie was divine. Even Beatrice, not easily impressed with anybody else's pie, was entranced by the quality of the pie.

Vera slurped her coffee while waiting on her chocolate coconut pie, then smiled at the waitress who brought it over to her. She would not look her in her eye. *She must be shy,* Vera thought.

"Thanks," she said.

The waitress nodded, gave a quick smile, and walked away.

Vera took a bite of her pie and nearly swooned over the

deep, rich chocolate set off by graham cracker crust, with a fine layer of coconut in between. A mile-high meringue topped it.

With the next bite, an image of her therapist invaded her thoughts. He was kind of boring and vanilla, she decided. And he wasn't helping her at all. Every session it was the same questions.

"How is the medicine working?"

"Fine."

"Have you had any indication of sleepwalking?"

"None."

"How are you feeling otherwise?"

"Just fine."

"Hmmm. How is business?"

"I'm hoping it will pick up."

"Do you like your new apartment?"

"It's fine."

"Have you had any strange dreams lately?"

"Not really."

"Any dreams at all?"

"Not that I remember."

"Hmm. Do you feel sad at all these days?"

"Sometimes," she would say and shrug.

Today she had told him something that would give him a little to chew on. "Sad? I don't feel sad . . . or anything. Why should I? I have a wonderful daughter, and we are both happy and healthy. I wish people would stop trying to project themselves and their sadness onto me."

"Well," he had said, "you seem to have everything in perspective. Have you given any thought to what's caused your sleepwalking incidents?"

"No. Have you?"

"I'd like you to think about hypnosis," he said.

That came from out of nowhere, she thought as she savored another bite of chocolate pie. Hypnosis, indeed.

"For what?"

"I think you are sadder than what you let on. Sometimes we can't look at our sadness. When we continue to push it inside, it has to come out other ways."

"But I'm not sad. I just told you."

"Can we give the hypnosis a try? At least think about it?"

She shrugged. "I guess so."

"I mean, a woman doesn't lose her marriage and almost lose her business, isn't questioned for murder without there being a little sadness, right? So, let's start to prepare for hypnosis."

"Whatever you say," she said.

But it irked her. Of course she was a bit sad from time to time and more than a bit angry at the way her life had recently shifted. But she was not one to dwell. What good would it do her to sit around and cry over her asshole ex-husband sleeping with a twenty-four-year-old woman on a nightly basis now? Or over the fact that her business was faltering?

She suddenly wondered if that was what people expected of her. And why she sometimes caught them looking at her like she had just landed there from Mars.

"That's her," she could swear she heard someone say.

"Are you sure?" another voice said in a hushed tone.

She turned around to see who they were talking about. The two women looked away. A little girl just then hopped up to her table.

"Miss Vera!" she said.

"Well, hi there, Kelly," she said, placing her fork down. "How are you?"

"Mama's paying for our pie," she said. "I'm good. I sure do miss you."

"Come back and dance with me anytime," Vera said.

"Mama says no. Says she won't have her money supporting a killer," Kelly said.

Just then, her mother came to the table and grabbed Kelly. "Let's go," she said.

"Nice to see you, Jane," Vera managed to say. She felt as if her heart was going to pound right out of her chest. Sweat beads formed on her forehead. Several customers were looking her way. A group of people shuffled by her and exited. One turned and looked at her out of the corner of her eye. No, Vera wasn't imagining that.

Vera lowered her eyes, looked at the remaining chunks of pie, and felt her stomach turn. She took some deep breaths, but it was pointless. The pie, which had once looked joyful, comforting, and delicious, now looked and tasted bitter.

Chapter 23

By Wednesday, the Department of Historic Resources had not gotten back to Beatrice. She was annoyed. She had a huge hole covered by an orange tarp in her backyard, and nobody was doing a thing about it. All she wanted was a pool for her and her family to enjoy over the summer. She sighed.

"Have you looked at the book yet?" Jon said as he walked into the kitchen with a bag of groceries and began to put them away.

"Oh, no," she said. "I promised we'd look at it together."

It sat on the kitchen table, mocking Beatrice the entire time that Jon was at the store.

He pulled up a chair and sat close to her.

"Jesus, Jon," she said, placing her elbows on the table. "Give me some room, would you?"

"Oh, sorry," he said and frowned. "Just get to it, woman." He raised an eyebrow.

She opened the tattered cover of the book. Its mildew scent made her nose burn. She could barely make out the writing on the page. "My Memory Book, 1871," was written in a beautiful, flourishing handwriting so faintly, but still there.

Light came through her lace curtain in patterned streams. A few dust particles flew around, but a hush came over the room. Beatrice clasped her hands, as if praying, and brought them to her lips. She almost didn't want to breathe. She wanted to savor each bit of this moment.

"Just lovely," Jon said in a whisper.

But there was no name there.

She carefully turned the next page. There, in the same script, was a name: Willa Rose McGlashen.

Beatrice gasped.

"What? What is it?" Jon asked.

"The McGlashens were one of the founding families of Cumberland Creek," she managed to say. "But we've never been able to prove that the McGlashen line had any progeny that carried the name. Looks like Emily may have been right. She may have come from our McGlashens."

"This is eighteen seventy-one, just after the Civil War. Maybe there are records," Jon said.

"Yes! Maybe those medals will tell us something! Maybe there was a McGlashen in the Civil War!"

Beatrice sat back a bit in her chair, mulling over the possibilities. A McGlashen connection in her backyard? The historical society had never been able to figure out where the old McGlashen place existed. Maybe her house had been built on top of it. Maybe the old foundation in her backyard was the old McGlashen place.

Jon touched her hand gently, as if to awaken her from her revelry. "Do go on, Bea. Turn the page."

The next page was translucent rice paper, but a face stared back at them through the paper. The paper swooshed quietly as she turned it. The next page held a photo of a beautiful young woman.

"Is this her? Is this Willa?" Jon wondered aloud.

"I don't know. . . . Could be her mother, sister, aunt. . . . Maybe it says something on the back."

"Initials WRM. Hmm. It would appear that this is Willa," he said, running his finger along the edge of the thick picture. "It's almost like a postcard, eh?"

"Yes, that's exactly what a lot of older photos are," she explained. "People would send them through the mail."

The woman looked to be in her late twenties. Since the photo was sepia toned, it was difficult to ascertain exactly the color of her hair, but it was dark and was pulled back into a severe bun, with a few escaping wispy curls on either side of her face. Her eyes were light and heavy lidded, as if she was tired or sad. Hers was a heart-shaped face, with high cheekbones and a high forehead. A slice of a shadow fell along her cheekbone line. Beatrice couldn't tell if it was rouge or just the lighting. Something about her gave Beatrice pause. She looked utterly . . . familiar. As if she'd just seen her yesterday. Now, who did this woman look like?

Her thick lips were almost in a frown, but not quite. Folks didn't really smile for photos then. And really, what was there to smile about? The years of the Civil War and just after were hard on the whole country. Especially the South. Even though the Shenandoah Valley was spared compared to Richmond and farther south, they'd certainly seen their share of destruction and death.

The woman's dress was plain and dark, just what you'd expect, with a bit of a poof or a hoop, not a huge one like that of the Southern belle of popular media. Full sleeves were gathered at her wrists, where a shiny fabric looked almost jewellike. One ribbon was tied at the neck.

Yes, the Civil War had been harsh on the families in the valley, but this woman looked like she had fared well. But then again, she was a McGlashen, of sturdy Scotch-Irish frontier stock.

She stood on a patterned carpet, next to a velvet settee.

"I bet this is a formal photo," Beatrice said. "Like in a studio somewhere. But where?"

Jon shrugged. "There's no marking. She is very uncomfortable looking."

"What? What do you mean?"

"She looks unhappy. I don't know. The dress, maybe, looks uncomfortable for her."

"Yes, maybe you're right." She smiled. "But you know I don't think I've ever seen an old photo where anybody is smiling."

Just then, a knock sounded at her front door.

"Hello!"

Vera and Lizzie had arrived a little earlier than what they planned. Damn. Beatrice gathered the book, slid the photo back in it, and gingerly slipped it into a kitchen drawer. If Vera knew about it, she'd certainly make sure that Beatrice turned it over to the state immediately. Beatrice and Jon had talked about it and were not sure what they wanted to do with it. Although ultimately, they would probably donate it to the state, like the rest of the artifacts, for now it remained a delicious, mysterious secret that she and Jon shared.

Chapter 24

Another half day of school for the boys. Annie did not see the point in these half days of school. She waved to them as they rolled off in the school bus, and three hours later, she'd be back at the end of her driveway, waiting for the bus. She planned to proofread a section of what she had already written about the New Mountain Order. It would suffice for the day. Once the boys were home, all hell would break loose.

As she walked in the front door, her cell phone beeped.

"Hello," she said into it.

"Hey, Annie. It's Steve. How's it going?" said her newspaper editor.

"Fine. What's up?"

"I'm really curious about this Irish dancer that was killed."

"Me too," she said.

"Can you dig around and find out more about her? I mean, here she was, this famous Irish dancer, right? In Cumberland Creek. Gets herself killed . . . In the meantime, we find out she had this strange tattoo. Are you sure there's no link to the NMO?"

Annie hesitated.

"I mean, it seems sort of clear-cut."

"Too clear-cut, Steve. The murder didn't have any of the hallmarks of an NMO murder. Plus, several of its members are in jail, awaiting their trial."

"It's just too weird. All the way around."

"Yes, I've had similar thoughts. When I questioned Luther Vandergrift about Emily, he knew about her."

"There has to be a link," he said and coughed.

"My gut tells me no," she said after a moment.

"Hmmm. I know all about you and your instincts, but could you be in denial?"

"About what?"

"You're Jewish, Annie. I'm sure you don't want to believe in the possibility of another hate crime."

"Wait a minute. As far as I know, there have not been any hate crimes in this area. Sure, some vandalism and some threats. But none of the murders in recent years were hate crime related."

"So, how do we know this one is not? I'd really like a little more information about this woman."

"I'm a little uncomfortable with this. I'm the only Jewish woman in town. My kids have been picked on at school. I'm writing a book on the New Mountain Order. I've got conflicts of interest everywhere."

"Okay, Annie. Say the word and I will put someone else on it."

Her stomach sank. She and Mike could certainly use the money. They had just replaced the furnace in their 1958-built house, which placed them further into debt. Maybe it wouldn't hurt to write one more story, or series, about Emily McGlashen.

But then Mike might not be thrilled about it. He liked the money, but not the time she needed to spend away from him and the boys. Maybe she should talk to him first.

"Can I think about it?"

"Okay. I'm giving you a few days to think about it. If I don't hear from you, I'll give the story to someone else," he said.

After she hung up the phone, Annie started cleaning up after breakfast. When the last dish was rinsed and placed in her dishwasher, she stood and looked around her pink kitchen. Very vintage. She loved every piece of it. It was so different from the kitchen she and Mike had when the lived in Bethesda, which was sleek and modern. She leaned up against the counter, and it creaked. She didn't miss that kitchen. In fact, the only thing she missed was her closet where she kept all her shoes.

Annie's cell phone blared.

"Annie? It's Adam."

"Yes?"

"The Greenbergs are trying to reach you. They couldn't find your number."

"Where are they?"

"At Emily's apartment. Do you have that number?"

"Yeah, yeah, sure. They gave it to me," she said. "It's odd they would contact me. I wonder what they want."

"I wondered the same thing," he said. "But they sounded upset."

"Upset? Maybe I should just go over there. . . ."

After she was buzzed in by the Greenberg family, Annie hit the elevator button. Sixth floor. She made her way to the right door and rang the bell. A weary-looking Donald Greenberg answered and led her into the living room. He was wearing a long white cotton shirt with flowers embroidered around the collar.

The place was a mess, with boxes and trash bags scattered everywhere. It reeked of pot.

"Can we get you some herb tea, coffee, anything?" he said with a tired smile.

"No, thank you," she said, smiling.

"Please sit down," Rachel Greenberg told her. She patted the couch space next to her, so Annie sat down beside her. The woman had been crying. Her eyes were red and swollen. Or maybe she was stoned?

Rachel still didn't have a bra on, and her shirt was revealing. Annie didn't go around checking out other women's breasts, but the woman was big breasted. It was hard not to stare.

"What's wrong?" Annie asked in a hushed tone. They had lost their daughter. What else could set them off like his?

"My daughter and I . . . Well . . . sometimes I think I wasn't a good mother to her—"

"Rachel—" Donald began.

"No, no, no." Rachel placed her hand up. "But then I look into my heart, and I know I've done my best to teach her right from wrong. Sometimes your best isn't good enough. People make mistakes."

Annie tilted her head and leaned in toward her.

Donald held a journal. Was that Emily's journal? Why hadn't Bryant confiscated it?

"We just now found this. You can take it to the cops, if you want," Donald said, as if her were reading her mind. Odd.

"Usually, we would keep this in our family. We're ashamed. But we'd like to find some justice in our daughter's death." Rachel paused and took a deep breath. "Emily was having an affair."

"I had no idea. I never saw her with anybody," Annie said, almost to herself.

"There's a reason for that," Donald said, sitting down on the arm of the couch, surrounded by filled boxes and trash bags from cleaning his dead daughter's apartment. "She was seeing a married man."

Chapter 25

"So," Vera said after swallowing a chocolate-covered pretzel. "Once again, we have a married man cheating on his wife. I see a pattern here. Are any of them true to their wives?"

"Mine better be," DeeAnn said, holding up her scissors. "Or snip, snip, snip."

After the giggles died down, Annie cleared her throat. "But seriously," she said. "Had any of you ever seen her with a man?"

"I tried not to pay attention to her," Sheila said after a moment. "I really didn't like her. But I can't remember ever seeing her with anybody but dancers and other women," she added and then paused. "I'm printing off these fabulous borders. This is one of the great things about hybrid scrapping. These borders are free. I am printing them and am going to use them in a traditional scrapbook."

"It's kind of strange that she was unattached, come to think of it," Paige said after a moment. "Emily was young and pretty, in great shape, and didn't have a boyfriend. I guess I never gave it much thought."

"She wasn't easy to ignore," Vera said after cutting a photo into a heart shape, sitting back, and admiring her work. "Just perfect. Sometimes pictures just speak to you. This one needed to be a heart shape."

"I know exactly what you mean," Sheila said, reaching for the pretzels. "And other times you just don't know what to do with them."

"I find myself taking photos that I think will look good on a scrapbook page, you know?" Vera said and laughed. "Sometimes those are the best pictures, too."

"Here's something you can do with washi tape," DeeAnn said, holding up a photo that she had taped onto the page. The washi tape, which was acid free, came in many fun patterns and colors. This one was a black-and-white houndstooth pattern and framed the photo nicely against the red floral page, while at the same time providing an adhesive.

"Cool!" Sheila said. "Love washi!"

"So can't the police find out who she was seeing? Cell phone records? Computer records? That kind of thing?" Paige asked Annie after a beat.

"Yes," Annie responded. "It takes a lot longer to sort through all of that than what *CSI* shows on TV. Besides, the Cumberland Creek Police Department is seriously understaffed. The population has exploded, and the department hasn't yet caught up. They have some new people starting next week, I think. I'm going over on Monday to help, if I can."

"They are going to let you do that?" Vera said.

"Well, I'm covering the case, you know? And no, they usually don't let reporters do this kind of thing, but I think they really need the help."

"Oh, Annie, c'mon. You are kidding yourself," Vera blurted. "Bryant just wants to get you alone."

The room became silent. DeeAnn cleared her throat,

Sheila looked up from her laptop, and Paige looked down steadily at her scrapbook page.

"Maybe," Annie said, finally breaking the silence and the tension in the room. "But don't worry, Vera. I can handle him."

"I'd like to handle him," DeeAnn muttered. "What a hunk."

A few of the croppers laughed. But Annie didn't. Neither did Vera, who had strong feelings about spouses cheating on one another. Vera was just sick to death of it. The older she became, the more she saw and she hated it. And there was her own ex-husband, the father of her child, living with a twenty-four-year-old in Charlottesville, while she struggled to make ends meet. She found it true that some men just couldn't get their heads straight, simply thinking with their little one and not their big one.

She knew that Annie was attracted to Bryant and that she was struggling. What she needed to do was stop covering the case, back away from Bryant, and concentrate on her husband and family. She could see that so clearly, but Annie was her friend and she wanted to support her. And she was usually so smart. How could it be that she was confused about this? She wasn't sure what she should say or do to support Annie. Vera tried not to be too judgmental or harsh. But Vera saw things very simply: *If you are married, you are married. That is that. If you don't love your spouse anymore, get out of it. For God's sakes, don't drag another person into it before you are finished with your marriage.*

"Things are rarely as black and white as they seem," Annie muttered, then finished her beer.

"Sometimes they are exactly as they seem," Vera said, closing the scrapbook she was working on. "I'm exhausted. I need to collect my daughter and get home."

"Why isn't she staying with Bea?" Paige asked.

Vera shrugged. "She is getting funny about the bedtime thing and wanted to come home tonight. She said she wanted her own bed. So Mama is looking for one just like it to put in her room there. Until then . . ."

Vera was surprised to see Elizabeth wide wake. She'd hoped that her daughter's bedtime struggles would give way to sleepiness. No such luck. Lizzie talked all the way home in the car. The child was a fount of energy.

By the time she finally got Lizzie down, Vera was too exhausted to take a bath or to go downstairs and take one of her pills. She climbed into bed with her clothes on and slipped off her shoes. Ahh, bed.

She woke up what seemed like fifteen minutes later, her clothes clinging to her in the most uncomfortable manner. And so she peeled them off and reached for her nightgown at the bottom of the bed.

After what seemed like another fifteen minutes of sleep, Vera awoke. Lizzie cried. Vera lay there in the dark and listened. Was Lizzie crying, or was she dreaming? She rolled over as quietly as she could manage in the old creaky bed, which her mom had dug out of the attic for her.

Oh, she loved the quiet and the dark. The child didn't cry again, and she dozed off into a warm sleep.

Her feet were cold. The floor was drafty. A cry. A wail. "Mama!"

Suddenly, she was holding Elizabeth. How had she gotten there? Lizzie looked up at her with a red and contorted face wet with tears, as if she had been sobbing for quite some time. "Mama?"

Vera sat down in the rocking chair and wrapped her arms around Lizzie. "Shh, baby. It's okay. . . ."

But Vera wasn't sure that it was.

She glanced out the window, saw the shadows of the old fire escape there. She really wanted to have that thing removed. Why was the window open? Had she forgotten to close it? Or had she just opened it?

She peered out at the indigo blue sky; the full orange moon was still there. The wall glowed with the dusky blue light. The princess clock in the corner said it was 4:00 a.m.

How had she gotten into this room and not remembered it? How long had she been here? And what was going on with her daughter?

She brushed Lizzie's hair off her forehead. Lizzie was calmer now, and her sobs quieted, but the child burned with fever. She didn't look right, not at all, and Vera was certain it wasn't just because she had been crying.

Chapter 26

Beatrice and Jon had just finished an early breakfast and cleaned up. Oh, it was so easy and quick to clean the kitchen when there were two of you. Beatrice kissed Jon on the cheek.

He smiled. "What was that for?"

"I just love you," she said, feeling her old, somewhat bitter heart cracking open just a little more this morning. It was going to be a wonderful Sunday. She and Jon were going to look over the memory book this morning, and then she would get ready for a big Sunday dinner. The new couple in town was joining them again, and Beatrice planned to share her old music with the professor. Not too many people were around that appreciated it any more. A shock of excitement moved through her.

"Let's get the book out," Jon said, his dark eyebrows lifting and his hands rubbing together.

They had been entirely too busy to look over their treasured book. It was delicate and fragile, and they certainly didn't want Elizabeth to get ahold of it. And they weren't ready to share it with anybody yet.

Beatrice sat the book down gingerly on her dining room table. They used this room only on Sundays. Even though she had stopped going to church years ago, she still liked to maintain some of the Sunday traditions she held dear, like big Sunday dinners.

Jon wrinkled his nose as she cracked the book open to the picture. "Musty," he said. "Willa."

Beatrice smiled. Lawd, this man loved intrigue almost as much as she did. The old book looked splendidly shabby against her lacy red crocheted tablecloth. Oh, that Mrs. Lokomski was a talented woman with the crochet hook.

She turned the page to find what were probably pressed flowers, too crumpled and old for identification. The next page held nothing but a lock of the brightest red hair she'd ever seen, including her own from when she was a child. A weird sense of foreboding came over her: The last time she'd seen a clipping of red hair like this was in Cookie Crandall's scrapbook of shadows, as she called it. And the young women who were murdered last year each had beautiful red hair.

She had never understood the Victorian fascination with things like clipping hair and fingernails and saving them, for she was not much of a sentimental person. But this lock of hair sent senseless ripples of fear through her, but then a feeling of awe came over her, as well. This hair belonged either to Willa or to someone she loved. It was tied with a lacy ribbon. A girl. Sometimes the passage of time, or the acknowledgment of it, sent Beatrice's head spinning. Was it the old lady in her? Or the quantum physicist? She felt her eyes stinging.

Her moment was interrupted by a phone call. Jon jumped to answer it.

"Yes, I see," he said into the phone in a voice an octave higher than usual. His French accent was more pronounced, the way it was when he was upset. Beatrice turned to look at him. His face showed it. There was something wrong.

"Yes, yes, yes," he said. "We'll be there just as soon as we can." He hung up the phone, frowning.

"What is it?" she said, standing.

"Now, Bea, everything is okay. Vera rushed Elizabeth to the hospital earlier this morning. She is there now. She had a horrible fever and is with the doctors now," he said.

"Elizabeth? Fever? She was fine when she was here. What on earth?" Beatrice felt her heart race. As she shut the book in front of her, she said, "We better get dressed and go to the hospital. How is Vera?"

"She sounds exhausted," he said, already climbing the stairs.

"Of course," she said, almost to herself. "Of course, she's exhausted."

Beatrice and Jon dressed quickly and quietly in their own rooms.

"Did they say anything at all about what they think is wrong?" Beatrice asked him on the way to the hospital.

He shook his head. "Just that they are testing her."

"I'm trying to rack my brain and remember if she ate anything at our place or if she acted strangely at all," she said.

"Me, too, but I don't think so," Jon said, pulling into the parking lot at the hospital. "She was her normal vivacious self."

"Yes, you're right. And with children, things come over them quickly. She could have been exposed to something days ago. Who knows?" Beatrice said. "I'm sure Vera is trying to figure it all out, as well."

"And Elizabeth is in good hands," he said, shutting off the engine.

"Yes, of course, and Vera did the best thing bringing her here," Beatrice said, getting out of the car.

But with each step toward the hospital, Beatrice remembered losing Ed here. She hated the place, the memories, the loss. She gathered her strength. "Oh, God, Goddess, ruler of the universe, if there is anybody out there, please watch over our Lizzie," she whispered as she opened the door. Jon's arm went around her and squeezed her shoulder.

The first person Beatrice saw was Sheila in a mismatched sweat suit, looking very much as if she had just rolled out of bed. Paige was sitting in a chair with her legs crossed, knitting. She looked up at Beatrice and nodded.

"Where's Vera?" Beatrice asked.

"Behind you," came her daughter's voice. Beatrice turned, and Vera sank into her mother's arms. "Oh, Mama, I've never been so scared in all my life."

"There, there," Beatrice said to her armful of daughter, who was sobbing as if she were two years old. "Come on, now. Sit down."

Jon slipped onto the seat next to Paige. After Vera settled into a chair, Sheila handed her a coffee. "Can I get you some coffee, Bea?"

Beatrice shook her head. "No. I want to see Lizzie. What's going on? Where is she?"

"She's sleeping," Vera said. "Finally."

"Where's her father?"

"I've left messages on his cell and at his office," Vera said and shrugged.

Just then a ruckus erupted in the hall around the corner and a bedraggled Bill came bounding over to them.

"God, what has happened to Elizabeth?" he said, panting.

"She's sleeping now," Vera said.

"Where've you been, Bill?" Beatrice asked.

He flailed his arms around. "I just got the message. My cell was turned off."

"I'm so sorry, Bill. I just thought you needed some sleep," came a voice from behind him.

Vera stood up and looked around Bill's bulk.

Good God, Bill had brought his girlfriend with him. And as she stepped around Bill, Beatrice almost gasped. She looked like a child. She also looked almost exactly like their new neighbor, Leola. How odd.

Chapter 27

"Hey, what's going on?" Annie walked into the scene at the hospital. Vera was pale, standing with her arms crossed; Beatrice looked confused; Jon and Paige were in the corner, Paige engrossed in her knitting project; and Sheila had her finger in Bill's face.

"What's wrong with you, Bill Ledford?"

"What? Wait." said the young woman, butting in. "He does have a life."

"This is his child we're talking about, young lady. Bill is a father. I don't expect you to understand. What are you? Sixteen? When there is an emergency, Vera needs to reach him. You need to realize that Bill has responsibilities," Sheila spat.

The young woman rolled her eyes and crossed her arms. "Who is this witch, Bill?"

"Whoa!" Annie stepped into the circle. "Bill? You better take your friend somewhere where she can cool off." The next thing she knew, Jon was at the young woman's elbow.

"Let's you and I get a cup of coffee," he said.

"Wait, who are you?" she said as she was being dragged off.

That Jon, you couldn't help but like him.

Annie turned to face a fragile-looking and pale Vera, who sat in a slump next to Beatrice on a small couch.

"Why would he bring her here?" Vera said to Annie. Never mind that he was standing right next to her.

"That's my daughter in there," he said.

"Well, well, well," Beatrice said. "Maybe you should start acting like it. Get your house in order, Bill, or I'll see to it that you never see Lizzie again."

"Now, Mom—" Vera began.

"Listen," Beatrice said, "someone's got to say it. You're acting like an ass, Bill. You're living with a woman who's nothing more than a child, you rarely see your daughter, and you bring the woman you're living with to the hospital where your ex-wife and her family and friends are gathered? What is wrong with you?"

Annie wanted to shrink away into the corner. This was a moment that best happened behind closed doors, with just their family. She made eye contact with Paige and Sheila, who nodded. The three of them slipped off together into another lobby of the hospital.

"They think it's meningitis," Paige said after they were situated.

"Where would she have been exposed to that?" Annie wondered out loud.

"Who knows? As I tried to tell Vera, kids just get sick. I know. I've had four of them. Dusty had meningitis when he was fourteen and is fine, but for a three-year-old, it's scary," Sheila said.

"But they aren't sure?" Annie asked.

Sheila nodded. "No. Big ole fancy-ass hospital and they still aren't sure."

The three of them sat there, each in her own thoughts. Paige knit furiously. Sheila's foot shook impatiently. Annie noted the man passing by in a wheelchair, then a woman with a cane. A voice paging a doctor came over the intercom.

New modern art hung on the walls, which used to be filled with paintings of barns and flowers. Now Annie found the modern art a bit more comforting.

She had been in Cumberland Creek for only three years and in this hospital way too many times. When she was shot and stuck in the hospital, she suffered a real turning point. For a while, she mostly focused on her family and the book, and things were doing well. But now, once again, she found herself sucked into a murder investigation.

Strange that she had left D.C. for a simpler, more peaceful life. She sometimes marveled at its twists and turns, which always led her back to murder.

Later that day, after dinner, Annie left to go and help Bryant out at the station. She had told him she would, so she felt it was the right thing to do. When she showed up, the officer at the desk said he wasn't there.

"Where are you?" Annie said into her cell.

"I'm on my way. Make yourself comfortable in my office."

Several boxes were piled on Bryant's desk. Annie looked in one of them. It was stuff from Emily's apartment. She gathered that the laptop on the corner of his desk was Emily's. She pressed the space bar, and the screen popped up. Hmmm. Interesting. They'd been able to figure out the password for at least one of Emily's e-mail accounts. It looked like Bryant was systematically going through each one. Well, since she was here, she could continue to do that.

Should she?

Hmm. Of course she should.

She clicked on the first one. *Junk mail. Delete.*

But the next one was from a familiar name. Leo Shirley.

He was just plain bad news. He'd been a menace to the town since he was a kid. As an adult, he'd gotten away with everything as they were unable to make any charges stick. He was squirrelly. Always skirting the line between legal and illegal.

Em—
Please, please, please, let me explain. You know that I am married. I want to leave her, but I'm afraid she knows too much . . . and it would ruin me.

Wow, there it was. So Emily McGlashen had been seeing Leo Shirley? That blew her mind. Emily had seemed to have her act together. Why would she bother with the likes of Leo Shirley?

The office door flew open. He stood there, looking at Annie. His hands were on his hips, and he was frowning. For some reason, his shoulders looked particularly broad; and his pants, a little too tight. Annie almost blushed and looked away.

"So, did you see the e-mail?" he asked.

"The one from Leo? Yes," she said.

He came over and leaned over her.

God. She could smell him. What was worse, she could feel the heat just pulsing off of him. He was so close, so close to her.

"The bastard has an alibi," he said, reaching over and almost slamming the laptop lid down. "And he claims the e-mail was not about them seeing each other. Damn!" He was seething. "I thought this was it. And I thought we finally got Leo, ya know?"

Annie rose from the chair. "Oh, that's too bad," she said,

reaching for a box and then placing her hand on his shoulder. "We'll find out who killed her. Should I start here?"

His blue eyes met hers, and a bolt of something almost like electricity was exchanged between them. He moved toward her. Her hand found its place around his neck as he pushed her against the wall. He was lifting her off the floor with a brute strength, and her legs wrapped around him, as if she had no control over them. These legs, were they hers? This mouth, was it hers? His lips met hers again, and she found herself sliding into a deep, pulsing place, before she had the strength to pull away.

"Adam," she breathed. "Stop."

"Yeah," he said with a deep guttural tone. "Just one more kiss."

"No. This is . . . not right," she said, stepping away from him.

As she left the office, she dared not look back at him. Her legs were shaking, and she could barely move. But she just had to find the will to keep moving forward to her house, where her husband and children were.

Chapter 28

Vera was exhausted and hungry. Everything in the snack machines at the hospital looked too small. She could eat the ass end out of a bear right about now. She smiled to herself. She loved those old expressions from Beatrice's cousin, who Vera called Aunt Rose. Didn't make a lick of sense.

Vera lost track of time. She slipped a few quarters in the machine, opting for a package of crackers. It dropped down onto the shelf, and she reached in and pulled it out.

When she turned around, Bill's girlfriend was standing in the room. It was just Vera and the young woman in the little room that held snack machines. Vera took a deep breath and looked her in the eye. It was hard to believe that the woman who stood before her was twenty-four, for she looked even younger.

"I followed you in here, Vera," she said, her manner softer than it was with the others in the waiting area. "We need to talk."

There was something cold about the way she looked at Vera. Her skin was like fine porcelain, her eyes like blue glass, and she was so young looking that it made Vera ache.

Vera forced a polite smile. "We do?"

"You know I didn't break up your marriage," she said matter-of-factly.

"Yes, of course," Vera managed to say, wishing Kelsey would lower her voice. This was personal, not to be hashed out in a public place. Didn't she get that?

"I know we probably won't be friends, but I don't want to make things uncomfortable for Bill," she said, looking away, lifting her chin.

Vera's heart sank. The childlike woman thought she was in love with Bill. "You are Bill's midlife crisis," she wanted to say. "Nothing more. I am the mother of his child. The one who told him to leave and never come back." *How odd to be standing in front of a woman who was now sleeping with the man you used to love.*

"It's just going to take a while for us all to get used to . . . things," Vera finally said, gathering herself. "My main concern is Elizabeth."

"Oh, yeah, yeah, sure. I know. I'd love to get to know her," she said, looking like she was not more than twelve years old herself in that moment, with enthusiasm sparking her eyes. She was wearing similar garb to Leola, a long, tight denim skirt and flats. Were they back in style and Vera had just missed it?

Vera's heart began to race. This woman with her baby? She didn't think so.

"We'll see," Vera said, fiddling with her crackers, trying to open them. "Plenty of time." Hopefully, this young woman would be out of Bill's life soon enough and this would be something she'd not have to think about. Not today. Not tomorrow. Not ever.

Vera's pulse continued to race. She wanted Kelsey to move out of her way. It was a tiny snack enclave, and she was feeling like a caged animal. It was difficult to keep composed. It seemed like no matter how she shifted, Kelsey shifted with her. She couldn't get around her gracefully.

"Um, so you are a law student, Kelsey?" Vera said, wishing once again that Kelsey would move out of the way.

"Last year," she said, smiling. "It's pretty intense."

"Yeah, I remember what it was like for Bill," Vera said.

"He's actually a pretty good teacher," she said and bit her lip. Nervous habit?

"I imagine," Vera said, wanting to say, "Let's hope he's a better teacher than a lawyer."

"My parents and my uncle and aunt, well, they really hate me being with Bill. They say he's too old for me," she said, digging in her pocket and pulling out her wallet. She moved toward one of the snack machines, providing Vera with the perfect opportunity for escape.

"Well, good luck with everything," Vera said and walked out of the snack enclave. *Because you are going to need it.*

When Vera rounded the corner, she saw Bill sitting there and rolled her eyes at him. "Ass," she said under her breath.

"What?" he said, following her into Elizabeth's room.

She ignored him and just kept walking by with her crackers, heading into Elizabeth's room, where Beatrice and Jon already were. Elizabeth slept soundly.

"What?" Bill asked again.

"Never mind, Bill," Vera said.

"What's wrong with you? Why are you acting like this? Why are you treating me like an outsider?" he said.

Vera raised an eyebrow and glared at him.

"What makes you think you're in charge of her?" Bill said, Kelsey coming up behind him.

"I'm her mother, Bill. I am in charge of her," Vera began.

"Well, you're going to need more than that to eat," Beatrice said, looking at Vera's crackers and ignoring Bill. "Why don't you go to the cafeteria?"

"No, Mama, I'm not leaving her," Vera said as something tightened in her throat. No. She wouldn't cry, not with Bill and Kelsey here. No, she wouldn't. She turned and looked out the window. Sometimes it was hard to look at a sick child. Elizabeth was so pale, so still, that she looked as if she were dead. Vera couldn't let her mind mull that over. She couldn't.

The other thing she couldn't really think about—not now—was that she didn't remember how she'd gotten into Elizabeth's room. She'd forgotten to take her pill. What woke her? Was it Elizabeth's cry? Her cold feet on the floor? The breeze coming through the window? Why was that window open? She never left windows open, but maybe she'd forgotten to close it, just like she'd forgotten to take her medicine.

She looked out past the hospital parking lot to the mountains, the same mountains she grew up looking at. When she was small, she often prayed when looking at the mountains, and in her mind she imagined God as a mountain. When Beatrice found out that she thought the mountains were God, she had smiled. "Well, it makes a kind of sense. And who's to say the mountains aren't God?" She was blessed to have a mother like Beatrice. Even with all her oddities and grouchiness, Beatrice was a good mother.

Vera turned around and looked at Beatrice, who was already looking at her. "Mama, have I told you . . . thanked you . . . for being such a good mother?"

Beatrice looked dumbfounded. Her eyes watered. "Vera," she said softly after a minute. "You been praying to that mountain again?"

Chapter 29

Beatrice didn't think she'd ever been so scared in all her life. And that included when she lost Ed. To see her grand-baby so small, so weak, so sick was only part of it. As if it weren't enough. But there was Vera, who was acting oddly. It was as if she had something to hide. And what could that be?

Beatrice looked up and saw a doctor walking in the room. Good Lord, he looked familiar. Could it be? Now, wait. Doc Green passed away last year. Didn't he?

"Hi there," he said, Bill trailing him. "I'm Dr. Green," he said to Vera.

As she turned to face him, his face lit up.

"Vera?"

She smiled.

God, her daughter was pretty, Beatrice thought, and this Dr. Green knew it.

Bill noticed the attraction, too, and looked away, gri-macing.

"You any relation to Doc Green from Bluestone?" Bea-trice interrupted.

"Yes, Mama. This is his son," Vera said. "I remember

you from the investigation about the abandoned baby. How is she?"

"As far as we know, she's doing fine, Vera," he said. "Her grandparents have taken right over."

Bill cleared his throat.

"Ah, yes," said Dr. Green. "I have news about Elizabeth."

"I just hope it's not meningitis," Vera said.

"It's not. Believe it or not, it's the flu. I think she'll be all right. According to her chart, her temp is coming down. I'm glad you brought her in. The flu in small children can be deadly, but she's going to be fine."

Vera grabbed him and flung her arms around him. "Thank you," she said, then pulled away, looking slightly embarrassed. "Sorry."

"Anytime a beautiful woman wants to hug me, that's quite all right with me," Dr. Green said, his face red. "I do have some other news for you," he added. "We ran blood tests, of course, and the tox report suggests that Elizabeth has been exposed to lead. Any ideas about that?"

"Lead?" Bill said. "What?"

"Have you moved recently?"

"Yes, Elizabeth and I live in an apartment over my business," Vera said.

"Could that place have lead in the paint?"

"Vera! You didn't test it?" Bill said.

"It must have slipped my mind. . . ."

"Damn," Bill said.

"Now, just hold on a minute," Beatrice said to him. "You didn't test it, either, now did you? You were too busy in Charlottesville with your new hussy to help Vera move at all."

Bill's face turned angry red. He stormed out of the room.

"The truth is, I thought about it. The place is old. It just slipped my mind," Vera said.

"Don't beat yourself up over it," Dr. Green said. "The exposure has been minimal, but you need to find another place to stay and get that taken care of."

"Stay with us," Jon said, getting out of his chair next to the window. "No arguments! No!" He stuck his finger in her face.

"Yes, sir," Vera said and smiled.

"Here's a list of contractors for you," Dr. Green said, handing her a paper.

"I knew your daddy," Beatrice suddenly said. "My Lawd, you look just like him. He must have been proud of you."

"I like to think so," Dr. Green said, straightening up. "I remember Ed, too. Dad and Ed had a lot in common, were pretty tight."

Beatrice nodded. "Indeed. Well, I'm glad you're taking care of Elizabeth."

"We'll try our best," he said, his beeper going off. "I have to run," he told them, looking back over his shoulder at Vera. "See you later?"

She nodded. "I'm not going anywhere." Their eyes met in an awkward moment. Elizabeth stirred and mumbled.

Oh, those little cooing baby noises. Beatrice loved to hear them.

Sheila appeared in the doorway. "Brought you something to eat," she said, her arm full of containers.

"We all did," DeeAnn said, coming up behind her.

The next thing Beatrice knew, Sheila, DeeAnn, and Paige were bringing food into the room. Beatrice helped herself to some corn bread, beans, and rice. And, oh my, that potato salad was good.

Elizabeth rolled over onto her side as DeeAnn's laughter sounded through the room. Paige told a funny story. Beatrice wasn't paying attention. She was suddenly thinking about Willa Rose and her memory book, which she'd left sitting on her dining room table.

Bill and Kelsey sat on the fringes of the room, not taking any food offered.

"Wonder where Annie is?" Paige said.

"I tried to call her," DeeAnn said. "Voice mail."

Beatrice looked up and nearly gasped when she saw him in the doorway. "What are you doing here, Bryant?"

"Hello, Beatrice," he said, standing against the door-jamb. "Vera, we need to talk."

"Okay," Vera said. "In private? Or is this okay?" She gestured.

"This is fine," he said, walking into the room "Your neighbor was robbed last night, and we're talking to all the neighbors to see if they noticed anything suspicious."

"Robbed?" Sheila squealed. "First murder, now robbery. What's this town coming to?"

"But remember," Vera said, "Emily McGlashen was robbed before she was killed."

The room was in a stunned silence.

"True," Bryant said after a few minutes. "That's one reason I need to know if you saw or heard anything strange."

Vera bit her lip.

"Vera?" Beatrice said. Yes. Vera was definitely hiding something. "If you know something . . ."

"Look, it may not be anything . . . but I could have sworn I never opened Elizabeth's window, and it was open when I went into her room this morning."

"Let's get someone over to your place immediately just on the off chance. We can't be too careful," Bryant said, reaching for his cell phone.

Suddenly, Bill was standing at Vera's side. Kelsey sank back, looking smaller than before, a rumpled heap on the chair. Beatrice sat back down next to Jon and wondered what would happen next.

Chapter 30

"Annie, I've known you my whole life, you know? You're my sister. I know there's something wrong. Spill," Josh said.

Annie was scrubbing out the kitchen sink, phone to her ear. The boys were off to school, and Mike was off to work. If she didn't get an objective opinion about this Adam thing, she thought she might lose her mind. But could her brother be objective?

He was a trained listener, a psychiatrist. But he was also her brother, her brother the "swinger," who branded monogamy unnatural. She always thought it was an excuse for an extended adolescence. But here she was. She still loved her husband but was lusting after Detective Bryant.

"Annie, you gonna make me guess?" he asked.

"It's just that, um, it's so personal. I'm a little uncomfortable about it. It's so not like me," she said.

"Does this have to do with Mike? Is he, um, having problems?"

"I wouldn't know about that. . . . I mean, there has not been time for us . . . , so, um, I just don't know," she said.

Josh breathed into the phone. He was losing patience.

"It's just that I'm finding that I'm attracted to someone else," Annie said finally.

Silence.

"Did you hear me?" she asked.

She heard him breathe out. He was smoking. He had never even tried to quit.

"Yeah," he said. "So? You're attracted to someone else. You haven't acted on that, have you?"

"Not really, but he has. I mean, he's kissed me twice," she said with a stab of regret or shame or something else dark and bitter moving through the center of her.

"And you let him?" His voice was raised.

"Yes. But I ran off both times, um, after . . ." Her voice quavered. God, was she going to cry? Throw up?

"Take a deep breath, Annie. Calm down," her brother said. "Okay, look. You know I don't go for monogamy. But I also don't go for cheating. I don't think you do, either. But I can see your situation. Mike and you are off your game. In walks this other guy. You find him attractive. He homes in on it. Happens every day. Tell me more about this man."

"Well . . . let's just say he's around a lot. I see him frequently."

"It's that Adam Bryant, isn't it?" he said.

Damn, he was smart.

"I told you about the way he was watching you at the Super Bowl party. I knew it."

"So?" she responded. If he could see it, could Mike? If so, why was he still having Bryant over?

"I know you've got to see him professionally sometimes, but does he need to be at your house almost every weekend?" Josh asked.

"I can't think of a good reason for Mike not to invite him. I mean, without telling Mike."

"This guy is a jerk. I'm just putting that out there," he

said. Annie could picture him holding back with his "professional" face, his tight-lipped, smooth, practiced face.

Annie laughed. "Is that your professional opinion?"

"Yes. And my brotherly opinion," he replied.

Annie started cleaning the kitchen counter. Squirt. Wipe. Squirt. Wipe. She loved her pink kitchen but hated cleaning it.

"He's really not as jerkish as he seems. He's all bristly on the outside, but it's a show. You know the type," she said.

"Humph, do I. Thank God for them, or I wouldn't have a job," he said.

She pictured him rolling his eyes and flicking his cigarette ashes into one of his huge ashtrays, which were always in need of cleaning.

"Okay, so statistically speaking, say, if you were to leave Mike for this guy, nine chances out of ten, it would not work. Could you ever really trust a man who is a cheater, even if it's with you?" he said, ignoring her statement about Bryant.

"I don't know. And I really don't want to leave Mike."

"But Mike is being kind of an asshole, too," Josh said.

"Yeah, kind of," she replied, her heart sinking. She took a deep breath.

"Here's what you do," he said after a minute. "Stay as far away from Bryant as you can. When he comes over, you go out. In the meantime, make plans for a romantic getaway with Mike. I'll spend the weekend with the boys. Let me know when. Okay?"

"Sure. I think that's a workable plan," she said, feeling a little better.

"I think you have to fight for your marriage. It's still worth something," he said.

Annie took a deep breath. Did Mike realize that? "You're right," she said.

"If things don't get back on track with Mike, you have no choice but to tell him, you know?" Josh said with a note of forcefulness.

"Yes," she said. But imagining that conversation made her stomach churn. Maybe it was possible to get things back on track with Mike and to ignore Bryant as much as possible. Maybe it was.

Kitchen wiped and clean. She stood back, looking over her clean kitchen, wondering how long it would last. Well, at least until the boys returned. She smiled. Now she needed to look over those transcripts of her interviews with the members of the New Mountain Order.

She picked up the stack of papers on her desk.

I didn't know anything about the drugs. I was just there because of Zeb. I really believed he was getting messages from God. I still do. He is a holy man.
How do you explain his illegal activities?
Illegal according to who? God? People like Zeb have a higher calling.

Annie pursed her lips. People were so gullible.

Chapter 31

"So when Bryant went through her financial records, he said he was amazed by how much money she had," Annie said. "So I started looking into it. She made good money, but a lot of it, in big chunks, was going to this person in Switzerland, and you just can't access those records quickly. No wonder she could afford to charge next to nothing for dance lessons."

"Switzerland? Who did she know in Switzerland?" Vera said, putting her glass of wine down next to her everbrimming Elizabeth scrapbook. She'd have to start another one soon. Now that she was staying with Jon and Beatrice, she had a bit more time to scrapbook.

"Yeah, I don't know, but she knew people from all over the world," Annie said and shrugged. "Strange. Maybe someone was blackmailing her. But for what?"

"DeeAnn, move that plate over. You are going spill that dip on your album," Sheila said, looking up from her computer screen.

"For God's sake," DeeAnn said. "I'm a big girl. I can handle my dip." But she moved her plate over, anyway.

The women sat quietly and listened to Adele singing in the background. Adele was Paige's new passion. The next thing they knew, Paige would start to sing her heart out as she was scrapbooking. Looks of amusement were exchanged.

A scratching noise interrupted the moment. Then a doorbell sounded.

"Who could that be?"

"Not Bea. She'd walk right in," Annie said to Vera.

"Yes?" they heard Sheila say.

And then a melodic, beautiful voice. "Hey, is this where the party is? Oh, dear, I'm sorry." She laughed. "I thought I'd gotten all the leaves off."

The woman was draped in leaves and dirt.

"It's quite all right," Sheila said. "Please sit down. I'm so glad you could make it."

Rachel laughed.

What was she laughing at?

"Yes, yes, yes," she said. "I'm Rachel Greenberg. Emily McGlashen's mother."

Vera looked at the other women, who were all looking at the person who had just waltzed into their crop. DeeAnn's eyebrows were in a crisscrossed worried line. Paige's head was tilted in curiosity. Annie sat back with her arms crossed. And Sheila looked uncomfortable.

"Oh, where are my manners? Can I get you something?" Sheila said. "Beer? Wine?"

Rachel wrinkled her nose. "No, I don't drink, but thanks. This is the place, correct?" She looked around at the women. "This is the crop you told me about?"

The women were confounded.

Sheila's hand went to her mouth, her eyebrows hitched.

"Don't worry, Sheila. You are too much of a worrier. A perfectionist is never really happy," the woman said, her voice softening a bit.

How would she know? Vera wondered.

"And you must be Vera, Elizabeth's mother?" Rachel extended her hand to her. "I understand our Emily was difficult."

Vera felt as if the air had been knocked out of her lungs. She couldn't remember how to speak.

"And Annie. The intellectual and hard-ass."

"What?" Annie said. "Rachel!"

"We found these journals of Emily's, you see. She wrote all about you all."

Her voice now had more than a hint of weariness. She frowned. Her eyes drooped with sorrow but had a look of hollowness to them. As Vera studied her more, a sudden shot of fear spun through her. How would she survive if something awful happened to Elizabeth?

Rachel had no bra on underneath that purple cotton shirt. And her eyes were lined with wrinkles. She wore a long pink cotton skirt with purple flowers.

"As I told you, none of us really knew her," Annie finally said.

"You know, I've wondered how much *I* knew her," she told them. "She was my daughter. I raised her. But she was always very different, and when she found out she was adopted, it was very hard, you know? I tried to stay close with her. But you can't push these things, man. She just wanted us to leave her alone. I had to respect that. I feel like I'm finally getting to know my daughter through her journals."

"I looked for family records—"Annie began.

Rachel cackled. "Oh, dear, we've never recorded anything. Modern life is full of such ridiculous time sucks. In the grand scheme of things, these things don't matter."

Annie leaned in close to her and noticed her glazed eyes, could smell the pot on her. How old was this woman? Fifty? Sixty?

"That's why I don't really get scrapbooking. I mean, who cares?"

"Those of us who are straight, that's who," Sheila said. "I've invited you into my home. This is what I do. I record memories. It matters to me."

"Does the recording matter? Or does the memory matter? Which is it? Because I have memories. Rich memories. But I don't think recording them means a thing to anybody, least of all me."

"Why did you come?" Vera said.

Rachel shrugged. "I wanted to meet you all after reading about you. So we feel differently about this memory-keeping thing. It's cool. I mean we are grown-ups and can disagree, right?"

Vera laughed. "You remind me of my mother. You should meet her soon. When will you be leaving town?"

Rachel shrugged. "We are in no hurry to get back. As I say, I'm beginning to feel close to my girl. I don't want to go. Not just yet."

Sheila snapped her laptop shut. "Let me show you some things, Rachel."

"Okay," she said gesturing with her hands up, as if to say, "Why not?"

Sheila walked over to a bookcase that was full of scrapbooks of all colors and sizes. Some were vertically aligned. Others were in horizontal stacks.

"I've recorded my children's lives in these books," Sheila said. "Pick any one of them, and it will tell you about them, what was happening in their lives, and it will also tell you a bit about me."

Rachel chose a mauve book and slid it out of the shelf. "And to what end?" she asked. "I mean, you have all these lovely books and photos, but what will happen to them?"

She opened the book and saw the label JONATHON.

"My youngest son," Sheila said. "I guess the 'end' of it all is that someday Jonathon and his children will have a touchstone to his past. Something that was made by his mother."

"Now, I do like *that* thought," Rachel said. "I have this quilt that my grandmother made out of dresses that belonged to her and her sisters when they were young. I love that thing, man. I love wrapping myself up in it and imagining which piece of cloth touched whose skin and what occasion they wore it on."

'It's really the same kind of thing," Vera said, coming up behind the two women as they looked over the book. "Except if you scrapbook, you can answer those questions for your kids. You have photos, of course, but you also can write about what was going on the day the photo was taken, or what was on your mind that day. We call it journaling. So you leave behind footprints through your scrapbooks," Vera explained, then paused. "I hope that Elizabeth will keep the scrapbooks I've made for her, and will find the same comfort you do in your grandmother's quilt."

Rachel turned the page on the book. "Your son likes music?"

"Yes," Sheila said. "Very different from the rest of my family. He plays the violin, as you can see."

"And whoa . . . those are some glittery, sparkly pages," Rachel said.

Sheila and Vera laughed. "Remember how I said my pages will tell you a little about me? Well, those years were what I call the glitter years."

"Oh yeah, how could we forget?" DeeAnn said and groaned.

Chapter 32

"Emily's mother?" Beatrice said, startled.

"We all have one, Ma," Vera said. "She said they were off the grid."

"Well, well," Beatrice said. She'd known plenty of folks who were "off the grid" when Ed first started practicing medicine. Most of them were deep in the hills and distrusted the government. Women birthed their babies, usually with the help of a midwife, and folks buried their dead after a preacher said a word or two. And the government never had cause to know these folks. But . . . today? It would be harder to manage. Suddenly her understanding of Emily had shifted.

"So Emily was adopted into this secular Jewish family who lived in a hippie commune, and when she found out she was adopted, she turned her back on them."

Vera nodded, then drank the rest of her water, walked over to the sink, and rinsed her glass.

"How did Lizzie do tonight?" Vera asked.

"She's done okay. Her temp has come way down. How was the crop?"

"Well, Rachel came in and talked about how memory keeping has no meaning in the universal grand scheme, or some such nonsense. Sounds like your kinda gal," Vera said.

Beatrice said nothing. She shrugged her shoulders. She sat at her turquoise kitchen table, relishing the silence, regarding her daughter as she looked out the window.

"What's that?" Vera stood at attention. "Is there someone at the door?"

Beatrice shot up out of her chair, pulling her robe closer around her. Who could it be at this hour?

When she opened the back door, she was shocked to see Leola, the woman who now lived in Vera's house. She was bloody and limping.

"Oh!" Beatrice said. "Come in!"

Vera, who was quick on Beatrice's heels, helped to get Leola to the couch.

"I'm so sorry," Leola managed to say. "Hate to wake you up . . ."

"We weren't sleeping," Beatrice said. "What happened to you?"

"I—I don't know," she said, then winced. "I mean, I was out for a stroll, and I don't know. . . . Maybe . . . I think someone pushed me."

"You *think?*" Beatrice said.

She nodded her head. "I know it sounds crazy, but by the time I got up and looked around . . . there wasn't anybody there. Yet . . ."

"Yet?" Vera said.

"I swear I felt someone push me," Leola said.

"Can I get you some water?" Beatrice said.

"Oh no, please," she said. "Can you just call my husband? I think I need to go to the hospital. It's my ankle." She pulled up her jogging suit pant leg and pulled back her sock.

"Oh my," Vera said, springing into action. "I'll get some ice. Mama, you can call her husband."

Just then, Jon came padding downstairs.

Beatrice waved him off as she reached for the phone.

"Please try to keep her calm," Leola's husband told Beatrice.

"What? Why?"

"She has a tendency to get a bit, um, hysterical," he said.

"Oh," she said, looking over at Leola, who seemed more like she was in pain than hysterical. Jon was approaching her, and Vera was placing an ice pack on her ankle.

"But who would have pushed you?" Jon said.

"I don't know," Leola said, wincing again. "It was dark. And whoever it was ran off very quickly. I was cutting through the alley."

A feeling came over Beatrice just then. A feeling she hadn't had in a long time. She felt her dead husband's presence. She could smell him. Was that him touching her hand? She looked behind her to see nothing. Yet she knew he was there. She knew to pay attention. This was a warning from him. But what was he warning her about?

Leola turned her face up at an angle, reminding Beatrice of Kelsey. She really favored her. Were they related?

"Leola, do you have any family around here?"

"No really," she said. "Just my kids and husband."

"Oh," Beatrice said.

"Well, there is my niece, but we hardly see her. Busy law student at U. Va."

"Her name Kelsey?"

"Why, yes. How—"

"I believe we met her at the hospital," Beatrice revealed.

"Wha—"

"It seems your niece is living with my ex-husband," Vera said, crossing her arms.

"Your Bill is the man she's been dating?" Leola's voice rose two decibels. Her hands went to her mouth in shock.

"Yes, I'm afraid so," Beatrice said.

"Well, that's just weird," Leola finally said, wincing, moving the ice pack around on her ankle a bit before settling it on one spot.

"It's a small world," Vera said.

She grimaced. "Yeah, there's that. Kelsey talks about him like he's Adonis, so handsome, so intelligent." She rolled her eyes. "You know how I feel about Bill."

Beatrice cackled. She couldn't help it. Leola didn't mince words.

"In fact, I told you I'd be happy to rep you if they ever charge you, Vera."

"With what?" Beatrice said, hackles up.

"Oh, Mama, don't worry."

"Now, wait. They haven't charged you with murder yet, and you're the only person that they can place at the scene of the crime?" Leola said.

"They know my daughter didn't kill Emily McGlashen, whether or not her purse just happened to be there, and let me tell you—"

"Your taxi awaits," interrupted Leola's husband, entering the room with a flourish. "Or should I say ambulance," he said as he regarded her black and blue ankle, so swollen that it hardly looked like an ankle anymore.

Chapter 33

Annie liked to spend Sundays with her boys, but today both of them had a birthday party to go to at the local YMCA, a pool party, and Mike never missed the opportunity for a swim.

"I'm hoping for chocolate cake," Ben said over breakfast that morning.

"Whatever kind of cake it is, you need to remember to be polite and thank the Meadows family for it," Annie said.

Ben shrugged. "Yeah, I know that, Mom."

"Me too," Sam said. "I wonder if there will be gift bags."

Annie sighed. All the recent birthday parties her boys had gone to had sent them home with gift bags with cheap little toys and candy in them. Her boys loved them. She and Mike hated them.

Mike mussed Sam's hair. "You know the party is about Frankie, not you."

Sam looked at him with his dark eyebrows lifted, as if to say, "So?"

"I like the Meadows," Mike said and then took a long drink of his juice. "I'm glad you boys found some good friends."

The family was new in Cumberland Creek, and Annie

liked them, too. The boys had other friends, of course, but Annie was never too certain about whom to trust with her boys. There was that incident at school last year, when Ben got into a fistfight over the Weekly Religious Education program. One of the children told him he'd go to hell because he didn't believe in Jesus. And there were other, less violent incidents. Like the time Sam couldn't go to a Christmas gathering because it was the first night of Hanukkah. Or the time Ben went to a friend's house and was served pork. Her boys were getting the message: they were different. She didn't want them to feel badly about themselves because of it. Even though they were not fully practicing, they still held fast to some Jewish traditions.

After the boys left, Annie spread her book notes out on the floor, grouping them into interviews, research, articles, and hunches. Mike always laughed at the hunch file. Funny, because at least one of those hunches always panned out for Annie. She would allow herself time to "play" with the evidence, what she felt about it, mull it over, and write about it.

One of these days maybe she'd write a book about her hunches. Of course, her editors would call it reporters' intuition. Cookie would call it psychic.

Some of the stuff that Emily's mother had spouted reminded her of Cookie. She decided she'd check Emily's mother and keyed in the name Rachel Greenberg. Of course, there was nothing online about her. She'd said they were off the grid. Annie smirked. What was the point?

Her computer screen froze. The thing was so old that she was certain she'd have to get a new one soon. Where would they get the money for that?

While she restarted her computer, she reached for another file and started leafing through it. *Oh. The Emily file.*

She glanced over the list of her financial information. Mostly it was just like everybody else's, with a savings account, credit cards, cell phone, rent, and so on. Just this one weird item, where she sent three thousand dollars a month to a bank account in Switzerland. Annie had e-mailed them and had yet to hear back. Who knew if they'd ever get back to her? She wondered if Bryant should just get the FBI involved. They might be able to get quicker answers than some freelance reporter. But she knew how he hated the FBI. And he had every right to after what they pulled on him during the NMO case.

Annie still wasn't certain that Cookie herself wasn't some kind of FBI operative. She and Bryant had discussed that possibility. Suddenly, she wondered if he knew that Emily's parents were still in town and it looked they were planning to stay. She reached for her cell. Then dropped it. *No,* she told herself. *He'll find out, and it won't be from me. Not today, when I have the house to myself, the whole day stretched out before me. A day where I really need to focus. Not Adam.* She pushed him from her mind.

Her cell phone buzzed. It was Vera.

"Hi, Vera," Annie said.

"Are you working?"

"I'm trying to focus. It's not easy today."

"Listen," Vera said, "Emily's mom gave me this great idea last night."

"Really?"

"Well, we were talking about retracing Emily's last day, you know the day of her murder, retracing her footsteps."

"Adam and I have already done that."

"Adam? Well."

"Um, I mean, Detective Bryant. You know who I'm talking about," Annie said.

"I didn't know you two were on such a first-name basis."

"Could we not get into this now?" Annie said after a few minutes of awkward silence. "What did you call for?"

"I think it might be a good idea to retrace my footsteps the night of Emily's murder."

"Why?"

"Look, Annie, I'm not a killer. You know it. I know it. But the whole town is talking about me. I had an incident at the Pie Palace. I have a business to run. A business with children involved. I'm worried about my reputation."

"How will this solve anything?"

"There's a part of me . . . ," Vera said and sighed. "There's a part of me that really wonders why my purse turned up in her studio. It bothers me. I just think if we could go back and sort of go through it, it might trigger a memory of someone or something. I don't know."

Vera had been giving this a lot of thought, which meant that Beatrice was right when she told Annie the situation troubled Vera deeply. But given Vera's fragile state of mind, Annie didn't know whether this was a good idea or not. What if she remembered something unpleasant? What would happen then?

"Have you talked to Bea about it?"

"Yes, she suggested I get my doctor involved and we try hypnosis, which, as luck would have it, we have already been working on. But I think that's a bit much, don't you?" she said and laughed.

"I think you should talk to your doctor and see what she thinks," Annie said.

"What? Why? I don't need to get the whole town involved."

"No. But you've been sleepwalking . . . under a lot of stress. . . . I think it's best."

Vera didn't argue before they hung up the phone. She sighed and went on to another subject. After finishing the conversation, Annie wrote two chapters of the book on the NMO, started supper, and took a bath, which was interrupted by her loud boys coming home late in the afternoon.

Chapter 34

"I don't understand it. Nothing was stolen," Vera told Detective Bryant over the phone.

"I know. I know," he said. "But my team has had a really thorough look at Lizzie's room, and we think someone else was there that night. You must have interrupted them."

She thought about her confusion that night, set off by the panic of Lizzie's high fever. By then, of course, nothing had mattered but getting her daughter to the hospital.

"But why would they want to rob me? It's common knowledge that I'm broke and I've moved into a tiny apartment. What could they want from me?"

"I'm not sure," he said after a minute. "Could be anything. Thieves will take stuff and sell it. It doesn't have to be money they are after from you. And they might not know you at all. So they don't know you're broke," he added and paused. "We've gotten a few fingerprints from the window and some hair."

"Hair?"

"Yeah, there was some hair on the carpet. Long strands of it. It looks like there was at least one woman in the room," he told her.

"A woman? In Lizzie's room?" Vera felt her whole body

react in a psychic fit. A strange woman in her daughter's room, perhaps looking at Elizabeth? Scaring Elizabeth? Oh, damn. If only she could remember something about that night. How she got in Elizabeth's room. What woke her? Was she responding to a noise? Or was she just sleep-walking?

"Now, if our perp has a record, the fingerprints will pop up on our system fairly quickly. The DNA test on hair? Well, that could take a while and may not lead anywhere at all, I'm sorry to say. But it's worth a shot. This might lead us straight to the robber. I've seen it before."

Vera sat at her mother's kitchen table. Beatrice and Jon had gone out for a walk and had taken Lizzie with them. She was glad to be alone with the news, if only for a few minutes. She needed to sit with all of this and make some kind of peace with it.

The timer on the oven went off. First things first. Strawberry muffins, made with fresh strawberries from her mom's berry patch, or what was left of it while the excavation was going on. She pulled the muffins out of the oven and nearly swooned at the smell. Her taste buds stood at attention.

She placed the muffin tin on the counter, allowing the muffins time to cool off, and looked out her mother's kitchen window, as she had countless times over the years. Such comfort in the view of a neighbor's well-tended home, spring flowers blooming everywhere, some in pretty pink flower boxes. Mountains in the distance, a backdrop for every scene in Cumberland Creek. Such comfort could be found at her mother's home, in her kitchen, looking out the window, with the scent of strawberry muffins filling her. Maybe she could stay here awhile longer.

Who was she kidding? Maybe she should stay here

forever. It would solve a lot of her problems. The money. Help with Lizzie. Safety.

But it didn't sit right with her to be in her forties and living with her mom and Jon. She should be on her own. *Should be.* Life wasn't supposed to be this way. It was against everything she had grown up believing. You worked hard, provided for your kids, and marriages lasted.

Surprisingly, a tear stung at the corner of her eye. What could she have done differently? Could she have seen any of it coming?

Oh, well. No point in going there. She shrugged and then began scooping the muffins out of the tin, placing them on a plate. None of it really mattered when she intently considered it. She'd done her best with the information she had. Now her decisions had to include what was best for Lizzie. Was it best for Lizzie to grow up here with Jon and Beatrice, in the same house she had grown up in?

The thought held a kind of comfort to her one minute, and the next it frustrated her. She wanted to be on her own with her daughter. She could do it. This was just a blip. She'd have to do something about the fire escape, the lead, and maybe keep Lizzie in her room with her until that happened. There was a way to settle her nerves about this. She just knew it.

Her cell phone buzzed. She answered without looking at the screen.

"Vera?" It was a male voice she didn't recognize.

"Yes, this is Vera."

"It's Eric Green. Dr. Green?"

"Oh, yes!" Vera had forgotten he said he'd call her. She'd not given it another thought.

"How's Elizabeth?"

"She's getting better. She's out on a walk with Mama and Jon. Her energy is almost back to normal."

"That's great news," he said. "Um, listen, we've talked a few times, and I think it would be fun for you and me to get together, say, for dinner one night?"

Vera's senses were suddenly overloading. Her heart raced, her palms sweat, and she felt the fluttering of nerves in her stomach.

"Vera?"

"Yes, yes, I'm sorry. Did you just ask me out on a date?" she blurted.

He laughed. "Yes, I think I did. Is that all right?"

"Yes, of course! And I'd be happy to have dinner with you. . . ."

"What's wrong?"

"Nothing really," she said, feeling herself blush. "It's just that I haven't been on a date in twenty years or so."

Did she just tell him that? Why was she so willing to spill her guts to this man? It was true that she hadn't been on a date in years. What she and Tony had been doing wasn't dating at all. They had basically been just sleeping together, trying to recapture their youth. And she'd not heard from him in months. Just as well.

He laughed again. "Well, you're in good company. It's been a while for me, too. Shall we say Friday?"

"Friday is good for me," she said.

When they hung up, Vera suddenly felt lighter. Even though she had forgotten he said he'd call, she was pleased he had remembered. That said something about the man. It probably would come to nothing, she told herself, but dinner with a nice man who happened to know her family very well was going to at least be a pleasant way to pass the time. One could always use a good friend.

Chapter 35

Lizzie and Vera were downstairs, romping around. Beatrice and Jon were hiding in her bedroom. They had sneaked the book into her room and had spread it out on the bed.

"Willa Rose McGlashen," Jon said, forming each word slowly. "I simply can't stand it anymore. Who was she?"

"I know!" Beatrice said, feeling like a twelve-year-old girl opening a Christmas package. Except that it was musty and spotted, which made it all the better to Beatrice. She cracked open the book to the spot where they had left off before, the day Vera called about taking Lizzie to the hospital. Thank God the child thrived.

Beatrice considered the handwriting in this book. It was so elegant and beautiful, with flourishes and so on, which made it difficult to read for modern eyes. But if she concentrated, her eyes became used to it.

Recipe for Christmas Pudding

One pound of raisins stoned, one pound of currants, half a pound of beef suet, quarter of a pound of sugar, two spoonfuls of flour, three eggs, a cup of sweetmeats, and a wineglass of brandy. Mix well, and boil in a mould eight hours.

Note: The best suet for this is that found around the liver. It's the same with mincemeat for pies. My grandmother always said that Mathilde knew her suet.

"She's a cook!" Jon said.

"Indeed," Beatrice said. "But who is Mathilde?"

He shrugged. "Someone Willa's grandmother knew. . . . Who was Willa's grandmother?"

"Oh, bother! We are going to have to go to the historical society. I was hoping to avoid that," Beatrice said.

"I thought you liked it," Jon said.

"I do, but I don't want to get anybody else involved. Bunch of busybodies over there. I already have strangers in my backyard. I don't know. . . . This feels private," she said.

He nodded. "I think you're right. This is something fashioned with Willa Rose's own hands. It's truly remarkable that it survived in the ground, in that box. And to think her hands touched this very book. . . ."

An appreciative hush fell over the room. The sun was gleaming through the bedroom windows, and fresh flowers sat in a vase next to Beatrice's bed.

Beatrice turned the page to one of complete handwriting, like a journal entry.

Papa says with Mama gone, I am to be the proper cook for the inn. But we get so few customers these days. They've moved the road farther west, and so travelers no longer come through. Of course, our old steady customers make the effort. Those that are left after this god-awful war between the states.

None of us will ever be the same.

Beatrice's heart sank. She was a Virginian, raised on Jenkins Mountain, educated at the University of Virginia, and this war was not so long ago. Even today there were remnants of it being found on playgrounds, at construction sites, and in farmers' fields. Looked like another, more visceral link to the war existed in her backyard. On her property. It made it all seem more real to her.

Jon tsk-tsked, as he always did when he found something appalling.

Beatrice smoothed over the quilt that she used as a bed-spread. Beatrice and her quilts. She loved them. Couldn't have a bed without them. Her off-white quilt was one of her favorites. She had read that this design was traced to the time of the Civil War. It was a "Gunboat" quilt. Southern women made these fancier appliquéd, medallion-style quilts and sold them for the war effort, namely, to purchase gunboats. Her quilt's medallions were stylized purple pansies, with a huge spray of them in the center and smaller ones in the corners. Funny, she was reading firsthand about the war and was sitting on a quilt whose design came from that time. A chill ran up her spine.

She wondered if the road that Willa Rose wrote of was Route 11, which used to come through Cumberland Creek. Or so they said. Roads shifted throughout history.

She turned the page to see some ads with drawings of women in fashionable turn-of-the-century skirts. She smiled. Vera used to keep a scrapbook full of magazine cutouts of women wearing clothes she liked. She was just a girl. Beatrice couldn't remember if she'd ever thrown those books out. They were delightful. How had she forgotten about them?

The dresses were brightly colored pinks and blues, and Willa had cut them out and pasted them onto the page, along with some cutout roses in between each dress.

She had drawn a little star and written beside one of the dresses. *I'd like this one in yellow. Papa says if business picks up soon, I can order it.*

Willa Rose loved to cook, was helping her family out, and longed for a pretty dress, just like most young women.

"That's a very pretty dress. I like the back of it," Jon said.

"Yes, that's a bustle," Beatrice said. "I don't imagine that would be easy to sit in."

Beatrice turned the page to another journal entry.

> *I am so bored. There are not many people around here anymore. The young people have moved to places like Staunton and Richmond. Sally and I sometimes sit on the front porch and don't see anybody. We marvel when we think of how it was here before the war. Now it is almost desolate. Papa thinks I should go to Staunton to visit family. But I know he wants me to find a suitor. I don't like to disappoint him, but there is only one man for me.*
> *And it's impossible.*

"Impossible?" Jon and Beatrice said at the same time.

"Very interesting," Jon said, grinning.

Just then they heard footsteps up the stairs. Beatrice closed the book and threw her shawl over it.

"Granny!" Lizzie's voice.

"Leave Granny alone!" Vera's voice.

"It's okay. Come in!" Beatrice said.

"Sorry to interrupt," Vera said as she opened the door.

"You're not interrupting at all. We were just sitting here, chatting," Beatrice said, gesturing with her hands. "C'mon in, Miss Lizzie. What are you up to?"

Lizzie plopped herself onto the bed, between Beatrice and Jon.

"Playing with Mama," she said.

"Will you two be available next Friday?" Vera asked.

Beatrice and Jon looked at one another.

"Sure," Jon said.

"Can you watch Lizzie?"

"Sure," Jon said.

"What's going on next Friday?" Beatrice asked.

Vera beamed. "I have a date."

"A date?" Beatrice stood so fast, the bed rocked Jon and Lizzie so hard that they tumbled over in a fit of giggles. "With who? Dr. Green?"

Vera nodded, her face tinged in pink.

Was she embarrassed? *Why on earth?*

"It's about time," Beatrice said. "And of course we will keep Lizzie."

"Now, Mama, don't make a big deal over this. It's just dinner. A pleasant way to pass the evening. You know I don't really trust men."

"Don't kid yourself, Vera. I saw the way he looked at you. There were definitely sparks. Don't shut yourself off from the possibilities. He comes from good stock."

Vera leaned against the doorway and smiled. "Well, well, well. It's been some time since you've given me dating advice."

"Maybe I should shut my mouth."

"What?"

"You've never taken my advice before. If you had, you'd never have married you know who."

Vera laughed and waved her off.

Chapter 36

So if I'm remembering correctly, the NMO lists a "pure heritage" as part of its precepts, Bryant texted Annie.

Damn him. He knew this was her time to be at the computer, writing. Why was he interrupting her?

She hit the IGNORE button.

C'mon, Annie! came the next message.

Okay. Yes. I am busy.

I know. But what does "pure hereditary lineage" mean?

For their purposes, it means no Jews, blacks, Hispanics, or any mixing of any of those sorts of people with their sorts of people.

Hmmm. Interesting.

And stupid.

Yes. But the place that Emily McGlashen was sending money to is a funky, funky adoption agency.

What?

This just in."

What?

Her cell phone rang. It was him.
She answered the phone. "What?"
"Sweet."
"Bite me. What's going on?"
"Emily was sending money to the Alicorn Agency. It's an adoption agency that specializes in 'purity.'"
"What? Whoa! And they advertise that?"
"Not in so many words. But the FBI has gotten back to me on this, and they've a contact there that's looking around for us."
"That is so weird," Annie said. "Why would Emily be involved with an adoption agency at all?"
Then she thought of her parents. Was this the agency that she was adopted through? But it makes no sense. She had wanted to break away from her past. Why would she give them money? Unless . . .
"I'd like to talk to her parents about this," she said.
"I've already done that."
"And?"
"This is not the agency they used. They have no idea what her link to that agency is."
Annie sat back in her chair, her blue computer screen glaring at her, as she mentally leafed through Emily McGlashen and what she knew about her. She grew up in many places, became an international dance champ, opened a school in Cumberland Creek, of all places, was

murdered in her studio, didn't like Vera, was sending large sums of money to an adoption agency.

"Could she possibly . . ."

"She was young and healthy. Maybe. Maybe Emily McGlashen has a child somewhere," he said.

An odd stinging sensation crept into Annie's gut. Call it another one of her hunches. But it was strong. Loud. This was a very real possibility. But what could this have to do with her murder?

"I don't know, Adam. This is very personal."

She thought of the Greenberg family. If Emily had had a baby that she wanted to keep secret and had given it up for adoption, how would her family react? Hadn't they been through enough?

"I know," he said, breathing into the phone. "I suggest we keep it under wraps, Annie, until we find out if it's a real possibility and if it had anything to do with the murder. There's no point in hurting her family more, unless we have to."

"I agree," she said, pausing a beat to reflect on the sensitivity from him. It was unusual. He surprised her from time to time. Like the day he handed her Cookie's scrapbook, or what was left of it. It was there that day, in Cookie's empty house, that she began to see him in a new light.

"How about that?" he said in a mocking tone. "We agree on something."

"Adam—"

"Now," he said, "when were you going to tell me about her parents still being here? About them thinking of staying?"

"The next time we talked, I guess. I've been working hard on my book. Sorry."

"It's a pretty big deal," he said. "Leaving the commune. Strange, don't you think?"

She sighed. "I don't know."

"What's wrong with you? Why aren't you grilling these people? They live in a commune, for Christ's sake. Don't you think it all has something to do with the puzzle of Emily McGlashen and her murder?"

"I'm busy," she said. "I don't have time for another project. I need to wrap up this book. You can handle it, can't you?"

"Of course, but I thought with all your curiosity . . . the way you cared about your stories . . . I thought there would be no stopping you."

"I'm keeping my fingers in it," she said. "I simply don't have the fortitude to take this on full force."

"Look, I know how you're feeling. I'll never forget the way you looked the day we met in Cookie's empty house. I saw it all over you," he said. "But also, I'll never forget the way you disappointed yourself by not thinking clearly about that investigation. It's the same thing I felt," he added, his voice quieter.

He was talking about the way they were both misled about Cookie's disappearance. How neither one of them read any of the clues properly and how it left them both reeling.

He was right. Her stomach started to twist and flip.

"But that's all in the past," she said, more to herself than to him. "You have a murder case to solve. And I have a book to write."

"Well, just think about it. I've talked to them already. But I know you might have some questions of your own," he said. "Gotta go."

His face came to her mind. She could see it so clearly

and almost felt the way she had felt when he kissed her. It was one thing when she thought this attraction was simply about sex. It was another thing entirely to think he really understood her. And very possibly in a way in which her husband no longer did.

Chapter 37

Vera sat in front of her laptop; it was new, and she was just getting to know it. She had brought it along to the crop because the croppers had all promised to try digital scrap-booking. They were setting aside their projects just for tonight so that Sheila could lead them through a tutorial, but not without a great deal of complaining, especially from Paige.

"Does everything have to be on the computer these days?" said Paige, the blue light from her screen reflecting on her freckled face. "Now our whole grading system is on the computer at school, and some of our elementary schools are going paperless."

"I think it's fantastic. Sam's class is heading that way. Think of it. By the time they get to college, textbooks might be all e-books," Annie said.

Sheila sighed. "Nobody loves paper more than I do," she said and nodded toward her color-coded stacks of paper. "But once you get used to digital scrapbooking, you'll see the place for it. I certainly won't give up on the traditional, but this is so much more efficient."

Paige reached for a pumpkin muffin. "What's the deal

with efficiency? This is supposed to fun and sloppy, and I don't know . . . inefficient."

"Jesus! What's with you?" DeeAnn said after taking a deep swallow of white wine. "Chill out, would you? We agreed to learn this, so just stop your bitching."

Paige sat back, crossed her arms, and smiled despite herself.

Vera opened up the file that Sheila had told her to open. "What's the big deal, Paige? Okay, now, Sheila, what do we click on?"

"Wait, wait, wait. I'm not there yet," Paige said.

Sheila waited a few minutes and looked up over her glasses, looking very businesslike, Vera noted. "Are we ready?"

From time to time Vera marveled at Sheila. They had known one another since childhood and had always been best friends, and yet they couldn't be more different. Sheila was wiry, serious, and organized; Vera was none of those things.

But she supposed they had the basics in common, with Southern roots, a good solid family foundation, and similar interests.

"My God, what am I eating?" Annie interrupted.

"Chocolate," Sheila said.

"Not just any chocolate," Vera told them. "That is some of the finest hand-dipped chocolate in the state of Virginia." One thing Vera knew was her chocolate, which had been a passion since she stopped dieting a few years ago.

"Mmmm. Mmm!" Annie threw her head back and rolled her eyes. "Oh, my God. It's the best thing I've ever eaten in my life!"

"What's that, dear?" In walked Emily's mother, who hadn't bothered ringing the doorbell this time, or taking a shower that day, based on the acrid scent permeating the basement.

"Oh," Annie said, suddenly looking pale. "Um, chocolate. Here. Have some." She held the box up to her.

"Oh, no thanks, sweetie," Rachel said, smiling. "I'm allergic."

"To chocolate?" Vera said. "I don't know what I'd do without it."

Rachel clicked her tongue. "Plenty of other vices in the world, ya know?"

And she used several of them, Annie reminded herself.

"Please have a seat," Sheila said. "Did you bring your laptop?"

Rachel laughed. "No, sweetie. I don't do computers. I always left the technical things up to Emily. She was a genius with it, you know."

"I didn't know that," Vera said. "I didn't think she even had a computer."

"Oh yes," Annie said. "She had one. The police have it. They are scouring it for clues."

Vera squirmed around in her seat. It seemed as if the energy in the room was shifting all over the place. Now it was definitely off. Or was it in her mind? The meds the doctors had her on gave her all sorts of weird side effects.

"Don't misunderstand me," Sheila said. "You are welcome to come to our crops. Have you changed you mind about scrapbooking?"

Rachel shrugged, trying to pull out something from her bag "Not really. But I'm getting kinda bored over there at Emily's place. Feeling hemmed in a bit. Not used to the walls, man. We live in a yurt back home. I needed a break from all the cleaning and packing, too. So I've been journaling in this book."

"What will you do with her things?" Sheila asked.

"We're giving it all away, of course. We've no need for it," she said.

"What the hell is a yurt?" DeeAnn said.

"It's a round, tentlike home," Rachel said and smiled. "We like living in a circle. And it's so light filled. I love light. Emily's place is so dark."

She finally stopped struggling and pulled the book out. It was a journal of sorts. She opened it, and there was a page with a photo of a very young Rachel holding a small baby.

"Emily?" Annie asked.

"Yes," she said.

The words *She kept this photo* were written in purple ink across the page. Something else was also written on the page, alongside the photo. *And I found it in a box of her things a few weeks after she died. I cherish the days of her babyhood. From the moment she learned to walk, she began her dance. The dance that took her far from home, far from us.*

"How did you make your paper look like this?" Paige said.

"I used tea," Rachel responded. "I teach art where we live. The kids love this trick."

"Have some cupcakes?" DeeAnn said, holding a plate up to her.

"Don't mind if I do," she said and smiled.

"What was Emily like as a child?" DeeAnn asked.

Rachel shrugged. "Pretty typical, except for her dancing. She was . . . extraordinary. There was a dance studio near where we lived, and I cleaned it so that she could have lessons. I wanted her to have ballet, but she wanted to do Irish dancing. I told her the only way she'd get to Irish dance is if she also did ballet. But she hated ballet."

The group quieted.

Rachel bit from her cupcake and swallowed. "You know, I always wondered about her birth parents. If they were athletes or dancers . . . because Donald and I, well"—she made a gesture at her thin body—"we're not very physical." She laughed. "She was different from the start," Rachel added, looking over the table. "If I'm to be honest . . . she was always so strong willed that it scared me."

Vera piped up. "She was a very strong-willed person."

"It sometimes seemed like she had no compassion, but she did. It was always in the most unexpected places, though," Rachel sighed. "Did she have no friends here?"

She looked around the group, at each face.

"Not really," Paige said. "In fact, we could not ever remember seeing her with anybody other than her dancers. We were surprised to hear she had a boyfriend. She was such a loner."

"That makes me sad. It was always the case, I'm afraid," Rachel said. "And I'd really like to find out who this man is. I mean, I don't care if he's married. . . . I'll be discreet. I just need to know him. Emily was madly in love with him."

The room stilled as all the croppers stopped eating and fussing with their computers, looking at Rachel. Half-empty wineglasses sat, half-eaten pumpkin muffins lay on their napkins, and computer keys remained untouched.

"She was a serious child. No matter what we tried, the streak of seriousness never left her."

Vera felt every word this woman spoke. Was it something about her voice? Something about her?

"Emily was always so . . . sensitive. Strong but sensitive. I never knew her to have a boyfriend, so I'm intrigued. It's funny. . . ." She paused and looked around the table at the scrappers. "I feel closer to her now than I have in years. Now that she's gone. Is it something about this place? That I'm reading her journals? I don't know."

Vera looked at Annie, whose big brown eyes were shimmering with tears. She looked as if she was caught between crying and ranting. Annie. She certainly was an odd bird.

"I don't know about anybody else," Annie said, "but I'd love it if you could tell us more about her."

"I'd love to dear," Rachel replied after a few moments. "But I'm afraid I've taken up too much of your time . . . away from . . . your scrapbooking. I'll be in touch with you soon."

And she was out the door before anybody could protest.

Chapter 38

Vera was not happy about it, but Beatrice insisted on having the Reillys over again.

"When I invited them, I didn't know you and Lizzie would be living here."

Beatrice leaned into the open oven and pulled out her roasting chicken, then slid it back in.

Vera felt the heat from the oven in a wave.

"So maybe Lizzie and I will go to DeeAnn's Bakery or something," Vera said.

"I won't hear of it." Beatrice stood up and slid off her oven mitt. "What is the problem? They seem like nice people."

"It's just awkward now that I know that Kelsey is their niece. I mean, how strange is that? And they are living in my house. The house I shared with Bill."

"Life is full of these things, Vera. You've been too sheltered."

"Sheltered?" Vera flung her arms around.

Jon walked in the room. "Wow, it smells very good in here."

Vera smiled at him. "Is Lizzie awake yet?"

He nodded. "Soon. She's getting to be a good napper."

"I think she's still in recovery mode," Vera said, reaching for cornmeal. She was making corn biscuits to go with their chicken. The menu also included collard greens with bacon drippings and corn. There would be strawberry pie for dessert, already in the refrigerator.

Beatrice saw that Vera had everything under control with the corn biscuits, and so she and Jon sat down for some tea on the back patio and looked out over where their pool would be. Should have been by now. But the state archeologist had hit the mother lode in Beatrice's backyard. She never knew who would come traipsing through her yard next. Most of them were nice young men, but a few of them had foul mouths and once left some soda bottles lying around. That would be the last time they did that. She grinned. *Bet they don't know a sweet-looking little old lady even knows words like that.*

"So have you given much thought to Willa Rose?" Jon asked.

"Yes, but not as much as you would think. But I did talk to Paige about it. I don't think she'd mention it to anybody else. With everything going on. Lizzie in the hospital. Them moving in. And now this business with Vera getting hypnotized."

"What? I missed something," he said. "Hypnotized?"

"Oh. Well, Vera wants to be led through the murder scene. She asked her shrink about it. He thought it would be best if she was hypnotized while they were doing it. It's very strange, if you ask me," she said.

"Well, that is strange. Did I hear that right?" a new voice chimed in. It was Leola Reilly.

"Hey, hello," Beatrice said. "Come in. Come in."

After they were situated on the patio, with Vera still in the kitchen, the conversation resumed.

"So they are going to hypnotize Vera?" Leola looked a little too concerned.

"Oh yes. Well, you know." Beatrice shrugged. She wasn't sure if she liked this woman knowing much of her business. "She's been sleepwalking, and they are just looking for the cause. Trying everything they can think of."

She looked at Jon, and he nodded. "Well done," his eyes seemed to tell her.

Just then Vera squealed, and a loud crash came from the kitchen.

When Beatrice arrived on the scene, Vera was helping a red-faced John Reilly up off the floor. He was slicking back his hair, which had been messed up a bit. A full head of gray hair.

"I'm so sorry," a flustered Vera said. "I don't know what got into me."

"What? What happened?" Leola ran to her husband's side.

"I—" Vera started to say.

"I'm sorry, Vera. I didn't mean to startle you," he said. "I came up behind her to get a good look at what she was doing, and the next thing I knew, I was on the floor."

Beatrice looked at her daughter and knew there was more to the story. "Never come up behind a Matthews woman," Beatrice said after a few moments. "We're tougher than we look," she added and managed a weak laugh.

"Now what can I get everybody to drink?" Jon said, breaking the tension. Jon led them all into the sitting room and took their drink requirements.

Beatrice watched him go, then spun around to face Vera, lifted her eyebrows.

"He pinched me, Mama," Vera said.

"Surely not!"

"Shall I pull my pants down for you to see the mark I'm sure he left on my bottom?"

"Humph," Beatrice said. "That's not necessary. But what on earth would get into a person?"

"Men, Mama," Vera said. "None of them are to be trusted."

She turned and poured her batter in the already warmed cast-iron skillet. It made a hissing noise.

What was the world coming to when a man pinched another woman while his wife sat in the next room? It was so crass.

Vera set the skillet in the oven.

"Now, give that about fifteen minutes," she said, almost to herself. She then turned around and said to her mother, "I hope you won't mind if I leave now. I told you I don't like these people. I'd rather not break bread with them. Lizzie and I will go out, maybe to Annie's or DeeAnn's, but I can't stay here."

What had gotten into Vera? There was a day when she'd have kept her mouth shut and stayed and helped out, like a good daughter. Well, she couldn't blame her for this. What right did he have to help himself to a feel of her daughter? She had no choice but to carry on with the dinner party; she didn't want to humiliate his wife. But she'd never ask them back here again. Beatrice took a deep breath. How would she manage not to throttle this man? Well, evidently, her daughter just about had. Beatrice beamed. She stood back and surveyed her daughter, a stronger Vera than ever before. Older. Wiser. A single mother. A woman who would not put up with a man pinching her bottom. Sometimes Beatrice caught glimpses of her daughter that almost took her breath away. She was so busy worrying about her that sometimes she forgot to see her for who she really was.

"Well, now," Beatrice said, "I think you should go when Lizzie wakes up. And I wish I could go with you. I can promise you he won't be welcome in this house again."

"Thanks, Mama," Vera said, kissed her on the cheek, and exited the room.

Chapter 39

"I have a bellyache," Sam groaned when Annie tried to wake him that morning. She felt his head, and he burned with fever.

"Okay, sweetie, go back to sleep," she told him. He slunk back into a sea of blankets, looking like a little rumpled ball.

Meanwhile, his brother was up, dressed, and hungry.

Mike was in the kitchen, pouring a cup of coffee. "What's wrong?"

"Sam's sick," she replied, reaching for the Cheerios box and a bowl. "I told him to stay in bed."

"This one will probably get sick, too," Mike said, reaching for Ben, picking him up, and placing him on a kitchen chair.

She sighed, placing the cereal bowl down in front of her son.

"You have work to do?"

"I always have work to do, Mike," she said, reaching for the cup of coffee she had poured herself before Sam called her back to his room. The coffee was already tepid. "Have you looked over your schedule?"

"Yeah," he said, sitting down, pulling his chair in closer to the table. "Ben, eat with a spoon, please."

"Ben!"

Yes, their child was lapping up his cereal like a dog.

"You know better," Annie said, tousling his hair.

He looked at them and grinned. "Sorry," he said.

"And?" Annie said to her husband.

"I just don't know when I can get away. Maybe two weeks. If the Grimsdale account goes well this week. Then I won't have to call on them that weekend."

"Well, Mike, I can't make reservations without a definite date."

"Yes, you can. Go ahead. Then we can cancel, if we need to," he said in kind of a business tone, which annoyed Annie. You'd think she was asking him to a business conference rather than a romantic weekend.

"Well, do you even want to go?" she blurted.

He shrugged. "Obviously, it's important to you. So yeah, I want to go."

Annie bit her lip. Ben was still there, finishing up his cereal. Was he going only to please her? Not because he wanted to spend time with her, get things back on track? Or didn't he realize they were as bad as what she thought they were?

"Oh, jeez," he said. "I've got to get going. An early meeting." He stood, then leaned down to kiss her.

"Have a good day," she said, standing and placing Ben's cereal bowl in the sink. She glanced at her son's Cookie Monster backpack with the lunch box attached. She had remembered to pack it, sign all the forms, and send the money for a field trip next week, for which she was still awaiting word as to whether or not she'd be chaperoning.

Later, after Ben was gone and she'd given Sam a dose of

Tylenol, she sat down at her computer to look up the Alicorn Agency. Very elegant Web site.

She clicked on the next page.

Our Heritage
Our Future
Our Partners

She clicked on *Partners*.

Ali Labs
Ali Genetics

Labs? Genetics?

So strange. An adoption agency partnered with labs? What were they doing? Growing children? What an absurd thought.

The agency's mission is to offer children to discerning parents throughout the world whose interests include maintaining genetic purity and raising children of the same ilk and stature.

The hair on the back of Annie's neck prickled.

It was right there in black and white. What was their definition of *genetic purity*?

Did she even want to know? And what was Emily McGlashen's interest in it? The coroner had confirmed that she was not pregnant when she was killed. Nor had she ever had a baby. Was she planning to adopt one of these children? That must be it.

Annie had read about successful women opting to adopt without a partner. She thought they were crazy, unless they had help. Single parenting was tough. Hell, parenting with two people was tough. She couldn't imagine embarking on parenting alone, although she had the utmost respect for those who did, like Vera. Even though Vera had a strong support system, when it came right down to it, she was alone.

But the question remained: what was Emily's interest here, and what did it have to do with her murder, if anything?

And . . .

There was this little piece of information that Annie could not seem to shake—that the NMO was also interested in genetic purity. A strange coincidence was that the investigation was leading her to an adoption agency and Emily was adopted.

No. Annie did not believe in this strong of a coincidence. There must be a connection.

She thought about Luther Vandergrift. Was Annie going to have to question him again? She dreaded it. Maybe she should take another tack. Look further into the adoption agency. The labs.

Man, it made Annie's head hurt. What a tangled set of circumstances. If she could just find the right thread to pull on.

"Mommy!" she heard Sam yell. Then came the horrible sound of him throwing up. She ran in the room just in time to see him and his bed covered in vomit.

"Mommy!" he cried.

"Hold on," she said. "Don't move. I'll get the shower going, and we can just rinse it all off at one time."

He sobbed, nodding his head, his face red from crying, and trying to stay as still as possible, difficult for any sick boy, but particularly this squirmy sick boy.

Poor boy. So sick. Annie hoped that nobody else would get sick, but even as she hoped, she knew it was futile.

She'd probably have Ben home tomorrow, as well. Maybe even Mike.

Annie held back the vomit she felt creeping up her throat. Happened every time one of the boys was sick. She could handle a lot of things, but puke was difficult. She'd find herself heaving soon enough.

Chapter 40

When Vera opened the door, long-stemmed red roses met her, along with Eric Green's grinning face, which popped up around them. "Hello," he said.

"Why, hello! Are those for me?"

"No, they're for me!" Beatrice said, coming alongside of her and laughing.

"Actually," he said, "these are for Vera." He handed them to her. "And these are for you, Ms. Matthews." He handed her a box of chocolates.

"Well," Beatrice said, "the boy's got class, just like his daddy. Come on in."

Eric laughed as he entered their home. "It's been a long time since I've been called a boy."

"C'mon in and have a seat. Can I get you something to drink?" Beatrice said.

"Thanks, Ms. Matthews, but our reservations are for eight and the restaurant is in Charlottesville. We'd better get going."

"Let me just grab my purse," Vera said, reaching for her handbag.

Vera's heart thumped. She'd always found him pleasantly attractive when she ran into him at the hospital, but she'd somehow not noticed his classic good looks. His hair fell in beautiful curls around his square face, and he had a dimpled chin, full lips, and those deep-set brown eyes. So intense looking. *Get a grip, Vera. It's just dinner. And remember, men are not to be trusted.*

She wore a new old dress she'd found at a vintage shop in Charlottesville. It was a black, slimming little number that reminded her of Jackie O. She donned red heels, carried her red bag, and wore red lipstick, which used to drive Tony crazy. *Tony.* Funny, she hadn't even thought about him in months, and this time last year they were sleeping together every chance they got, given that he lived in New York and she in Cumberland Creek.

He drove a Mercedes, which was the beige one that Bill had admired over the years in various parking lots, mostly at the hospital. There was only one in town, and this was it. She had had no idea. She sank into the plush leather seat. *Yes,* she thought, *I could get used to this.* And she felt so comfortable with him.

"You know, Vera, I've admired you for many years," Eric told her during dinner. "But you were always spoken for."

"Thanks," she said, noting the way the candlelight played against his skin. "I married Bill right out of college. Big mistake, I guess."

He chuckled and took a sip of wine. "Well, my crush goes way back to high school."

"High school? We didn't go to school together. . . ."

"No, but I saw you around, and our dads were good friends," he said. "I remember reading an article about you in the paper when you were dancing in New York. And before that . . . well, you were always in the paper for winning awards, being homecoming queen, and I can't remember everything else."

"Oh," she said, feeling her face heat up. Was she blushing?

And where had she been that she'd never noticed this Eric as a boy? Well, she always did have her head in the clouds, or rather on the stage. She didn't pay any attention at all to boys in high school. She did have a boyfriend, but nothing serious, just a boy to escort her to dances and parties.

"So, how is Lizzie?" he said, changing the subject, his dark eyebrows lifting.

"She is getting better, but she's still not quite herself," she said. "Easy to get down to sleep these days, and that's not like her."

"Active, huh?"

Vera nodded, noting the way his long fingers wrapped around his wineglass. A physician's hands. Hands that tended to the sick and traumatized. Just like her father's hands. She warmed.

"Where did you go to medical school?" she asked.

"University of Virginia. Where else?" he said.

"Oh my, yes. Where else?" she said. "Your daddy?"

He nodded. "I toyed with Princeton and even was accepted. But he wouldn't hear of it."

Vera bit into her chicken, which, next to her mother's fried chicken, was the best she'd ever had. It was so tender that it almost melted in her mouth. The asparagus served alongside was cooked to perfection, as well.

He reached across the table and grabbed her hand. "You are such a beautiful woman. I just had to tell you that."

Vera marveled at the sincerity of his remark, and the gesture seemed natural, as if they'd known each other for years.

Still, he was a man. Men were really not to be trusted.

He lifted her hand to his lips. She felt his breath with a soft kiss on her skin, and a tingle shot through her body.

Goodness. She needed to be cautious. She felt her heart stirring just a bit.

There was a little weariness behind his eyes.

"Late night?" she asked.

"Delivering babies. It's not something I usually do," he said. "But lately . . . well, I get house calls sometimes. And I've been doing some home deliveries."

"Home deliveries?" Vera said, thinking of her own birthing experience. "What's wrong with people?"

He just laughed.

"It seems to be in fashion with some younger women," he said, smiling. "What can I say?"

God, he was so handsome. Vera just wanted to bite his dimpled chin, but, of course, she held back.

Soft, jazzy music began to play, and several couples danced. The next thing Vera knew, she was swept away by her date, who happened to be a good dancer. She and Bill had never gone dancing. This was new, lovely, so divine, with their bodies moving together to the music. His touch was gentle but leading and strong.

Could she?

No. Of course not. Men were jerks. Led around by their interest in sex and not caring who they hurt in the meantime. Of course, some women were like that, too.

But when Eric grinned at her like that, it was hard to remember why she shouldn't trust him.

On the way home, she found out about his past. Divorced. No children. Just work and golf. She had always wished Bill had a hobby—other than the one that included his sleeping with young women.

When Eric pulled along the street and shut off the engine, she knew what was coming. Her heart raced. She started to sweat. He was going to kiss her. She didn't know quite what to do with herself. Should she lean into him? Open her mouth? Keep it closed? What if she had bad breath?

The moments between him stopping the car engine and him putting his arm around her were agonizing. But soon enough his lips found hers, and with just the gleam of the moon and a fading streetlight for light, they managed to find their way.

After necking in his car in front of her house like two teenagers, they said good night and kissed one more time. No, he wasn't Prince Charming, but this was a good start. A very good start.

After he drove off, she reached in her purse for the key and then dropped her purse on the porch. The door flew open. Beatrice stood there with her hands on her hips.

"Well?"

"Well, what, Mama?" She began scooting all the stuff into her purse.

"How did it go?"

"It was lovely," she said, then touched some unfamiliar item. She looked at her hand, and there was a miniature gillie fashioned into a key chain. She gasped. "Where did this come from?"

"What is it?" Beatrice leaned over.

"It's a key chain made from a tiny gillie," Vera said, holding it up.

"Well, what's it doing in your bag?"

"I've never seen it before in my life," Vera said, a jolt of fear moving through her. Or had she? No. She was certain she'd never seen such a thing.

She shoved it into her purse and looked at her mother, who was shaking her head.

"It's not over," Beatrice said, frowning. "I had hoped that when you moved in . . . Let me call Bryant."

"Do we really have to? What can he tell us? Okay. Someone dropped this in my purse, but when and where? How long has it been there?"

"Didn't he record all the items in your purse? He should be able to tell us something." Beatrice waltzed off to call him, leaving Vera holding her purse and sitting on the front doorstep.

She breathed in the chilly night air. It was a hell of an ending to a nearly perfect evening.

Chapter 41

"Whoa," Bryant said when he walked into kitchen
and saw Vera standing at the sink in her black dress and
heels. "Vera?"

When Beatrice walked in, Vera was smiling. Was she
just imagining that blush on Bryant's face?

"Well, are you going to get down to business, or are you
going to stand there, ogling my daughter?" Beatrice said,
pulling out a chair. "Sit down, Bryant. Can I get you something?"

"Um, er, no thanks. Can I see the object you found in
your bag?" he said, sitting down and clearing his throat. "I
barely recognized you in that dress. I've never seen you
dressed up. That's all."

Yes, he was obviously taken aback by Vera in that
black dress. Interesting. Once again, Beatrice found Bryant
intriguing. She used to not like him at all. But here he was,
youngish, good-looking, no wife, no relationship, that she
knew of. He was certainly dazzled by a beautiful woman,
so he probably wasn't gay. She reddened at the thought, as
if it were any of her business.

When the tiny gillie landed with a small thud on the
table, it was as if he was snapped back into reality.

"What is that? One of those Irish dance shoes?"

"Yes," Vera said. "I found it in my purse this evening, when I came home."

"From where?"

"I was at Luminosity with Eric tonight."

"Eric?"

"Dr. Green," Beatrice interrupted.

"Did you leave your bag at all tonight?" he asked.

"I've been thinking about that, and we did dance once. I left my bag at the table."

"Hold on," he said, dialing the buttons on his cell. "Can you get a guest list and a list of the employees at Luminosity tonight?" Pause. "If they give you any grief, tell them we can get a warrant."

"What will you do with the list?" she asked.

"This is where detective work gets exciting," he said and smiled. "We'll go through and see if any names look familiar. If anybody had a record, that kind of thing. If not, we'll need to start contacting people. What about this Dr. Green?"

"But he was with me, on the dance floor," she reminded him.

"Did he lead you onto the dance floor? Or did he come up behind you?"

She thought for a moment. "I remember the way his hand touched my back. . . . He must have been behind me."

"But why would he put ghillies in her bag? That makes no sense," Beatrice said. "It must have been a restaurant person."

"Not necessarily," Bryant said. "We need to check out this doctor."

"Someone that works at that restaurant could have killed Emily," Vera said after a minute.

"Does anybody from Cumberland Creek work there?" Beatrice said.

Vera shrugged.

"Let's not get carried away," Bryant said. "Your vandal or stalker might not be the same person as Emily's killer."

Did he just say stalker? Beatrice bristled.

The next day was a glorious spring day, exactly the kind of day that made Beatrice want to get her hands in the soil. But her yard was still too torn up from the pool construction. At least today they were working, and they thought if the weather held up, the pool might be finished in a week or two. They were confident that all the archeological finds had been found. They just weren't sure what any of it was or what it meant. And they would have to leave the old house foundation in place until they knew what it was. But for now they could ready the other part of the pool.

"You are losing your mind over that, aren't you?" Jon said, motioning to the pool area.

"Yes." She smiled. "I'm just eager to get the pool in. And get my life back. I want to get the landscaping and gardening started."

She spread butter over her pancakes. They were enjoying a quiet breakfast, with Vera and Elizabeth gone for the day.

"Well, let's do something today. Visit Rose? Go to the park?"

Just then the doorbell rang.

Paige stood on Beatrice's front porch with a beat-up manila folder.

"You found something?" Beatrice said, opening the door.

"Oh, boy, did I," Paige said "I can't stay long. Gotta get to the school at some point." She glanced at her watch.

"Well, come on in."

Paige sat at the table and spread out her papers, with Jon and Beatrice looking on.

"You've gotten this done quickly," Beatrice said.

"Evidently, someone had already been researching her, and the information was there." She placed her glasses on her face. "Now, this is very interesting."

"Go on, please," Jon said with impatience.

"Willa Rose McGlashen is listed in the Civil War directory as a war hero."

"What? But—" Beatrice started.

"Yes, yes, I know. Women didn't fight in wars. Well, that's a bogus notion. There were several women who fought in our Civil War. Of course, they pretended to be men."

"Is that what she did?" Beatrice said.

"No, dear. Willa Rose McGlashen was a spy of sorts."

"A spy?"

Paige nodded. "A spy for the other side. Some might call her a traitor."

Chapter 42

The Alicorn Agency, one of the most successful adoption agencies in Europe, announced that it has now placed all 197 displaced orphans in its domain. The agency has international offices scattered throughout the world and has an outreach team that travels to war-torn areas to help house, clothe, and feed children left homeless through the ravages of war.

Well, that's very cool, Annie thought. Maybe Emily was interested in helping children. If so, that would be the first kind facet to her personality that Annie knew about. But then again, she often wondered how well she knew anybody. Who would have thought that Vera's marriage would fall apart and her husband would be living with a very young law student? Who would have thought Emily McGlashen would meet her death by strangulation in her own dance studio? Who would have thought that she herself would awaken in the middle of the night because of passionate dreams about Adam Bryant?

Life was full of surprises.

Annie skipped over a few paragraphs—she could spot PR fluff from a mile away—to this.

> *To the allegations that the Alicorn Agency placed children with only the wealthiest families, even if it meant taking them away from their own country, a spokesperson says that there is no basis for these allegations. "We are striving to work with local officials and within all international law. The Alicorn Agency has an excellent record of finding homes for thousands of homeless children. We strive to keep them in their own countries, but sometimes international adoption is the only answer."*

Nothing about the labs. Hmmm.

Annie looked at the clock. *Okay.* Thirty minutes until the kids came home from soccer practice. She had plenty of time to make a connection with this reporter.

"*Baltimore Herald,*" the voice said on the other end of the line.

"Hi. I'd like to speak to Maya Simmeth."

"One moment please."

A very young-sounding voice came over the phone. "This is Maya."

"Maya, this is Annie Chamovitz, I freelance for the *Washington Herald* occasionally."

"How can I help you?" she said after a pause filled with the sound of a computer keyboard. She was Googling Annie. Now, that made her smile.

"I'm interested in the Alicorn Agency," Annie said after clearing her throat.

Maya guffawed.

"Pardon?"

Pause.

"Well, that was so long ago. And to tell you the truth, I don't remember much, except that something was really weird about it."

"What was weird about it?" Annie asked.

"Well, first, the name . . ."

"The name?"

"Yes. Alicorn."

"I'm sorry, but I don't follow."

"It has a mythological meaning. It's the horn of a unicorn."

"Humph," Annie said. The unicorn. A symbol of purity. Why hadn't that come up in her search?

"Yes," she said. "And you know they were freaks about reviewing my article before it went to press, which is why—"

"It seemed like PR," Annie interrupted.

"Nabbed," Maya said and chuckled. "Look, I can check into my files and get back with you. I'm on deadline and need to go."

"Okay, yeah, sure. I'd appreciate anything you can tell me," Annie said.

She sat back in her chair. What did any of this have to do with Emily? Anything? She grinned. She was investigating a murder, and here she was, looking up unicorns and alicorns.

She flipped through Web sites and checked her e-mail and saw an interesting ad. An Irish dance and music festival was scheduled to be the first event next weekend in the new amphitheater. It was a big deal for Cumberland Creek. The festival was being dedicated to Emily McGlashen. According to the ad, her parents would be there. So would the Reillys, who were also listed as one of the sponsors.

Chapter 43

Vera took a sip of wine, set her glass down, and finished telling the scrapbookers about her perfect date.

"So he kissed you?" DeeAnn said, then bit into a huge oatmeal cookie. "Not bad," she said as Vera nodded.

"Boy, did he ever. We made out in the car like two teenagers," she said, her face hot and reddening.

They laughed.

Sheila was hunched over her laptop. "I can't even remember what that was like," she said.

"I hear ya," DeeAnn said. "You know, these vegan oatmeal cookies are a lot better than I thought they'd be. I'm surprised."

Annie spoke up. "Why vegan?"

"It's this new baker I hired. Young. Made me start thinking about this vegan stuff. They have a point. It's probably healthier for us and the planet. But most of it has always tasted like crap," she said. "But the vegans have come a long way."

"Speaking of vegan, where is Emily's mother?" Paige said, her voice a whisper because she had a sore throat. "I went to the apartment, and they weren't there."

The room grew silent.

"Nobody knows. I've not seen her in a few days. Maybe she went back to wherever it is that she's from," Sheila said. "Oh my! That looks gorgeous, DeeAnn!"

"You think?" DeeAnn held up her page of cookies. "Cookie Love." She was working on her bakery scrapbook. She'd made a cutout cookie jar, which she'd placed on its side, with photos of her cookies coming out of it. The page was bright pink and sparkly. DeeAnn loved her pink.

"Check this out," she said, still holding up the page. She untwisted a pink ribbon from a clasp, and a flap opened. Inside the flap was a handwritten recipe card, which was an actual card that had been placed on the page—not one specifically made for scrapbooking. "I'm really getting into these hidden elements on pages. It's so much fun. And so easy to do. You just fold the paper or cardstock and place it on a page with the clasp and ribbon. But you don't even have to do that."

"Did you put the recipe card on after you placed the element?" Sheila asked.

"Not in this case, but I guess you could," DeeAnn said. She held up her work and admired it.

"They've not had a funeral for Emily? A memorial service? Nothing?" Paige asked after a few moments.

Nobody answered.

Vera glanced around the table at her friends, took them in. DeeAnn and her pink. Her shop had a lot of pink in it, too. Cocoa and pink. Every time Vera saw those colors together, she thought of DeeAnn standing behind the counter, fussing over some icing or scone or something. She was a great baker, an even better businesswoman. Vera admired her sense of business and needed to get some of that herself. She'd not raised the prices for dance classes in years, so she really needed to catch up to where she should be.

Now with the economy so down, her dance families—those that were left—were struggling, too.

Sheila was another good businesswoman. She opened her home to the crop every Saturday night. Of course, they ended up keeping her in business, buying all her paper, embellishments, and doodads. It used to be that Sheila's dream was to open a scrapbooking store, but no more. Now she wanted to create her own line of scrapbooking products. That would be amazing.

"I saw that there's going to be an Irish music and dance festival next weekend over at Riverview Park. They are going to use the new amphitheater," Annie said as she smoothed over the page.

"Really?" Paige said.

"It's the first event," Sheila said. "They are hoping to start an annual thing. In fact, they wanted to have it ready for the St. Patrick's Day Festival. Something happened to slow it down. Some permit problems or something."

Vera rolled her eyes. She knew that damned Dr. Reilly would be involved.

"Yeah. Interesting," Annie said after taking a swig of beer. "The festival is dedicated to Emily. Her students will be performing. Her parents are going to be there, along with the Reillys."

"That leaves me out," Vera said. "The bastard pinched my hind end while standing in my mother's kitchen."

"Well, how many times do we need to hear that story?" Sheila said, looking up from her computer and laughing. "Shouldn't stop you from going and having fun."

Vera waved her off.

"We're going," Annie said. "If anybody wants to hang out."

"You'll stick out like a sore thumb with all the blond-haired and blue-eyed people there," DeeAnn said.

"DeeAnn!" Paige said.

"Well, it's true!"

"I'm used to that by now," Annie said. "The Greenbergs are not blond-haired and blue-eyed, by the way. And besides, I'm counting on sticking out."

"You know, Emily colored her hair and wore blue contacts," Vera said. "Did you know that?"

Annie made a mental note.

Paige leaned across the table. "What's going on, Annie?"

Annie proceeded to tell the crop what she'd found out about Alicorn.

"So what do you think is going on, and how does this relate to the case?" Sheila asked.

"I have no idea," Annie replied. "But I just have a strange feeling about this."

DeeAnn groaned. "The last time you had a strange feeling, well, we ended up on the mountain, chasing a cult . . . and I ended up beating the living crap out of some weird cult dude." She smiled. "I'm in."

Chapter 44

Beatrice finished rinsing the breakfast dishes and placing them in the dishwasher—a new fancy-schmancy one, courtesy of Jon. She didn't really need such a contraption, but he insisted on her having the best of everything. The best according to Jon, that is.

He had gone on his morning walk while the first few men and women of the crew from the Virginia Department of Historic Resources gathered in Beatrice's backyard, discussing operations for the day. Vera and Lizzie had gone to some Mommy and Me program at the library.

When the doorbell rang, Beatrice thought it must be Jon, who always seemed to forget his key. She had always kept the front door unlocked until a few years ago. When she opened the door, she was surprised to find Annie standing there, smiling at her.

"Good morning," she said.

"Well, don't just stand there. Come in," Beatrice said, opening the door. "Coffee? I have a fresh pot."

"That would be awesome, Bea," Annie said, eyeing the scones and making herself at home at Bea's chrome and turquoise kitchen table.

"Cinnamon," Beatrice said, setting the coffee in a large mug in front of her. "Have one."

Annie smiled, leaning forward. "Sure."

"What's up?" Beatrice said.

"I wonder what you know about genetics," Annie said.

"Not my specialty," Beatrice said and took a sip of her coffee. "I mean, I know the basic stuff. That's about it. Why?"

"Well, you know, Emily McGlashen was giving money to this adoption agency in Switzerland that offers 'genetically pure' children," Annie said, then took a bite of scone, rolling her eyes. "Heaven," she said between bites.

Beatrice smiled, then knit her eyebrows. "Did you say 'genetically pure' children?"

Annie nodded.

"What's that supposed to mean?"

Annie shrugged. "I'm guessing you can adopt a child that's purely Irish or Jewish or Polish."

"Pshaw," Beatrice said. "Are there any pure people anywhere anymore? I doubt that. Well, if they have people buying babies on that basis, it seems like there's a bunch of suckers out there somewhere."

"Well, that's what I thought, too," Annie said. "But there's another side to their operation. A partnership, a lab of some kind."

Beatrice took a bite of scone and another sip of coffee as she looked at Annie, who was young, beautiful, and smart as a whip. Beatrice loved that she came to her to bounce ideas off. Kept her sharp.

"A lab? Like a . . . research lab?" Beatrice felt the wheels in her brain starting to turn.

"I'm assuming. I've been trying to track down this writer. I spoke to her briefly, but now she's not returning my calls. Anyway, she wrote a little fluff piece on them, and I thought she'd give me more info. Evidently, she had problems with the story. But how freaky is this? The name of the agency and lab is Alicorn, which is the horn of a unicorn—"

"A symbol of purity." Beatrice finished her sentence and raised an eyebrow.

Just then Jon walked into the house.

"Good to see you remembered your keys," Beatrice said, smiling up at him.

He smiled back. "Good morning, Annie." Then to Beatrice, he said, "What is the symbol of purity?"

"The alicorn, which is the horn of a unicorn."

"Alicorn?" he said. "Hmm, that sounds so familiar. Have I just seen that somewhere?"

"Well, I don't know if you don't know," Beatrice said, watching his slight figure as he walked to the sink and poured himself a glass of water. The glass clanked gently on the counter. A breeze tugged at her kitchen window curtain.

"You know, there are adoption agencies that specialize in Chinese babies, for example," Annie went on to Beatrice. "Or Russian babies. But to specialize in genetically pure?"

"And the lab . . . ," Beatrice said. "Are they creating pure babies? And according to whose definition?"

"My thoughts exactly."

"Genetically pure?" Jon said. "The last time I heard those terms was in connection with the war and Hitler. You weren't pure if you were Jewish."

"Jon!" Beatrice said.

"It's true, Bea. It's a matter of historic record," Annie said. "And I think that's why this has freaked me out so much. It certainly smacks of racism."

"But it all depends on your definition," Jon said. "If I'm Jewish, I may want a genetically pure Jewish baby. Or if I'm black—"

"We get it, Jon," Beatrice said.

"For me, the question is, what is the connection between this agency and Emily McGlashen?" Annie said.

"Maybe you should follow the money trail," Jon said, then leaned down to kiss Beatrice on the cheek. "Well, I'm off to get a shower."

"He's a bit cheeky this morning," Beatrice said, grinning.

"He's right, of course," Annie said. "I've tried to follow the money. The agency refuses to answer my questions. Privacy issues. But the police are working on it."

"Bryant?" Beatrice said skeptically. "I wouldn't trust that."

"I think one of the new guys is working on it," Annie said.

"You should have seen him eyeing Vera the other night," Beatrice said.

"The new guy?"

"No, Bryant. He came over when she found that weird little ghillie key chain in her purse. It was the night she had her first date with the doctor. Anyway. The man could barely keep his tongue in his mouth. Couldn't put a sentence together. It was kind of funny. Nothing overt."

Annie's face changed from alert to mystified and sort of fell.

What was that all about?

"Indeed," was all that she said.

"I've seen 'genetically pure' used other places, not just in reference to Nazis. Also the NMO. Remember?" Beatrice suddenly said.

"How could I forget?" Annie said, shaking her head as if she were shaking something off, a tick, an emotion. "But I can't seem to find a link . . . unless . . . Emily herself was the link."

"I'm not following," Beatrice said.

"I mean, she shows up dead. Murdered. We find out she's been giving money to this agency. And we also find out that she knew Luther, who researched her family before she came here."

"Well, sounds perfectly logical that there should be a connection. We're missing a thread. And what kind of connection could it be that needed to be severed so badly that Emily McGlashen is killed in such a brutal way?"

"That's the million-dollar question," said Annie, propping her elbows on the table and dropping her chin into her hand.

Chapter 45

It seemed as if the whole town had come out for the first Cumberland Creek Festival of Irish and Old-Time Music. The fact that a coldhearted killer was probably among them did not seem to faze them. Annie held on to Sam's hand, and Mike had Ben. A woman passed by them dressed like a green fairy, wings and all. Annie blinked, and Sam grinned.

They walked by food booths that were selling Irish brown bread and corned beef sandwiches, fish and chips, and oatmeal cookies. Another booth sold some food with cabbage in it, from the scent of it. Annie's boys wanted ice cream, and as they were standing at the booth, someone handed Annie a program. She stuck it in her bag and helped collect the ice cream cones.

They found a bench and perched themselves, listening to Irish music playing in the distance. It was a typical spring day in Cumberland Creek. The sky was bright blue, and dogwoods and cherry trees were in bloom, with their pinks and whites popping. A row of yellow forsythia skirted around the other side of the river.

The main show started in twenty minutes, which was plenty of time for the boys to finish their ice cream. In the meantime a group of young girls dressed in Irish dancing garb gathered at the far end of the park. DeeAnn, Paige, and Sheila walked up just as the boys were finishing their cones. They decided to head over to the amphitheater together so they could all sit around one other. They passed a man selling balloons, and in the distance a beautiful, colorful kite flew in the sky. The boys loved it.

Yes, Annie thought, *this is the kind of small town life we were opting for.* Maybe it was going to be okay for them. Maybe they would get through the school stuff okay. Maybe moving here was going to turn out to be a good thing.

She looked at Mike, caught his eye, and he smiled at her. God, she loved him. They had been through a lot together. Everything about him said it was going to be okay. He soothed her. She reached for his hand.

She wanted to get this book sent off to the publisher and take a break, work on the garden, spend time with the boys and her husband. Was it just a matter of where she placed her efforts? Rededicating herself, yet again, to her marriage, her family?

"What a gorgeous day," DeeAnn said and sighed. "Hey, boys, I've got some cookies."

"Great," Mike said. "They just had ice cream. They are going to need to run some of that sugar buzz off."

"That's your problem, not mine," DeeAnn said good-naturedly. "You want one?"

Mike shrugged and took one. "Okay," he said and grinned.

The boys thanked her and tucked in.

The band took its place and began to play. The boys just loved it and danced in their seats. Annie smiled.

She pulled out her program to see which band was playing. She then read over the program, where there was a list of

sponsors, which included the Reillys, but the main sponsor
was Alicorn. *Alicorn? Whoa! What?*

What were they doing here?

Annie's eyes scanned the crowd. Usually, corporate
sponsors had a booth set up or something to distin-
guish them.

"I'll be back," Annie whispered to Mike. DeeAnn followed her.

"What are you doing?" she asked when they were far
enough away from the music.

Annie pointed at the program. "This is the name of the
adoption agency Emily was sending money to," she replied
quietly. "I thought if I looked around, I might find them.
They would surely have a rep here or something."

"Let's go look over there." DeeAnn pointed to a group
of booths.

Sure enough, there was Alicorn, selling bottled water.
Finally, Annie would get to meet a person from the agency
in the flesh.

The young woman behind the counter wore a pink cardi-
gan over a white blouse. Her blond hair was pulled back
into a long ponytail.

"I'll take a water please," Annie said and handed her a
dollar.

"Here you go." The woman handed Annie the ice-cold
water.

"What is Alicorn?" Annie said.

"We're one of the sponsors of the event."

"No," Annie said, twisting off her bottle cap. "What
kind of business are you?"

DeeAnn was now standing beside her.

"We're an international adoption agency." The young

woman smiled at Annie. "Can I help you?" She turned to DeeAnn.

"Yes, I'll have a water," DeeAnn said. "International adoptions, huh? So if I wanted, say, a Chinese baby girl, I could come to you?"

"Certainly," she said. "If you're interested, our pamphlets are right over there." She pointed around the corner, and Annie and DeeAnn sauntered over to the stand.

"Isn't it odd that an adoption agency would be here in Cumberland Creek, sponsoring an event?" Annie said, as she picked up some pamphlets.

"Indeed," came a male voice from behind them. Annie knew the voice, but when she turned around, she was surprised to find Bryant in disguise as a farmer, complete with bib overalls.

"What are you doing here?" she managed to say.

"Same thing you are, I reckon," he said with a remarkably bad imitation of an Appalachian accent.

"Oh, Bryant," DeeAnn said. "If my husband heard that accent of yours, he'd pop you one."

Annie laughed, and Bryant shrugged. "Well, I tried," he said.

"So what do you know about these people?" Annie said in a low voice to Bryant.

"Not much, really, except that Emily donated money to them and that they are a weird adoption agency of some sort. What the link is, I just don't know, and nobody will tell us. We have some folks working on it. Nothing so far."

Annie's eyes scanned the pamphlets. Same verbiage as on the Web site. Wait. This was a little different.

Annie waited until the last group of water customers had left the booth. DeeAnn and Bryant were talking about the forsythia.

"Thanks for offering to answer questions," Annie said to the young woman behind the counter.

"I'd be happy to help, if I can," the woman said and smiled.

"What does this mean exactly?" Annie pointed to a line in the pamphlet. "Our labs ensure pure genetic heritage."

The woman frowned momentarily, then smiled pure saccharine. She cleared her throat. "One of our partners is a genetics lab where we test. You know, it's like your friend said. If someone wants a Chinese baby, it just helps to have the genetics test to prove the validity."

"Odd," Annie said. "I'd think the fact that they were from China would be enough proof for most people. Wouldn't you?" She tried to sound nonchalant, like a disinterested passerby who had suddenly happened on intriguing information.

"Well, yes," the woman conceded and looked away briefly. "But it's very important to some of our clients."

Bryant came up beside Annie.

"So it's just really a marketing thing?"

The woman reached for a handkerchief and patted her forehead, where beads of sweat were forming. It was getting to be a warm day. "Well," she said, "I suppose you could look at it like that. But that doesn't take away from the importance of it and the validity of it. All our children are genetically tested for all sorts of things. Our clients' peace of mind is always our biggest concern. May I help you?" she asked Bryant.

"Yeah," he said. "I'll have a water and a baby that's one hundred percent British."

Annie held her breath, and the woman almost dropped the slippery bottle.

A group of young women approached the booth. They were all pregnant, all fair, and sort of dressed alike, in long denim jumpers with white T-shirts, white tennis shoes, and socks.

Annie looked at DeeAnn, who rolled her eyes.

"What's that about?" Annie said to her as they walked back toward the amphitheater. "A group of pregnant women dressed alike?"

DeeAnn stopped. "Bryant is talking to them."

"Maybe they met at Lamaze class," Annie said.

"That many of them? All dressed like that? Weird."

"And look," Annie said, lowering her voice. "They are each being given a bag from the sponsors of the event."

DeeAnn's eyebrows went up. "Now, that is interesting. Could they be having babies for them?"

"You mean like human incubators? Harvesters?"

"Yeah, that's exactly what I mean," DeeAnn said.

Annie frowned, took a drink of water, but it didn't sit right in her stomach.

"You've been reading too many weird novels," Annie told her. Or maybe it was herself she was talking to.

Bryant found his way back to them.

"Interesting group of young women," he said.

"What's their deal?" DeeAnn said. "Why are they all dressed like that?"

"I'm not sure, but they all go to the same church, evidently. And I've seen other women dressed like that who go to that church," he replied.

"Are they Mennonite?" Annie asked.

"No," he said. "One of these start-ups. Been around for ten years or so. Think I should check into them?"

"I don't know. I just think it's an odd way to dress," Annie said and made a mental note to check on the group herself.

"Creepy," DeeAnn said.

Chapter 46

Vera, Beatrice, Jon, and Eric sat together in a row, chitchatting about the beautiful spring Cumberland Creek was having, about the ducks swimming in the rivers, and about the modern, sleek new amphitheater. Elizabeth was spending the day with Bill, which worried Vera. But he promised it would just be the two of them, that his girl-friend would be nowhere around. She caught Eric's eye, and they smiled at one another. He fit in with her family, even though he'd already excused himself once to call a patient. But because Vera's father was a doctor, she supposed she was used to that kind of thing, and it didn't worry her at all.

She scanned the crowd, and she saw Robert Dasher and his new wife, looking as if she were going to pop with the baby she was expecting. Vera sighed. She was so thrilled for Robert that he was able to get his life together after the death of Maggie Rae. She waved at them.

She also saw Emily's parents but was unable to get their attention. They were front and center to the stage, an honored position.

"Have you been sleepwalking anymore?" Eric asked her.

"I don't think so," Vera replied. "But I never really feel

rested. The medicine is supposed to help with the REM situation. But I'm not sure it has."

"Are you still going to do the hypnosis walk-through?"

Vera felt a chill travel up her spine. "I am," she said and swallowed. "Detective Bryant suggested that I do it. It will at least show that I feel I have nothing to hide."

Eric shrugged. "But you don't. Anybody who knows you knows that you'd never harm anybody."

"Damn straight," Beatrice chimed in.

"What she said." Jon poked at her.

Beatrice lurched back. "My, my, aren't you getting to be quite Americanized with your cocky attitude."

Jon grinned and shrugged his shoulders, pointed to the stage, where the musicians were taking their places.

Vera felt ill at ease about even being here, since so many of her previous dance students were performers in the show today. It was like looking at her failure in a way. A failure to compete with Emily. But she had been so unprepared for it, had never imagined that another dancer would come to town, let alone one who would go to such lengths to succeed. It wasn't personal, she told herself. It was business. But it still felt personal, and it hurt.

Her students were now Irish dancers leaping across the stage to the rhythms of the fiddle and the bodhran. Even though the rhythm and form were different, she saw the ballet in them, the way they held themselves, the way they pointed their toes. She gave them that. At least. Her heart swelled.

She closed her eyes. The sound of the fiddle slowed, and it seemed to vibrate deep within her chest yet lift her spirits. She opened her eyes and looked out over the river to her mountain. *What next?*

* * *

The next morning Vera woke up with the scent of eggs and ham teasing her nose. Bless her mother. She had made her favorite breakfast. As she padded down the stairs into the kitchen, she smelled the biscuits. Beatrice and Jon were already awake. Lizzie was still asleep.

"My last meal?" Vera said and smiled as she looked over the mounds of food on the table.

Beatrice grinned and answered the doorbell. In walked Annie and Sheila.

Soon enough Vera's doctor, Dr. Long, was there in Beatrice's living room. He brought in another doctor, who explained that he was certified in hypnosis and so on and so on. Vera had no idea what any of it meant. She just wanted to get to the bottom of it. She looked up at Beatrice, Annie, and Sheila, standing close by, and the detective on the other side of the room.

"Well, how the hell am I supposed to relax with all of you looking at me?" she clipped.

"Yes, you all need to leave until she is under, but we'll see you later. Wait outside. Once she's under, you can follow along quietly," the doctor said, getting up from the couch.

Beatrice grumbled, but the others moved along to Beatrice's front porch without comment.

It took very little time for Vera to get settled in the chair in her mother's living room.

"Just relax, lean back in the chair, and concentrate on my voice," he said, fiddling with his tie a bit.

"Oh, damn," she said.

"What?"

"I have to use the bathroom," she said.

He bit his lip. "Okay."

She felt more relaxed somehow when she sat back down in the chair.

"Okay, listen to my voice," he said.

It was a nice voice.

Had she remember to shut the light off in her bedroom?

Ten.

Nine.

Okay. What is supposed to be happening here? I feel nothing.

Eight.

Seven.

"I hope you are feeling a little more relaxed."

Six.

Yes, she was. But she was certainly not "under." Just a little more relaxed.

Five.

Four.

Three.

"Vera, your arms are feeling heavy."

She tried to lift them, and darned, they *were* heavy.

Two.

One.

One moment she was completely relaxed. The next, she was asleep and dreaming. Walking. She was wide awake and accompanying the doctor down the streets of Cumberland Creek. Everything had been planned according to the doctor's instructions. They would walk her through her evening the night of the murder in hopes that her relaxed, "hypnotic" state, along with the physical triggers, would help her to remember something useful. Emily's studio door was already unlocked, since they were certain she'd lead them to it.

Walking and walking. Dreaming and walking.

"Is this the street you walked along from the parade to your home?"

Vera looked up at the sign. It was blurry. She blinked. "Walnut, yes."

"What do you see?"

"The girls look so pretty all dressed in green. Everybody is going home. The streets are littered with glittery green confetti," she said.

"Where do you go next?"

Vera turned and walked toward her apartment.

"Where is your bag?" the doctor asked.

"I have it around my shoulder."

"Are you certain this is the street you walked along?"

"Yes, but wait—"

"What?"

"I decided to cut across Main Street here," she said. "I heard a strange noise coming from Emily's studio."

"What kind of noise?"

Silence.

"Vera? The noise?"

"It was a . . . a . . . muffled scream," she said. "And I ran for Emily's studio. Someone needs help."

They entered the studio. A low, guttural sob escaped from Vera. She felt like she couldn't see.

"Vera? What is happening?" a male voice said to her.

"Where are the lights . . . ?" Her hands searched around the walls. Her bag dropped.

Trying to see in the darkness. The mirrors. A sudden glint of light. That horrible gurgling sound. Eyes looking up at her. A slice of light. Then gone.

"Who's there?" Vera said, almost out of breath.

"Look closer," the doctor said. "We are in the studio the Friday of Emily's death. What do you see?"

A hand stretched out to her and dropped to the floor with a thud.

Where were the lights in this place? Her hands went to

the walls once again in search of the switch. The shard of light captured the face again.

The face looked up at her.

It was the face of evil.

Vera felt fear shoot through her, every cell in her body lit. Something deep, primal in her became unleashed. It rose and twisted inside of her. Sweat poured from her. She was so frightened that she could not move. *Feet, move,* she told them. But they betrayed her and stood firmly rooted. *Lungs, breathe,* she told them, and suddenly she could no longer breathe.

"Air," she said before collapsing on the floor of Emily McGlashen's studio.

Chapter 47

"Good God!" Beatrice screamed and ran to a sobbing Vera, cradling her. What had her daughter seen that night? What horrible act had she witnessed? No wonder she behaved like a wounded animal.

"Step back," the doctor told the others. "She needs air."

He crouched over and spoke very softly. "Vera, remember I told you that when I clap, you will awaken and will remember everything."

"Really?" Beatrice said. "Does she need to?"

"I'm afraid so, Bea." Bryant stepped forward.

The doctor clapped three times, and Vera's eyes flew open. She looked around the room and buried her head in her mother's lap. Beatrice's heart raced. Jon was behind her, his hand on her shoulder.

"Vera, darling," Beatrice said, having trouble finding words, "you need to pull yourself together."

But when Vera looked back up at her, Beatrice barely recognized the look in her only child's eyes. Haunted? The light and vibrancy that usually came from her had vanished

"Doctor, what the hell?" Sheila yelled.

"Has something gone wrong?" Annie said at the same time.

"Calm down," the doctor said. "Sometimes this happens. What she saw was devastating. . . . She's remembering and sifting through repressed images. It could take some time. A few hours at least."

"But what did she see? I mean, I was having a hard time figuring it out," Sheila said.

"She saw Emily McGlashen's murder," Annie said after a moment, then turned to the detective. "Does this clear her?"

Bryant frowned. "Is that what you heard? Because I'm not so sure . . . Doctor?"

"It's hard to say at this point. Let's give her some time," the doctor said.

"Indeed," Beatrice said, helping Vera to stand. "Now, get out of my way. I'm taking my girl home."

Beatrice and Vera left the studio. The others trailed behind them. Once they reached the house, Beatrice and Jon helped Vera up the stairs, and she fell into bed with all her clothes on.

A few hours later, Vera came down the steps of the home in which she'd grown up, looking a little tired, but that haunted look was gone. The detective, the doctor, Annie, and Sheila were all still there, milling around, playing cards, watching the digging in the backyard.

"So, what happened?" she asked them. "Did we find out anything at all?"

Dr. Long stood. "You mean you don't remember anything?"

Vera looked at him with a blank expression. "No. I'm sorry. But you taped it, right?"

He nodded. "But I'm not sure it will do you much good

to listen to it. We'll try it tomorrow. Sometimes listening to it triggers the memories. How does that sound?"

"To tell you the truth, I don't want to do this anymore," Vera said. "I'm sorry. I don't want to disappoint, but I just don't think I can help."

"Vera—" Bryant began.

Jon spoke up. "If you have the evidence to arrest this woman, then do it," he said in a voice Beatrice had never heard before. Strong. Forceful. Well, well, well. "If not, please stop harassing her." He gestured toward her. "I'm no doctor, but Vera is certainly ill over this matter. Gentlemen, I suggest you leave."

"I better go, too," Annie said. "It will be time for the boys to be home soon. Vera, call me if you need anything," Annie added and hugged her.

"Well, I'm not going anywhere," Sheila said and plopped onto the couch as Annie, Bryant, and the doctors left.

Vera sat down next to Sheila, who reached out and took her hand.

Later, Sheila took Vera out for pie, leaving Jon and Beatrice in a quiet house with Lizzie sound asleep upstairs.

Beatrice took a sip of her chamomile tea. Her nerves were shot, seeing Vera like that. "Thank you, Jon, for getting rid of everybody today."

"Eh," he said. "It was nothing. She is really like a daughter to me by now." He looked out the window. "When did you say they were pouring the concrete for the pool?"

Beatrice sighed. "It was scheduled for tomorrow. But canceled by the state. I don't know what's going on."

"I must admit that I'm disappointed that we don't have

our pool yet, but this history business is very exciting, yes?"

"Yes." Beatrice suddenly remembered that they hadn't read over the report that Paige brought them. "What did we do with that folder?"

Jon went off in search of it as Beatrice leaned back in her chair, Vera still on her mind. What had she witnessed? Vera was a strong person, and getting stronger every day. *But when one witnesses a horrific thing, who knows how the body and mind will react?*

With Vera, it is repressed and comes out in her troubled sleepwalks. What will become of her?

"Bea? Are you okay, dear?" Jon interrupted her thoughts.

"Yes," she said. "I was just thinking about Vera."

"I know," he said softly. "Let's think about something else, shall we?"

He forced a smile. Goodness, he was trying to cheer her. You had to just love a man like that.

He reached for her quilt and placed it on her lap. Its warmth spread through her.

"Let's look at all this stuff. It's a wonderful treasure," he said. "Willa Rose McGlashen was born in about eighteen fifty, the eldest child of William McGlashen Jr., and Eleanor Jenkins," Jon read.

"Jenkins?" Beatrice said. "Now, that's an old name, but I didn't think they ventured far off the mountain. Hmmm. Born in eighteen fifty. That makes her in her twenties when she dated that journal."

Jon continued reading. "The McGlashen family ran the first inn, or 'ordinary,' in the town of Cumberland Creek, first known as Miller's Gap. Hans Mueller or Miller and his family were among the first settlers of the region. His daughter Mathilde married a McGlashen. None of Hans's sons survived."

"Aha," Beatrice said.

"By all accounts Willa Rose was an extraordinary young woman. She helped her aging parents run the inn. As the innkeeper, she was in a perfect position to help during the war, and she did by passing messages for spies during the War Between the States. In one case, at great risk to her life. This was during a journey to Manassas, when she traveled as a young man with a freed slave named Ez, son of the family's kitchen helper."

"Ez?" Beatrice said. "She mentions Ez in her journal, doesn't she?"

Jon nodded. "She mentions his death. She grieves for him. She also mentions his child, Billy. Remember? She adopted him, or whatever they called it then."

"Billy? Ah yes. I remember. It was such turmoil after the war. Must have been awful. There were orphans, widows, young man disabled. It was horrible. What else does it say?"

"Willa never married. She spent her days keeping the inn. Historical records show that there were several deaths in the area, which could have been TB or TB related. There is a death record for Mary, Ez's mother, but no mention of the child, Billy, that Willa Rose adopted. It's mentioned in the record that Willa died at the Shenandoah Home for the Mentally Disturbed and is listed as a lunatic—"

"What?" Beatrice interrupted. "What happened to her? She had this useful life, then suddenly loses her mind?"

"Maybe it was something like . . . How do you say? Dementia?"

"But what about the child? No mention?"

"Here's a note from Paige. There was a Bill McGlashen

that was listed in California in nineteen twenty. She is not sure if this could be our Bill, but she is checking. There were no other McGlashens in the state of California and one family listed in Pennsylvania, but no William there."

"Well, that's fascinating. Emily McGlashen is from California."

Chapter 48

"So I set up a tour of the lab when I found out that it's in Virginia," Annie said and then took a bite of a strawberry shortcake cupcake. "Oh, my *Gawd,* this is good."

DeeAnn looked pleased. "Thanks, Annie. Do you need me to go with? Ya know, in case there's any trouble?"

Sheila spoke up and crossed her arms. "That's just what she needs."

"Thanks for the offer, but I don't think so." Annie smiled. "I'm just going alone, disguised as a potential client for one appointment and as myself for another. Even Bryant doesn't know I'm doing this. And I don't want him to, because it may not lead to anything at all. What they are doing is legal. I'm just hoping I can find the link between them and Emily."

"Emily was very into her heritage in a strange way," Paige said while cutting out a picture.

"What do you mean?" Annie asked after swallowing a piece of her cupcake.

"Well, I thought it was kind of creepy. She really thought that having a certain bloodline made you better than anybody else," Paige replied. She smoothed over a border she'd just placed on her page. "She used to talk about that all the time at the historical society meetings."

"Other people are like that sometimes, too. The Daughters of the American Revolution used to be," Sheila added.

"I sometimes think a lot of people in the town are like this. And I've been thinking about why this kind of thing bothers me. It's almost a subtle form of racism," Paige said.

"It is? To be proud of your heritage?" Sheila said, looking up from her computer.

"Well, there's a fine line between being proud and thinking you're better than everybody else because you're Irish or French or . . . white," Paige said. "That's all I'm saying."

"But you know what? It fits," Annie said. She patted her page and then turned it. She loved the fresh, empty scrapbook page almost as much as she loved a blank piece of paper. The possibilities were endless. "This is an adoption agency that has a lab partner. Emily was giving her money to them. They are a sponsor of this Irish music event. There is a link. We've just not found it yet."

"The ironic thing is that Emily McGlashen most likely had what she would think is tainted blood," Paige said. "She probably is a descendant of Bill McGlashen, an adopted black boy who started the McGlashen line in California."

"What? How do you know that?" Vera said.

Paige's face turned red. "I've, ah, just been digging around a bit. That's all."

"You're hiding something," Vera said, laying her scissors on the table.

"Why didn't you tell us this before?" DeeAnn asked.

"Well, it's not even that big of a deal," Annie said. "We probably all have some African American blood in us. C'mon."

"No, it's not a big deal, for heaven's sake," Vera said.

"What *is* a big deal is that Emily McGlashen would be turning over in her grave." She grinned. "She was all about genetic purity."

Sheila was hunched over her laptop, as usual. She sat up straight. "I knew this ancestry membership would come in handy. Look, there is a William McGlashen in California in the nineteen twenty census. He and his wife are listed as what? What does that say . . . ? Mulatto. What is that?"

"It's an out-of-date term for a mixed-race person," DeeAnn said.

"Well," Sheila said, "it doesn't look like they could be any relative of Emily McGlashen, who was just as white as you and me."

"Emily's hair was colored. Remember? And she wore blue contacts. Besides, genetics are a tricky thing," Annie said. "Who knows what is in the mix? Many of us right here at this table might be surprised about what kind of blood runs through our veins, even me. We know we came from Eastern Europe. But who knows before then? The whole world is just one big mixing bowl, when you think of it."

"Which is why," DeeAnn said, "this agency is so suspicious to me."

"I feel the same way," Annie said. "How can they prove that a child is absolutely one hundred percent English or German or whatever?"

"Seems the only way to prove such a thing would be to grow one yourself," Vera said.

The room filled with an uncomfortable silence.

"I've thought the exact same thing," Annie finally said. "Could it be?"

"Designer babies are all the rage," Paige said. "Randy and his partner have been looking into adopting a child. I don't think they are ready for it, but he's never listened to me about anything else, so . . ." She shrugged. "He was telling me how some of these agencies do a lot of genetic screening and testing."

"Yes, but isn't that just for disease?" Annie asked.

"I think it used to be. Not anymore. And it's not just gender, either. They talk about eye color, intelligence—"

"Intelligence?" DeeAnn interrupted. "You mean you can order a smart baby?"

Paige nodded. "I suppose."

"Well, now, that's where I went wrong. I bred with my own husband, the old-fashioned way. No wonder my kids are so weird," she said and laughed.

"But seriously," Vera said, "you wouldn't change them, would you? You never know what you're going to get, of course, but ultimately, even though kids are a brew of your genetics, they end up being their own people. I think it's great. Sloppy, yes, but magic."

DeeAnn shook her head. "Spoken like a new mother. Talk to me in twenty years," she said and smiled.

But Annie was beginning to catch a further glimpse of what made Emily McGlashen tick. She was adopted by a secular Jewish family living in a commune. She rebelled when she found out she was adopted. Which twisted into this obsession she appeared to have with genetic purity. She was such a believer in it that she gave a lot of her money to this agency. But what was she hoping to accomplish? And could this have led to her death?

Chapter 49

Vera was up and down all night, with fitful dreams that she couldn't really even remember. In her sleep, she would tell herself, *Remember it. This is important.* But the moment she woke up, all memory vanished.

Sort of like the hypnosis.

Was she really, truly losing her mind?

She pulled her comforter closer to her. *Five a.m. Great.* Lizzie would be up soon. The quiet house would be filled with the noises of her daughter.

She thought about last night's discussion, and images of her own daughter played in her mind. You couldn't get a more perfect blending of two people. She and Bill had made this girl, and she was so much like them both. It was more than the shape of her nose or the color of her hair and eyes. It was the way she laughed, the way she knit her eyebrows when she was trying to understand, and how she tilted her head when she was listening.

Could she love an adopted child as much as she could her flesh and blood? Of that, Vera was certain. Loving a child was the easiest thing she had ever done. It wouldn't matter if he or she was blood.

Vera's family had settled in the area generations ago; it

had never occurred to her that this was an important thing. It just was who they were. So when Emily McGlashen came to town, making claims, Vera was amused. Who cared? What relevance did it have to everyday life? None that she could see.

"Mama! Mama!"

There was Lizzie. Vera smiled. Yes, she was tired, bone weary. But she loved Sundays with her daughter.

Later that day, her mother interrupted her playing with Lizzie. They were playing with blocks and fashioning a magnificent pretend village.

"Vera, Detective Bryant is here to see you," Beatrice said as she walked into the room.

"To see me? Really?"

Beatrice nodded. "I'll stay with Lizzie. Better that she stay here."

Vera's heart sank. Was he going to arrest her? Why didn't she remember the details of what she witnessed that night? Why did she not want to even try again? It might be the only thing that would save her.

As she walked down the stairs, her legs were shaking slightly. Oddest feeling. Bryant and Jon were sitting on the sofa together, chitchatting. The scene didn't appear to be tense at all. Maybe she was wrong. Maybe he hadn't come to arrest her.

But when he looked up at her, Bryant's face was stern. "Hello, Vera. Please sit down."

"No. I won't sit down. If you're going to take me to jail, let's just get it over with. I didn't kill her, I swear." It spewed from her. "I couldn't kill anybody, whether I was sleep-walking or not—"

"Vera," Jon interrupted, "the detective is not here to arrest you."

"Then what?" she said, sinking into the chair.

"We have news," Bryant responded. "And it's not pleasant."

"Okay," she finally said. "What is it?"

"We know who has been trying to set you up. She claims she didn't kill Emily, though."

"Of course!" Jon said, folding his arms.

"*She?* Who?"

"First of all, you should know that this person is young and, I think, very confused about some things," the detective said. "And you should know that there is a personal connection."

"With whom? Me?"

"Yes. And Bill," he said.

Vera leafed through her brain. Why, almost everybody she knew also knew Bill. He had told her nothing.

"Oh, for God's sake, just tell me who it is!" she finally said.

"It's Kelsey, Bill's girlfriend," the detective said.

The room stilled.

Had she heard him correctly? The young woman her ex was shacked up with had tried to set her up for murder? Well. That was just too good to be true. She grinned, then allowed a bubble of nerves to spring deep from within her guts and escape as laughter, unattractive, snorting, crying, freeing laughter.

"Vera?" Jon finally said. "Are you okay?"

She calmed down but looked at the detective, who was also trying to stop himself from laughing, probably.

"I'm sorry," she said finally, after taking a deep breath. "It's just too much."

"Yes," Bryant said.

"How did you—"

"We found her sneaking around your place a few nights ago, so we brought her in for questioning and DNA testing, which went very quickly this time. Usually, it takes forever. But we have a small new lab in our office now," he told her.

"Sneaking around?" Vera said.

Bryant nodded. "And she's confessed to all of it. Except the murder."

"Of course she killed Emily," Jon said. "Why else would should be doing this to Vera?"

"Jealousy," Bryant said. "She saw an opportunity to get you out of the way."

"But I am not in her way. She can have Bill." Vera waved him off.

"Ah yes," Jon said. "She can have Bill, but not all of him. You have the most important part of him, Elizabeth."

Shock tore through her. "Elizabeth?" She remembered that strange night when she woke up next to her daughter crying in the crib.

"We don't know if that is the case," Bryant said, "but let's just say that Kelsey is a troubled young woman."

Vera snorted. "No kidding. I mean, why else would she be with Bill?"

"Spoken like a true ex-wife," Bryant said and smirked.

Chapter 50

When Annie learned the DNA lab for Alicorn was in Chesapeake, near Virginia Beach, she took the boys out of school for a few days and she and Mike made a midweek getaway. It wasn't exactly the kind of romantic trip she had had in mind when she and Mike first talked about it, but maybe that would come later. And maybe this change of scenery would do them all good.

The green hills and valley gave way to flatter and grayer terrain the closer she and her family drove toward the eastern shore of Virginia. Only a few hours away, but the area felt so different, looked so different.

The boys each had a book and were quiet for most of the trip. Traveling was getting to be easier with them. Mike turned up the radio when one of his favorite Beatles songs came on. "Yesterday" blared through the minivan. Annie smiled at her husband.

It was going to be okay. Wasn't it?

This trip proved that she could work her career around her family. They were cool with it. Excited. They had museum and fishing plans. She was thrilled.

Later, though, as she drove off for her first appointment and left her boys with their fishing gear at the dock, her guts pulled at her. She would miss it. If her boys caught a fish, if anything funny or sad or sweet happened, she would miss it.

She swallowed her bottled water hard and blinked back a tear.

The tour was uneventful. The building was establishment gray. The office workers seemed friendly and polite, and the views of the labs were pristine. Workers in friendly white coats, goggles, and gloves.

"We run these tests to give our clients peace of mind," the tour guide said. "We want to make certain that all our children are healthy and exactly what our clients want."

"What if you find a disorder or something in the tests?" A man Annie hadn't noticed before stepped forward. But he looked vaguely familiar.

The tour guy cleared his throat. "Our policy is always honesty. We tell the potential family and leave the decision up to them, of course," he said.

"How can you be certain of a child's heritage through these tests?" Annie asked, noting the odd look the other questioner gave her.

"Because there are certain genetic markers, for example, that we see in population strains," he replied.

"Still," Annie continued, "there are very few genetically pure populations these days. That is what I am interested in. I want a child of my heritage only. It's important to me that my children have Jewish blood."

"Well," the man said, reddening, "we can discuss your personal situation at a later time. Suffice it to say that we are at the leading edge in science and genetics technology. We do our best. In the meantime, we are just about out of time. Any other questions?"

There was a group of six individuals. Two couples. One was Asian. The other white. Then there was Annie and this familiar-looking man, who was African American. He made eye contact with her again and smiled.

In the parking lot she heard someone call her name and turned to see that same man.

"Annie? Annie Chamovitz?"

"I'm sorry. You look familiar, but . . ."

"It's Herb Ross," he said. He lowered his voice. "On assignment."

"Oh," she said. "I see. The beard and the glasses . . . effective."

"You want to get a cup of coffee?"

Oh boy, did she ever. What was an investigative reporter doing here? She glanced at her watch. She'd have to call Mike.

"Okay, sure," she said. "I just have to call Mike. Excuse me."

Mike didn't pick up his cell phone, so she left a message. Had he left it in the hotel room?

Herb and Annie found the nearest coffee shop and planted themselves there with mugs of steaming coffee and a plate of muffins.

"Listen, I hope you don't mind my asking, but I thought you had kids. What are you really doing here?" he asked. "Are you on a story?"

"You're right. I do have kids," she said. It had been years since they had worked in a newsroom together. He had left and worked at another paper. Funny that he knew anything about her having kids, but word did get around. "And I really don't know if I'm on a story or not. But at this point, I'd have to say no."

"What's that supposed to mean?" he said, laughing.

She explained to him why she was there. He whistled low, eyebrows lifting.

"I gotta tell you, Annie, what your hunch is telling you

is correct. Emily McGlashen was a board member of the Alicorn Foundation."

"Foundation? I've seen nothing about a foundation."

"No. You wouldn't. It's a behind-the-scenes foundation. Nothing illegal. They just don't mention it. They've been collecting funds for research for years."

Annie took a long drink of her coffee. Emily McGlashen was full of surprises. Even dead. "What exactly are they researching?"

"You see, this is where it gets dicey. It's not illegal in the U.S., but it is in some of the other countries Alicorn does business in."

"What?"

"Embryonic research."

"What do you mean? They are creating embryos and what?"

"They are attempting to create perfect babies. Health. Intelligence. Gender. Ethnicity."

Annie's stomach lurched. It was true that reporters didn't want to retch in front of police, but it was also true they didn't want to do it in front of another reporter. She took a deep breath.

"Excuse me," she said and made her way to the ladies' room.

Her next appointment was the following day, with John Reid, the president of Ali Labs. The office building was adjacent to the labs and was warm and inviting, decorated with wood and brass. The receptionist greeted Annie with a professional and friendly demeanor.

When Annie walked into John Reid's office, she was a little surprised by his youth. He couldn't be more than forty-five. So blond that he was almost albino, but not quite. His blue eyes were framed by darker eyelashes. One sweeping look told her that he was moneyed, educated, and considered himself powerful.

"Good morning, Ms. Chamovitz." He stood and shook her hand.

Pleasant demeanor.

"Good morning," she said and then sat down in the overstuffed leather chair. *Nice.*

"I've taken the liberty of doing a little research." He smiled at her. "I hope you don't mind. But I see that you've done some interesting reporting."

"Yes, thank you," Annie said, a little taken aback. "And I've done some research on you."

He laughed. "Not me, surely. Perhaps Ali Labs?"

"More like it, yes." She grinned.

"What can I help you with?"

"Well, I'm interested in a previous board member, Emily McGlashen."

"Terrible what's happened to her," he said.

"Indeed," Annie said. He seemed genuinely distressed. She sat back in her chair. "Can you tell me about her involvement here?"

"Well, she was a board member of our partner company's foundation. That much I know," he said. "But I don't know much else about her."

"Are you certain? Because it seems that she was passionate about Alicorn. I can't imagine you hadn't met and known each other."

"Oh, we met," he said and grimaced. "We didn't exactly get along. I felt that she was unethical in some of her leanings."

"What do you mean?"

"Well, the whole business with accepting money from this strange group . . . Oh, what was the name of it ? New

Mountain Order. That's it. I couldn't get behind it," he said. "Unfortunately, many of the board members don't care where the money comes from as long as the research is funded."

Annie's heart leapt. Did he just say the NMO helped to fund Alicorn?

"The NMO was a supporter of Alicorn?"

"No, not the adoption agency. Ali. The lab. We are partners and are funded separately. And the research is where the money is these days."

Annie nodded.

"I told Emily that I wanted nothing to do with those freaks," he said with vehemence.

"But she secured the funding, anyway?" Annie asked.

"Highly inappropriate." He nodded. "But the NMO, as far as I know, proved me wrong. They gave us the money and went away. I really thought they could have other interests."

"What would that be?"

"You know about them," he said. He had done some research on her.

"They are bigots. Pure and simple. I thought they were interested in starting a freaky Aryan race in our labs. But so far, nothing. They've been the perfect supporters, giving us money and leaving us alone," he said and shrugged. "You just never know about people, do you?"

No, you didn't, Annie thought. It was just as she had thought originally. The NMO was a huge red herring in this case. The organization was scattered and disorganized since its leaders were gone. She agreed with Bryant in theory that this case led right to the NMO's door. But all the hard evidence? None of it pointed to them.

Chapter 51

"But what does any of that have to do with her death?" Beatrice asked Annie over the phone.

"I have no idea," Annie replied over the sound of her boys and the rushing of waves.

"It's the strangest thing I've heard, that they are trying to create designer children. But it fits her personality, doesn't it?" Beatrice said.

"I wonder if she stepped on someone's toes. I mean, this is a sensitive area. This research has all kinds of moral and ethical implications," Annie said.

"Good science gone bad," Beatrice said. "It started out to help families. . . ."

"Ben, put that sand down now! I'm sorry, Bea. I've got to go," Annie said.

Beatrice sat back in her chair and thought over the past few days. Bill's live-in lover had been arrested for trespassing, harassment, and conspiracy. After the police found strands of hair in Elizabeth's room, she fell apart and confessed. From what Beatrice understood, the young woman confessed almost immediately. She was trying to frame Vera, Bill's ex-wife and Beatrice's very own daughter. What was wrong with people? Beatrice had never liked that young woman, but she felt sorry for her for the desperate and twisted attempt at getting attention. Beatrice and Vera had yet to hear from Bill. Not a phone call. Not an e-mail.

When he was her son-in-law, she knew he cared for Vera and was good to her, but she never really understood what Vera saw in the man. None of her business, ultimately. But when they broke up, it was still sad, especially since after all these years, they finally had gotten pregnant. She couldn't blame Vera for not wanting to work it out with him. The fact that he lived with such a young and disturbed woman gave Beatrice fodder to outright despise him. What a fool a middle-aged man could be.

Annie's news was startling. Not so much that Emily was a member of this group, but more that such a group and such a science existed. But it was good to know that at least some of the people involved in it were trying to be ethical.

"Would you like a sandwich, Bea?" Jon said, walking into the room.

"Yes, and after that more of that strawberry-rhubarb tart you made," she said.

"It turned out well," he said. "I just love that rhubarb."

It was one of his discoveries in the United States. They didn't have it in France, or at least not in Paris, which was where he had lived most of his life. He was smitten with rhubarb, making jams, pies, tarts a few weeks back and a cake just last week. It was one of the plants that grew freely in Appalachia.

Jon made her a ham sandwich, and they settled at the table.

"What are we going to do about the hole in our back-yard?" he said and grinned.

She shrugged. "The man is supposed to get back to me

this week about what's happening. We'll get our pool. Don't worry."

"I am not worried," he said and shrugged. "If we don't get it this year, in time for summer, maybe next year?"

Next year? Lawd, the man had plans to stay awhile. Beatrice's old heart fluttered.

Just then her doorbell rang. When Beatrice opened the door, she was surprised to see Leola.

"Hello. C'mon in," Beatrice said.

"I'm here to see Vera," Leola said.

Well, that was polite.

"I'm sorry," Beatrice said. "Vera and Lizzie are out for the day. Can I help you with something?"

"I just wanted to ask her why she's pressing charges against my niece," Leola said.

"Your niece? Oh, that's right," Beatrice said, just then remembering the family connection.

"I mean, you don't think it's because . . . well . . ."

"I think it's because the woman was in her home in the middle of the night and she's been trying to frame her for murder," Beatrice said. "I believe I'd press charges, too."

Leola's mouth dropped.

Jon came up behind Beatrice. "Hello, Leola. Please come in."

She shook her head. "I don't think so. I just don't understand why Vera would want to press charges against Kelsey when she's just so troubled. It feels bitter."

Beatrice cackled. "Look, if you think Vera in any way wants Bill back into her life that way, you can think again. She's moved on."

"I wish Kelsey would move on, too," Leola said. "But Vera should drop those charges."

"Why should she?" Jon said. "She tried to frame her for murder. I hope they lock her up!" he said emphatically, twisting an imaginary key in front of Beatrice's face. "Now, if you will excuse us."

He shut the door in her face.

"Trash," he said, wiping his hands together. "Good riddance."

"Now, Jon, we don't do that in this country. You just don't shut the door in people's faces," Beatrice said, trying to be stern.

He shrugged. "Such is life, *mon amour*. You can't like everybody. What was she doing here? I don't put up with such nonsense, and neither should you."

"Well," Beatrice said, "I was handling it just fine."

"Yes, you were," he said. "I'm sorry for stepping in, but she needed the door slammed in her face. Some people . . . well . . . How do you say? They are illogical, and you must not waste your energy."

"I get that, Jon," Beatrice said, unsure of how she felt. She had never needed anybody to stand up for her. She wasn't sure if she liked it or not.

She looked at her man, eyes sparking, smile on his face.

Well, he was cute, and he could make a mean strawberry-rhubarb tart. She thought she might just keep him.

Chapter 52

Vera had just slid Lizzie into the "baby" swing at the park. Lizzie laughed and pointed at the ducks. When Vera turned around to look, Leola was walking toward her, with her hands on her hips.

"Well, hello there," Vera said, stepping behind the swing to start pushing Lizzie.

"Don't hello me." Leola glared at her.

Confused, Vera smiled at her. "I'm sorry. Are you okay?"

"I'm livid!" she screamed. "Why are you pressing charges against Kelsey?"

Vera's heart nearly stopped. Was everybody looking her way?

"Maybe this isn't the best time to talk about this," Vera finally said.

"Mommy?" Lizzie reached for her.

Vera lifted her out of the swing and grabbed her bag.

"We'll talk later," Vera said.

"We'll talk now," Leola said, stepping in front of her.

Vera was at least a foot shorter than Leola, and she had Lizzie on her hip. What did she want? To fight?

"What do you want from me?" Vera said with an even tone.

"I want you to drop the charges," Leola replied. "She's just young and foolish. She meant no harm."

Vera bit her lip. Kelsey had tried to frame her for murder. And she had been in her daughter's bedroom in the middle of the night. Kelsey would have let her hang for the murder. Vera was certain of that. But this was not the time to get into it with Leola, whose face was so contorted with anger, Vera was shocked by the change in her appearance.

Best to try to make peace. Mollify her.

Vera smiled as best as she could and shrugged. "I'll talk to my lawyer about it."

"Who would that be?" Leola said.

Vera just looked at her. She didn't have to tell this woman anything. Who did she think she was? She turned to walk away, and Leola grabbed on to her arm so hard that it made her squeal. Vera twisted around to face her, and her daughter squalled just as her tiny little hand reached across and smacked Leola hard across the face.

"Oh, Lizzie! I'm so sorry. Lizzie, we don't hit," Vera said, looking at her daughter, not knowing whether to feel embarrassed or proud.

A tiny red handprint spread on Leola's startled face.

"Let that be a lesson to you, Vera. We never know what our children are capable of," she said, with tears forming in her eyes. Finally, she walked off.

"Bad lady," Lizzie said. "Bad, bad, bad."

"Yes, Lizzie, but we don't solve our problems by hitting people. Remember that," Vera said. "Okay?"

"Okay," she said. "Sorry, Mommy. Look! There's Daddy!"

"No, that's not Daddy," Vera said, watching as the man came closer. A dark, slumped-over, dirty-looking man. But as he approached, he yelled Lizzie's name. Yes, it was Bill. Good Lord. Wasn't this just a banner day?

Lizzie fell out of Vera's arms and into her father's.

"Well, hello, Bill," Vera said through clenched teeth. First Leola, and now Bill was making an appearance. Could the day get any worse?

"Hey, what's with the attitude?"

"Leola just nearly assaulted me," she said.

"Huh," he replied. "She's got quite a temper."

"Yes," she said. "But nothing like Lizzie's."

"What do you mean?"

"Liz smacked her across the face. Hard. Where has she seen that done, Bill?"

He shrugged. "Kids do that. She probably saw another kid doing it."

Vera looked off into the distance, not wanting to watch Lizzie fawn all over her father. The man who lived with the woman who had tried to set her up for murder.

"Hey," he said to Vera. "We need to talk."

Vera smirked. "Now? You want to talk now?"

"I just wanted to say I'm so sorry about all of this," he said. "I know it's been hard on you."

Vera just looked at him. Is that all he had to say?

"You have to believe me. I didn't know anything about it. I never would have—"

"Daddy, swing!"

"Just a minute, Lizzie. I promise we'll swing."

"Look, Vera," he said. "Kelsey has had a kind of rough past. Has all these insecurities. And she is intimidated by you. Jealous, I guess."

"Oh, for heaven's sake, why is she jealous of me? I'm the ex-wife. She is living with you. She has you. I don't get it," Vera said.

"Vera, don't you know how together you appear to someone like her? How beautiful you are? How much I still love you?" His hand went to his mouth. "Sorry. Didn't mean to say that."

"Really, Bill," Vera said. "Are you going to stand there and tell me you are living with this young woman who is crazy about you and you still love me?"

He nodded.

A fireball of anger formed in the pit of her stomach and moved through her body. She concentrated to keep it from erupting there at the park.

"You are despicable," she said, taking Lizzie from him. "We need to go. Sorry. You can swing with Daddy some other time."

"But—" Bill began.

"Bill, please stop," Vera said. "We've known each other for a long time. And I can honestly tell you that . . . well . . . I don't know who you are anymore."

He looked as if she had slapped him.

"Vera," he called after her as she started to walk away. "Kelsey might have done all this stuff to you, but I'm sure she didn't kill Emily."

Vera swung around. "Are you, Bill? Because from where I stand, it seems like she's perfectly capable of it."

Chapter 53

"Well, this is an interesting turn of events," DeeAnn said as she cut out a photo.

"Indeed," Sheila said, leaning over her computer.

"Well, I hope they lock her up and throw away the key," Vera said. "Honestly, what have I ever done to the woman?"

"It's obvious she's not right," DeeAnn said. "And then there's you." She turned to look at Annie. "What's wrong with you?"

Annie shrugged. "I've got a lot on my mind."

"Like what?" DeeAnn asked.

She told them her story about Alicorn. "I'm waiting to hear back from my friend about some questions he's digging into. But suffice it to say, I can't find a connection at Alicorn, other than the fact that Emily was a board member of their foundation and was constantly giving them money. And there is an NMO connection. She got money from them to give to the labs. But I can't see how it plays into her death."

"I can see how it might. You know, maybe some of these political right-wingers took issue with what they are doing," Paige said.

"But usually when that happens, the group is making a

very public statement. Nobody has stepped forward to claim it. You know? And she was strangled. That's a very personal way to kill someone," Annie said.

"What does Bryant say?" Sheila asked, taking a sip of her wine.

"I haven't talked to him," Annie said and went back to working on her parents' black-and-white album.

"Why not?" Sheila said.

"I just haven't had the time," Annie said. "We just got home last night."

"I think you better talk with him soon," Sheila said.

But Annie didn't want to talk with him. It was easier to think when he wasn't around. She wasn't helping with the case anymore. She was just working on a possible story. No reason to divulge what she knew. None of it was evidence, at this point. She took a long drink of her beer and thought about her last conversation with her brother, who now thought that she'd developed an alcohol problem.

"If you've been drinking every time he's been around and all these sparks have been flying, I'm telling you the problem is not you. It's the booze," he had said.

She had laughed him off. But the night they first kissed, she had been pretty drunk. She had found herself sitting at the bar way too long because she was afraid to stand. It was one of those nights she felt she just had to get out of the house alone, and all of her friends were busy. She decided to stop in the bar for a few drinks and realized she had too much.

She didn't know that Bryant was even there. She'd just ordered a coffee to help sober herself up, and he came up behind her, pressed himself into her back, and breathed onto her neck. She remembered his smell—bourbon and a deep muskiness that seemed to pull her to him. When he kissed her neck, all her senses spun. She had not been kissed like that in years. The next thing she knew, she was kissing him back. Never mind that they were in a bar just outside of town and anybody could have seen them together.

If the bartender had not interrupted with her coffee, Annie was almost certain she would have had a sweaty and hot time of it in his car. And she wasn't proud of that. She loved her husband. She liked the kiss, liked the way it made her feel, and that tore at her guts.

"Have you looked into that church?" DeeAnn asked and then took a bite of a muffin.

"Yes," Annie said. "It's not an official church of any kind. No denominational leanings, so it doesn't seem to have any documents related to it at all. I called the minister, and he was friendly enough, invited me to a service, but said that they are an interdenominational group rather than a church. But he did say they are Bible centered."

"I know what that means," DeeAnn said. "They are taking the good book literally."

Annie took another drink of her beer and looked around the table. Vera was mostly gray now and said she didn't have time to bother with her hair. Also, she didn't cake the make-up on anymore. According to Annie's eye, Vera looked better than she had in a long time. Maybe she was sleeping better these days. Sheila was becoming more and more successful with her digital designs. One daughter was in college; the next was heading off to school next year. Her boys were still in middle school. DeeAnn hadn't changed much since Annie had known her. She had always been a successful business owner, had always looked like a baker, with strong, muscled arms, and had always had a wisecrack or two. These days, Paige was unusually quiet, which usually meant she was trying to keep a secret.

"What have you been up to, Paige?"

Paige glanced up at Annie and shifted in her seat. "Nothing unusual to report." She started fussing with the plate of chocolate chip cookies.

"Are you going to eat one of those or not?" Annie asked.

"Leave me alone, Annie," Paige snapped.

Annie laughed. "It's true. You're hiding something."

"What is it?" Sheila looked up from her computer.

"Maybe she's pregnant," DeeAnn said and elbowed her.

"Pregnant?" Paige said. "You know that ship has sailed."

"Maybe she has a secret crush or lover," Vera offered.

"Pshaw," DeeAnn said. "She's all about Earl."

"Well, he *is* my husband," Paige said, affixing a photo to a scrapbook page. "Such as he is." She grunted. "And there's nothing interesting to report there, either."

The group laughed.

"But something is going on with you," Annie said.

"Well," Paige said, "yes, there is. I'm doing some research on the side. Very exciting research. But I promised I'd keep it a secret."

Vera dropped her scissors. "From us? Really?"

"Especially from y'all," Paige said.

The room quieted.

"Why?" DeeAnn said. "I think you should just tell us what's going on."

"Are you kidding? She'd kill me," Paige said.

Annie grinned. With that statement, everybody at the table knew exactly who she was talking about.

"What is my mother up to?" Vera said.

Chapter 54

"Are you home so soon?" Beatrice came walking into the foyer, where all the scrappers were gathered. "Well, what are you all doing here?"

They just looked at her. All of them did, that is, but Paige.

"Well, I suppose you're here to see it, then," Beatrice said, resigned.

"How could you keep this from me, from us?" Vera said.

"Never mind," Beatrice said in a hushed tone. "I have company."

"Company?"

"Yes, come on in. Emily's mother is here," Beatrice said. "We're sitting out on the porch. It's a nice warm evening for April."

"What is she doing here?" Vera asked.

"Came to introduce herself, and we started talking, and one thing led to another," Beatrice said.

"Well, maybe we should leave," Annie said.

"Why, dear?" Beatrice said. "Her daughter is dead. Where is your sympathy? What is wrong with you people?"

Annie's face reddened.

"I tried to help," Sheila said. "I just don't know what more we can do."

"The police still haven't found the murderer," DeeAnn said. "What can we do?"

"I think it's about her healing. This reaching out to us. She's having a rough time," Beatrice said.

"Do you know anything new, Annie?" They heard Rachel's voice before they saw her coming. "Do you? Do you know anything new?"

The woman who stood before them was the same woman who had come to the crop and whom each of them had seen throughout the town, but she was not as composed—and she had just barely been composed before. In fact, she was a mess. Beatrice saw it in their faces; they were shocked.

"Now, dear," Beatrice said. "Let's go sit down and drink your chamomile tea."

Jon had gone to bed hours ago with a headache. Just the scrapbookers and Beatrice and Rachel gathered. They formed almost a circle on Beatrice's screened-in porch, which looked out over her piles of dirt in the backyard.

Rachel sipped at her tea and sniffled, holding a tissue to her eyes every now and then.

"Have you found out anything new?" she asked Annie again.

"Sort of, but I'm not sure it means anything in terms of finding her killer," Annie replied. "She was heavily involved with that adoption agency—"

"Her adoption agency?" Beatrice interrupted.

"No, that's been gone for years," Rachel said. "Go on," she said to Annie.

"She was on the board, worked as a fund-raiser, and gave money to them. She was passionate about genetic purity," Annie said.

"So strange," Rachel said. "We didn't raise her to be like that. In our commune, we had so many interracial families that loved her. I don't get it. As my husband says, it's probably all a part of her rebelling against us. But why? I don't understand it. We were a happy adoptive family."

"The man I spoke with also said that one of the groups she took money from was the New Mountain Order," Annie said.

"The New Mountain Order?" Rachel said and blinked.

Annie explained who they were.

Beatrice's heart sank. What would she feel like if Vera died and she found that she had never really known her?

"Tell me something," Beatrice said. "Do you think she could have been involved with those people?"

"Well, I know that she paid for someone to do research, but I can't imagine . . . ," Rachel said, then stared into the distance. "Wait," she said suddenly. "The man she was seeing. His name began with an *L*. Do you think it could be Luther?"

Beatrice's mouth dropped.

"Unbelievable," Vera squealed.

Annie looked perplexed as all the women sat forward in their chairs.

"No, I don't think so. Luther isn't married," Annie said.

"Yes, that's right," Rachel said, her eyes clearing up from the muddled, tear-filled way they were just moments ago. "And this L is definitely married."

Chapter 55

After Rachel left, suddenly claiming exhaustion, Vera turned to Beatrice.

"Now, Mama, what's going on with you? Why are you keeping this old memory book a secret?"

Beatrice looked from woman to woman in the group. Her eyes shifted back and forth. "I don't want it to be taken off to some museum. And I don't need all you busybodies poking around in my stuff."

"Huh," Sheila said. "If it was found in your yard, you have the say-so about where it goes, correct?"

"Yes, but I've given Virginia most of it. I handed over most of the stuff. What good is it to me? But I can't part with this book. Not yet, anyway," Beatrice said.

"I don't know about you all, but I want to see this thing," Annie said.

Beatrice waved her off. "Some other time. Now, let an old lady go to bed."

"You're not getting off that easy," Vera said. "Give us the book. You don't need to supervise. What are we going to do? Steal it? Burn it? C'mon, Mama."

"Well, I know how trustworthy you are," she said and shot a glare toward Paige.

"I tried," Paige said, shrugging.

"Humph," Beatrice said. "Well, all right. Follow me."

"Remarkable," Annie said as Beatrice placed the book on the table. "It's in such good shape."

"Paper products in those days had less acid in them," Sheila said. "It must have been in an airtight container."

"It was," Beatrice said. "Well, as far as we could tell. It was a chestnut trunk, and it was placed under a baby doll."

"Doll?"

"Yes, the historian we spoke with loved the doll. He showed us the hole in the back, which was used to smuggle drugs back and forth during the Civil War."

"Civil War? I guess this site is historically significant," Annie said.

"Well, yes and no," Paige said. "There are Civil War sites all over the area. And there is a direct link to Willa Rose and the Civil War. But I suspect this property goes back to when the area was founded."

"Who is Willa Rose?" Vera asked.

"She's the young woman who owned this book," Beatrice answered. "Willa Rose McGlashen, born eighteen fifty, died sometime about nineteen ten. She was a spy of sorts during the Civil War. In fact, she was awarded medals for bravery."

"Is she related to Emily McGlashen?" Annie asked.

"Maybe," Beatrice said. "We've not been able to prove that William, who grew up here and left, is actually related to her."

"We found a William McGlashen in California earlier this evening," Sheila announced. "He and his wife were both listed as some strange term. . . . What was it? Anyway, he was mixed race."

"Mixed?" Beatrice said. "Not according to what Willa wrote. Well, wait. She never really mentioned it. Just that she adopted the child. Mary, the kitchen helper, was the grandmother, and Ez was the father."

"What beautiful dresses," DeeAnn said as Beatrice flipped the page.

"A dream page of sorts," Sheila said. "It's heartbreaking, isn't it?"

Vera had to admit it was. Looking over the scrapbook felt almost like a sacred task. A young Willa Rose had placed some of her hopes and dreams onto those pages. Pretty dresses. New recipes she wanted to try. Books she listed that she wanted to read. Vera couldn't help but wonder if she had ever read all those books, or if she had ever gotten that yellow dress. For as they flipped the pages, Willa Rose was becoming more grim. It was the war. It was amazing she survived and even more amazing that the book survived. Vera blinked back a tear.

"Vera?" DeeAnn said. "You okay, hon?"

"It's just sort of sad. Here we are, looking at her book. Did those dreams ever come true? What became of her? And of her William?"

The room quieted.

"That's one of the reasons I love history so much," Paige said and smiled. "When you actually see something like this . . . you gain such an appreciation for the lives that came before us. They weren't just characters in a history book."

Just then a wind came through the open dining room window. Beatrice's lace curtains billowed. Some of the pages in the book wafted and paper went flying.

Beatrice shut the window. "Boy, what a breeze. Cold."

Annie gasped. Vera and the others turned to face her.

"This is amazing," she said. "Disturbing."

She held a fragile newspaper clipping and read it to the group.

"Ez Kingston, son of Mary, was found hanging from an oak tree at the crossroads. Nobody has stepped forward and claimed they committed such a heinous act to a loyal member of this community. An investigation into his murder is pending."

"Murder?" Beatrice said.

Annie kept reading.

"He served as a soldier and fought bravely. Recently he had been accused of cavorting with a white woman. The witness claimed they saw her only from the back and were never able to get a view of her face. He refuted their charges."

"So he hung because of a woman," Paige said. "A white woman."

"Could it be?" Vera said. "Could Willa Rose be the one?"

"Why not?" Beatrice said. "Willa Rose. No wondered she lost her mind after William left. He was all she had left of Ez."

"If this is all true, and we find a link between Emily and William, well, can you imagine? Emily was in an awkward position, then, building her creds on this pure heritage of hers," Vera said.

Chapter 56

The scrapbookers settled in at Beatrice's house. She had just made a peach pie, and they were eating pie in the kitchen and looking over the memory book in the dining room. Jon and Elizabeth were both upstairs, asleep, so they tried to be quiet in their conversations.

When Annie's cell phone beeped, she just about jumped out of her skin.

"Hey, Annie. It's Herb."

"Hey," she said, slipping outside the kitchen and sitting on a stair. "What's up?"

"I've been digging around. Going through some files," he said. "Files that I'm not supposed to have. Get my drift?"

"I think so," Annie said, realizing that he had probably stolen them. As long as she didn't ask, she wouldn't have to know where they came from.

"Emily McGlashen was an egg donor, like you suspected, and they were trying to find the right sperm donor."

"And?"

He breathed into the phone. She was certain he was having a cigarette. The night was chilly, and she was beginning to shiver. She watched a cloud cover the moon.

"I have three names here. Luther Vandergrift. Know him?"

"Yes. He's in prison."

"Okay. Well, then, he didn't kill her, did he?"

"No."

"Then we have John Reilly. Know him?"

John Reilly? The professor who pinched Vera?

"There must be a million John Reillys," she said, thinking aloud.

"This one is a professor of business . . . claims to be one hundred percent Irish. And he's on the board, not of the foundation, but the labs. "

Annie groaned. "Is that right?"

"Yes. And how stupid is that? One hundred percent Irish, my ass," he said. "But anyway. He was listed as a sperm donor. Several occasions and attempts. I'm not sure what happened. I can't tell from the notes as to whether it was successful."

"Well, Emily wasn't pregnant," Annie said. "I checked with the coroner. Nor did she have any pregnancies."

"There is one more name," he said. "This guy's a lawyer. So be careful."

"A lawyer? Local?"

"Yes. His name is Bill Ledford."

Annie almost dropped her phone.

"Are you certain?" she asked him.

"That's what it says. Several donor attempts and was scheduled to make a few more, ah, deposits. You know this guy?"

"Yes. His ex-wife is a good friend. He's kind of an asshole," she said, standing up from the cold stairs. "But I can't see him having the balls to kill anybody. Or even what his motive would be, you know? Donating sperm is one thing, but murder is another thing."

He snickered. "For most of us, yes."

"Okay," she said. "What do I do with this info?"

"First, keep it to yourself," he said. "Nobody wants to know their asshole ex-husband is donating sperm to create a designer baby."

Good point, Annie thought. *Especially Vera, who appears to have a lot on her mind these days. What would be the point?*

"But what I would do is find out more about this Reilly character. He seems the most likely candidate, since you know Bill and the other guy is already in prison."

"His wife is a bit of a nut job. She's a lawyer and is very confrontational. She approached Vera yesterday at the park," Annie said and explained why.

"That Bill guy doesn't seem right to me, either," he said. "Let's not write him off. What is a guy like that doing living with a twenty-four-year-old who has been terrorizing his ex-wife?"

"Midlife crisis. He's all about his dick," Annie said, then caught herself. She was talking just like she used to back in the day. She never said the word *dick* anymore. She flushed at the idea of it, yet at the same time she sort of liked the way it felt to say it.

"Poor guy," he said. "That's an awful place to be in your life. I was there when I was eighteen." He laughed.

"I need to go," Annie said, realizing that DeeAnn was looking out the window at her. "I'll call you if I find anything out."

"Okay. I'll do the same," he said.

She walked back up the stairs just as the moon was coming out from behind the clouds, shedding more light on Beatrice's mess of a backyard. Piles of dirt. Tents set up. Soon there would be a pool here, on top of what was one of the first places of record in the Shenandoah Valley. Time marched on. Places were of the here and now.

She opened the door and walked back into the warm house.

"It's getting late. I should be going," she said and picked up her bag.

"Wait," Vera said. "Who was on the phone? You were out there a while."

"It was my friend Herb. He's been snooping around the lab, came up with some possibilities for me."

"Well," DeeAnn said, "are you off to see Bryant?"

"No. I don't have anything conclusive yet."

"You should probably still talk with him," DeeAnn said.

Annie took a deep breath. Maybe she was right. Maybe he had a right to know what she had found out. More important, maybe he could add something to the investigation. Maybe she should stop by the office and see if he was around. It was inevitable. Maybe she should just get it over with.

Chapter 57

The police station was unusually quiet for a Saturday night. Annie knew that Detective Bryant would most likely be there, because he had confessed once that he caught up on paperwork on Saturday nights and liked being at the office for any Saturday night incidents. A workaholic. The only day of the week he took off was Sunday.

"Hello, Ms. Chamovitz," the woman behind the desk said. "Can I help you?"

"Is Detective Bryant in?"

The woman nodded. "I'll let him know you're here."

Annie wound her way through the halls, noticing new desks and a cleaner environment. It was coming together. They were finally getting the funding to hire more officers and renovate the offices a bit.

Bryant's door was open and his back was to her when she walked in.

"Adam?" she said.

He turned and looked up at her. He looked as if he hadn't shaved or showered or slept for days.

"What's with you?" Annie said.

"Oh, uh, nothing." He frowned, rubbed his face. "I'm just not sleeping well these days."

"Are you okay?"

He looked up at her with a world-weariness that nearly broke her heart. He shrugged. "You're not here to check on me, are you?"

"Ah, no," she said. "May I sit down?"

"Of course. Now what's up?" he said, sitting back in his chair.

"I wanted to let you know that I visited Alicorn's genetic labs the other day," she said. "I didn't find out anything, but I have a friend who is working on a story about them."

"What kind of story?"

"A story about creating designer babies."

"What does this have to do with Emily's case? Anything?"

"I'm not sure. She was an egg donor and was obviously wanting to use their services to make a baby," Annie said.

"Hmm. Interesting. You think someone offed her because she wanted to make a baby in an unnatural way?"

"No. But there is something fishy about all of it."

He chortled. "Always is when it comes to murder."

"There's something else, and I hope you will keep this to yourself."

"Annie—"

"Listen, Adam, this is a very delicate situation. We're dealing with babies, life, death, sperm—"

"What? Jesus."

"My friend has some files."

He looked at her with more interest. "Can I use those files as evidence?"

"No," she said.

"You journalists." He stood. "Doing illegal stuff in the name of a story." He sighed.

"If you don't want to know, I won't tell you," she said, starting to stand up.

"Wait, I don't have to use it in court. I might be able to make it work some other way," he said.

"Look, don't give yourself a hernia," Annie said. "It might not be anything. But I have the names of some donors."

She took a pen and paper and wrote them down, slid the paper closer to him.

"Well," he said. "I'll be damned."

Annie leaned back in her chair. "Thoughts?"

"Well, we can rule out Vandergrift. But the other two? Between you and me, I don't like either one of them, personally."

Annie frowned. "I'm not sure I can see either one of them as murderers."

Adam thought a moment, rubbed his scruffy chin. "You'd be surprised. I often am. We humans . . . sometimes . . . we are hard to read. We do stupid things."

Annie tilted her head. Was he talking about this case, or was he talking about them?

"Annie . . ." His voice lowered. "We need to talk."

She took a deep breath. "Go on."

"I'm sorry. I've been so stressed out, and it seems like . . . this attraction between us . . . I just could not avoid it. It was way out of line. It won't happen again."

That was not what she had expected to hear. A mature, sensitive Bryant spoke to her. She wished it were that way for her. She had been seriously tempted by him. A big part of her, her ego, to be sure, wanted to hear him professing his undying love for her. Could she just walk away and pretend the attraction didn't exist, that it didn't shake her to her core?

"I, um, ah—" she began.

"You don't have to say anything. You never did. Why start now? We kissed. I'm an idiot. I thought there was something there. Sometimes you seem so unhappy with Mike. I thought I had a shot. My mistake. Could we just please drop all of it . . . ?" he said, his face turning bright red.

She looked away, feeling the breath leave her. He was hurt. She had hurt him. But she had done nothing to lead him on, had she? What could she say to him? That yes, she had thought about him? Lusted after him? Was shaken by him? But. She loved her husband. She loved her children. The life they had created. It was worth fighting for.

"So, let's move on to the case. I'll run a background check on Reilly. We pretty much know all there is to know about Bill Ledford, but I'll run a check on him, anyway," he said and smirked.

"There's something else. Might not be worth mentioning. But I thought it was strange," Annie said. "The Greenbergs are still hanging around."

He jumped to attention. He sat more erect, looked more alert. What was going on?

"I've been talking to Rachel a lot. She's painted quite a picture of her daughter. From her point of view, Emily had a fabulous family life, growing up on the commune. When she found out she was adopted, she went kind of berserk and rebelled. They think she was still rebelling."

"At her age?"

Annie nodded.

"But she also admitted that Emily was difficult and was a loner. Rachel is still on a quest to find her daughter's lover. She thinks his first name begins with the letter *L*."

Adam bristled. "I can't get into that with you right now."

Annie's stomach sank. There was that feeling again. Her gut instinct pulling at her. There was no shaking it.

He knew way more than he was telling her.

Chapter 58

Vera loved her naps with Lizzie. Sundays were all about playing and napping and eating. She lay snuggled in the bed with her daughter. She had never been happier. Being a mother was the best thing that had ever happened to her. It was also the hardest. How could that be?

She listened to Lizzie's breathing. Rhythmic. She thought about the conversation at one of the last crops that focused on genetics. She wondered about the mixing of her and Bill's blood and genetics in their daughter. Lizzie was the only good thing that had ever come of that relationship. Why had she spent all those years with him? Almost all of her youth was spent on him. It was maddening. She tried not to think about it.

Then his girlfriend had been stalking her. *Lovely.* Kelsey had preyed on her by trying to make her feel like she had lost her mind. Trying to set her up for murder. What kind of a person did that? And what would Bill see in a person like that? She meant it when she told Bill that sometimes she wondered if she knew him at all.

They had met in college in New York City and had been astounded that they had grown up not fifty miles from one another. His family, like hers, had been in the area for generations. He could trace their roots back to the *Mayflower*. She could never be bothered. Who cared about all that? What was important was the here and now.

She brushed a piece of Lizzie's red hair off her face. For a moment, she swore she could see Beatrice in her daughter.

That wouldn't be such a bad thing, would it? Beatrice would be a great role model for any young woman, and this one had her genetic code in there somewhere. Vera had often thought that if her mother had been born a little later, she'd be queen of the planet by now. As it was, she had still accomplished a great deal in her life. Vera was proud of her. Maybe Lizzie would inherit some of Beatrice's intellectual prowess.

Later that afternoon Detective Bryant stopped by.

"Can I come in?"

"Certainly," Vera said, opening the door.

"What do you want?" Beatrice said when she saw him in her foyer.

"I just wanted to touch base with you about a few things," he said.

"Well, come in," Vera said and led him to the couch, where they both sat. Beatrice stood with her hands on her hips.

"Can I get you anything? Iced tea?" Beatrice said.

"That would be fine. Sans poison, of course," he said as he grinned at her, referring to the time Beatrice was poisoned and threw up all over Tina Sue and Zeb's front porch.

"Don't tempt me," she muttered, walking off into the kitchen.

He didn't look well. It looked like he hadn't shaved in days, and she wondered if he had been showering at all.

"Everything okay?" Vera asked.

"Yes," he said. "I just need to clarify a few things with you."

She smiled and leaned forward.

"You are still under suspicion for Emily's murder. I know you think Kelsey did it, but she has a rock-solid alibi. So you are it at this point," he told her.

Her heart pounded. She swore he could probably hear it. Sweat rushed to her forehead. "I thought I had been cleared because of the hypnosis walk-through."

He shook his head. "No, I'm sorry. I was there, and I'm still uncertain about what you saw or what you think you saw. Was it someone else? Or was it you seeing yourself? And I found out that we need an unbiased expert to witness it for the court."

"Oh," she said, now focusing on breathing.

"So I wondered if we might try it again. Maybe this time it would be clearer. Maybe you'd remember."

"I just don't know," she said, suddenly feeling tired. So tired she swore she could sink in the couch and sleep sitting up.

"What's going on?" Beatrice said, walking into the room with a pitcher of iced tea and several glasses.

"We'd like Vera to do it again," the detective said.

Beatrice poured the tea. "Do what?"

"Go through the hypnosis," he said.

"Absolutely not!" Beatrice said. "You saw what happened to her."

"I did," he said. "And I wouldn't ask it, except that I'm getting pressure to make an arrest. All the evidence leads to Vera still. I don't know what else to do to try to clear her. We have hired a specialist, a forensic hypnotist, to work with your doctor on this."

Beatrice handed him a glass.

Vera was afraid her mother would pour it on him and was happy to see that she didn't. Not that it hadn't happened before. With teachers. With other parents. Even with her teenage friends.

"What do you think, Vera?" Beatrice said.

"I think I don't have much choice, Mama," Vera said.

Beatrice's brows knit as she turned to Bryant. "I want you to know that if anything happens to her, it's your balls. I'm holding you responsible."

"Understood," he said.

"Oh, Mama," Vera said and waved her off. Had her mother just said "Balls" to Detective Bryant? That thought warmed her. Same old Beatrice.

A huge smile cracked on Bryant's usually stern face. DeeAnn was right. He was a handsome man. But only when he smiled, which wasn't often.

Chapter 59

"Well, you have to wonder who the outsiders are," Beatrice said.

"I'm not too thrilled to know the police want a few other people there to watch the hypnosis. I'll feel like I'm on display," Vera said. "But what can I do?"

"I hope you're under and things are in hand before they bring the others in," Beatrice said, pulling out a cherry cobbler from the oven, its scent filling the kitchen and making both of them nearly swoon.

"What do I smell?" Jon said as he walked into the kitchen with Lizzie on his hip.

"Dessert for dinner tonight. A cherry cobbler. Nancy gave me a bunch of cherries. This recipe is actually from Willa Rose's book," Beatrice said, then turned away from Vera, who looked surprised.

"A recipe?"

"Oh yes," Jon said. "There were several."

"Difficult to follow, though," Beatrice said. "No measurements to speak of."

"Mama, why are you keeping this book? You know, it really belongs to the state."

"They have everything else," Beatrice said.

"They won't miss it," Jon said, shrugging.

"So? What will you do with it?"

"I don't know. And here's the thing. . . . That book is special. I can't explain it. But I feel like I have it for a reason. I sort of feel a connection to it. A connection to Willa Rose, too," Beatrice said. "Well, that needs to cool off. I need to sit down for a bit, and then I'll get supper."

"Lizzie and I can do that, Mama. Go relax," Vera said and waved her off. Beatrice shrugged and went outside.

Out in the garden, or what was left of it, Beatrice was finally alone with her thoughts. These days she liked to daydream about Willa Rose, what they knew about her and what they didn't. She was born before the Civil War into a family that helped settle this area. They owned an inn at one of the busiest crossroads. She somehow managed to impress enough politicians or soldiers so much that they trusted her, a woman, to help spy, carry valuable information from one place to the other. Remarkable.

Most remarkable, though, was that she somehow fell in love with Ez. But maybe it wasn't that remarkable at all. Young women and men had been falling in and out of love for generations, most of them not caring whether their families or their culture supported it. But to be a white woman in love with a black man during the Civil War and shortly after it, well, it was so romantic. And also dangerous. As it turned out, very dangerous for Ez.

What was he like?

What was she like?

How did they meet?

How deeply had they loved one another?

These thoughts rolled around in her mind. *I am an old romantic fool. And this is one of the many things Jon has done to me.* She smiled. Beatrice was in love for the second time in her life. Blessed twice.

Now, if she could only see that for her daughter, she'd die a happy woman. Poor Vera. First, there was Bill and all his shenanigans. Then this Tony character in New York, whom Vera had never even brought back to Cumberland Creek. Now there was this doctor, Eric. He was a nice guy, and Vera seemed to like him, but she didn't seem to be smitten. Oh, well, time would tell.

Truthfully, the only person Vera had ever seemed smitten with was Lizzie. Land sakes, maybe that was enough. Who said you had to have a man in your life to be happy?

Love was good, but it was also the cause of pain, turmoil, and sometimes death. *Look at poor Ez. A man who fought against slavery. A man who was given freedom by the government, only to be lynched by his community for loving a white woman,* she thought before she sank into her chair and dozed off.

She woke up, startled. *Oh, damn.* She'd been dreaming about Willa Rose, hadn't she?

A thought came to her as crystal blue as the sky. *This book belongs to her family.* Were the Greenbergs still in town? Was Emily's birth family the McGlashens who were spawned by Willa Rose and Ez? It certainly looked that way, but Paige was still researching.

"Well," Jon said as he walked up to her, "are you ready for supper?"

"Supper? How long have I been sleeping?"

"A few hours," he said, shrugging. He sat down. "Are you feeling well?"

"Yes," she said. "I'm fine. I was dreaming about Willa Rose."

"Really?"

"I don't remember much about it," she said. "But I awoke with the thought that I'd like to get this book in the hands of her family."

"We need to prove that the McGlashens are indeed her family."

She nodded. "I never really cared for Emily McGlashen. She was so mean to Vera. It was unnecessary, and I've always thought there was more to it than the dance studios competition."

"What do you mean? What could it be?" Jon said.

"I've no idea," she said. "But even so, it was a cruel way to die. I wouldn't wish it on my worst enemy."

Jon nodded. "Quite right." He paused. "Has there been any break in the case?"

"I don't know. The last I heard, Annie and Bryant were up to something. God knows what."

Chapter 60

Annie was working on deadline. The first draft of her book on the NMO was due next week. Files and papers were scattered all over her bed. *Taxes, taxes,* she thought. *Where did I put the tax file?* She searched all over her bed and finally found the folder she was looking for. Okay the NMO was a nonprofit and tax exempt. She scanned down the forms in front. Suddenly the word *Alicorn* leapt off the page.

"What?" she said out loud, even though she was completely alone in the house.

The name John Reilly was listed with the other board members.

She dialed Bryant.

"Yeah?" he said into the phone. "What's up, Annie?"

"I can't believe I overlooked this. I have evidence of a link between Alicorn and the NMO."

"We knew that was the case," he said. Suddenly his voice was crisper, more alert. "Nothing wrong with that. I mean, nothing illegal about it." But then he grew quiet on the other end of the line. "Do me a favor and copy that for me," he said, then breathed into the phone.

"Have you checked out Reilly?" Annie asked.

"Yep," he said.

"And?"

"Annie, this part doesn't concern you," he said.

"What do you mean?"

"I mean I can't tell you a thing about what I'm finding out these days. It's all conjecture at this point. What I have is hunches. Scattered pieces of information and evidence. I'm looking for that moment when everything comes together. Or that moment when something clicks. Right now I feel like we are building a strong case, but I have no idea where it's leading," he said.

"You can't tell me about Reilly?" she asked.

"No, I can't. But feel free to dig around yourself. Well, knowing you . . . you'll do that, anyway. I'm surprised you haven't," he said.

"Well, I have found out that he was on the board of the lab. The same time as Emily McGlashen was on the board of the foundation," she said, looking at the papers scattered all over her bed, which was her makeshift office. She was met with silence. "I'll try to get you a copy of this soon."

"Good," he said and hung up.

Bryant was not behaving in a copacetic manner. He wasn't his usual prickly self, nor was he coming on to her with sweet and sexy words, for which she was grateful. But he seemed reticent, and it troubled Annie. Her gut told her he was hiding something, but she didn't have the time to follow up, with her deadline closing in on her. It was all she could do to feed and bathe her boys. And forget about cleaning. As soon as she finished this book, she was going to clean her house. Top to bottom.

So close to finishing this book. Well, it couldn't hurt to do a brief Google search on Reilly.

U Va. Professor of Business Receives Prestigious Marketing Award.

"The Links between Old-Time Appalachian Music and Irish Music," by John C. Reilly.

Annie eyes scanned farther down.

"On the Irish: Always Superior," by J. W. Reilly.

Was J. W. Reilly John W. Reilly? She clicked on the article. No photo. But the bio stated he was a professor of business. It must be him. She read over the article.

He wrote about literature, art, and so on and sort of poked fun at the idea of any one group of people being referred to as superior, even though the Irish clearly had their act together, according to him.

Well, that was a relief.

Just then her doorbell rang.

When she answered the door, half expecting to see the postman, she was surprised to find the Greenbergs.

"Hi. Come on in," Annie said, embarrassed that her house was such a mess. Toys were scattered about; books and papers were piled on tables and in corners. At least the kitchen table was relatively clear.

"Thank you," Rachel said.

"Please sit down," Annie said. "Can I get you something?"

"No thanks," Rachel said, sitting on the couch. "We just came by to thank you for helping us out a few weeks back. We're getting ready to leave."

"Today?" Annie said.

"No," Donald replied. "Probably by the end of the week."

"Do you know if the police have any leads?" Rachel asked.

"Not really," Annie said. "But I do know they are working on the case. Have you found anything else in Emily's papers?"

They looked at one another and shifted in their seats.

"We found another hidden journal," Donald said.

"We'd rather not talk about it," Rachel said, taking a deep sigh. "Emily was never an easy child, and she grew into a complicated woman. She was hard on us. She was hard on everybody. We wonder as her parents . . . what we could have done differently . . . but there comes a time . . . when you just have to accept that people are people, and there's not much you can do, even as a parent."

Where was this conversation going?

"But we loved her and would have continued loving her if she had given us a chance. We would have been more a part of her life. She assumed that we couldn't deal with it," Rachel said.

"I don't understand," Annie said.

"Evidently, Emily was gay," he said.

"Gay? But I thought you said she was involved with a married man?"

"We assumed it was a man. It turns out that it was a woman," Donald said.

"She was involved with a married woman?"

They nodded.

"Do you know who?"

"We think so," said Rachel. "That's why we're here."

Chapter 61

Dearest Em,

Please forgive me for writing to you about matters of
the heart, for not facing you, my love. I do not have the
strength. For now, it's best that we have no connection.
My husband is getting suspicious. I found him looking
at my e-mails yesterday. He keeps badgering me about
sex, and I simply can't do it.

I know that it seems easy to you for me to pick up
and leave my family for you, but it's complicated when
you have children. I promised myself I would not be like
my selfish bitch of a mother, who left us alone with my
father. Children need their mother. I cannot turn my
back on them. And, if he knew about you and me, it
would be a battle for me to keep them. I don't want to
place any of us in that position.

I've been pleading with you to not make me choose.
And all along it was there, in front of my face. I love
you, but my choice is clear. It has to be, for now. I can't
ask you to wait for me. You are so young, beautiful, and
talented. You really must put me behind you.

With all my heart,

L.

Annie slipped the letter back into her bag as she approached Vera's old house. Sad. The Reillys were not really keeping it up. The shrubs were overgrown, and the flower beds needed weeding.

She rang the doorbell, and Leola answered.

"Thanks for agreeing to see me," Annie said.

"No problem. I've got a few minutes to spare, though I do have an appointment in a bit," Leola said. "Please come in. Can I get you anything?"

Inside the house was exactly as Vera had left it. It was as though Leola and her family were not even living there.

"Temporary quarters," Leola said, observing Annie looking around in shock. "What's the point in redecorating? Not really my thing, anyway. Please sit down."

Annie sat down on Vera's old, beautiful plush blue couch. Leola sat in the chair across from it.

"What can I help you with?" Leola said, perched on the edge of the chair, folding her hands over her knees. White knuckles. Ruby-red nail polish.

"I'd like to chat with you about Emily McGlashen," Annie said.

Leola's eyes lowered to the floor. She nodded. "What can I tell you about her?"

"I understand your husband was on the board at Alicorn with her," Annie said.

"Oh, that." She waved her hand. "Yes. They were both so into that place."

"Why?"

"Well, Emily was adopted, you know, and so these matters were important to her," Leola said.

"And your husband?"

"An old friend of ours got him involved. He needed to be on a board for his résumé. Once he was on the board, he liked it. And he and Emily saw eye to eye on many things,"

Leola said, sitting back in her chair, relaxing just a bit. Then she crossed her legs. "They were both into Irish music, for one thing," Leola added and smiled.

"Well, yes, I know that," Annie said. "But let me be clear here. What was their involvement together on the board?"

"Hell, I don't know. We never talked about that kind of stuff. Didn't interest me in the least."

"Do you know if they ever disagreed about anything?" Annie asked.

"Let me think," Leola said. "There was something about some funding that John didn't like. Funding from some group . . . oh yes. Emily hired that Luther to do some research for her. Turns out he was a member of that group, the New Mountain Order. When he found out she was on their board, they gave it some money. John didn't like it. He said it was stepping on the toes of another project or something. . . . I don't remember exactly."

"Nice suit," Annie said.

"Thanks," Leola said. "As I said, I've an appointment soon." She looked at her watch.

"Yeah, usually you don't dress like this," Annie said and smiled. "What is it with all the women around here dressing in long jean skirts? Long jumpers and stuff?"

Leola shrugged. "Modesty," she said. "The church we go to is really into it. I don't dress like it for work, though."

Annie nodded. *Modesty? Hmmm.* There sat Leola, made up to the hilt, in a beautiful formfitting suit and a low-cut silk blouse.

"Are you sure I can't get you something?" Leola asked during the awkward silence.

"I'm fine," Annie said. "Can I ask you something?"

"Sure," Leola said, leaning forward, white knuckles no more. Yes, she felt much more at ease with Annie. Her body language told her that. So now was the time to zoom in on her. Annie felt a little sympathy, but she set it aside.

"How long had you and Emily been lovers?" She looked Leola squarely in the eye.

Leola's jaw grew firm, and her face flamed red. "What are you talking about?" she spat.

Annie reached into her bag and pulled out the letter that Emily's family had given her.

"This is what I'm talking about," Annie said. "I've not gone to the cops about this. But if I did, I'm sure a handwriting analysis would tell us exactly who wrote this. I'm sure it was you."

Leola just looked at her. Her mouth hung open slightly and her eyes were moving back and forth, as if she was trying to find the right words.

"Besides that," Annie said, "this is extremely personal. I don't know what purpose it would serve. Unless it has to do with her murder. I don't think you killed her. You loved her. That much is clear."

Leola lost her composure as she looked into Annie eyes. She began to unravel with a shudder. She bit her lip.

"What do you want from me?" Leola said at last.

"I want to find out who killed her. I'm betting that you do, too. Maybe we can figure this out together," Annie said.

Leola sighed. "I'll do anything I can."

Chapter 62

When Vera woke up, she was standing next to her mother's bed with something in her hand. Something sharp, metallic, gleaming.

Beatrice wasn't stirring.

The moonlight shone through her lace curtains onto Beatrice's wrinkled skin.

"Mama?" Vera whispered. What had she done?

Beatrice didn't stir.

Vera gingerly reached for her mother's shoulder and shook her.

"Mama?"

Beatrice sat straight up. "What's wrong, girl?" She switched on her light. "Vera?"

Vera stood in her nightgown, perplexed. What was she doing here?

She had gone to bed early. She had been thinking about Detective Bryant. She had fallen asleep quickly. What was she doing here?

"I . . ." She held up the object she'd been carrying.

"What are you doing with a pie slicer?" Beatrice said.

Vera shrugged.

"Are you sleepwalking again?" Beatrice said, sitting up farther on her bed, reaching for her glasses. "Oh!"

It was then that Vera noticed the blood on the sleeves of her pink nightgown.

"What!" she exclaimed. "What have I done?"

"Now, now, just calm down," Beatrice said, getting up from the bed.

Vera scanned herself. . . . A burning, stinging pain came from her lower arm.

Beatrice grabbed her wrist. "You cut yourself. That's all," Beatrice said. "That thing is sharp."

"Yes," Vera managed to say as Jon entered the room.

"What is happening?" he asked, bleary-eyed.

"She cut herself," Beatrice said. "Go back to bed, Jon. I'll take care of this."

He shrugged. "She cut herself at one thirty in the morning?" He looked at both women. "Very well. Good night."

Beatrice looked frazzled.

"Please, Vera, sit down over there and I'll get you cleaned up."

After Vera was cleaned up and a bandage was placed on her wrist, a wave of weariness overcame her. "I'm so tired, Mama."

"Listen, Vera," Beatrice said, "we need to get to the bottom of this. You can't live your life like this."

"I know, Mama."

"We'll call the doctor in the morning and see if he can adjust your medicine, okay?"

Vera nodded. "I can't remember coming into your room."

She looked around at her mom's room. The quilt-covered bed. The stacks of hand-crocheted and knitted afghans. The books. The doily-covered tables. The paintings. Her jewelry box, one that she had had since Vera was a girl. It had held such magic then. In fact, this whole room had. Her mother's closet, most of all. She used to find such comfort here.

"I realize that," Beatrice said. "Do you remember anything at all?"

"I just remember thinking about something before I went to sleep. Bill and Kelsey, for one thing. And I thought about Leola."

"Well," Beatrice said, sitting down on her bed, "I imagine that was quite a confrontation. I don't reckon you'd be dropping those charges."

"Hell no, Mama," Vera said. "And the more I think about it, the thing that disturbs me the most is that night she was in Elizabeth's room. What was she doing there? And then for Bill—" Her voice cracked. "And then for Bill, the man I lived with most of my life, the father of my daughter, to approach me about it . . . the way he did."

"It's another heartbreak," Beatrice said.

Both women sat quietly with their own thoughts.

"Bah, that thing between Bill and Kelsey won't last. You know that, don't you?"

"It doesn't really matter to me, Mama. I think what my gut is telling me is that I don't want my daughter around him as long as she is in his life."

"Vera—"

"I mean it, Mama," Vera said. "I hate to take her from her father. But Bill is making bad decisions. I don't want Elizabeth caught up in it."

Beatrice's lips gathered, as if she was trying not to speak.

"I know she loves her daddy. The way I loved mine. It hurts. But I think I'm going to need to talk to another lawyer about this."

"What made you come to this conclusion?"

"My whole life has brought me to this conclusion," Vera

said, rising from her chair, listening for the same old creaks in the floorboards that had been there since she was a girl. She stopped. "You need to get those floorboards fixed."

Beatrice waved her off. "Go to bed, Vera. I like my creaks." She sank into her bed as Vera walked out of her room.

Of course, Vera stopped in Elizabeth's room to gaze at her as she lay in her bed.

Only the bed was completely empty.

Vera blinked her eyes. Was she seeing things? Dreaming? Still sleepwalking?

She blinked again. No. Elizabeth was gone.

"Mama! Jon!" she screamed into the night.

Both came stumbling into the room.

"Where's Elizabeth?" Beatrice said.

"The window is open," Jon pointed out. "Someone has taken the child."

"I'll call the police," Beatrice said.

Jon reached for Vera, who was swooning. The room was swaying. She was trying to keep her footing. She leaned on Jon, whose eyes were wide, hair standing straight up. Jon. What a good guy.

"Find my baby," she found the strength to say before it all went black.

Chapter 63

Annie was sound asleep when sirens jarred her awake.

She reached for Mike, who was already halfway sitting up, struggling to untangle himself from the bed.

"What the—" he said.

And Annie's cell went off.

"Shit," he growled.

"It's Bea," Annie said. "Yes, Bea?"

"Annie." She sounded strange. Was she crying? "Someone has taken our baby girl. Someone has Elizabeth. The police are here. They are searching . . . already."

"Be right there," Annie said.

"What the hell?"

"Mike," Annie said, placing her hand on his shoulder. "It's not the paper. It's Elizabeth. She's been taken."

"Good God," he said after a moment. "What can we do?"

"I need to get over there . . . for Vera. For Bea. I'll call you later if there is anything you can do. Can you get the boys off to school?"

She leapt out of the bed and slipped on her jeans. Years of practice enabled her to dress quickly in the dark room. Mike turned the light on.

"Well, that makes things easier," she said.

"Damn," he sighed.

"What?" she said, slipping off her nightshirt and reaching for her bra.

His eyes lingered on her breasts. "Sometimes I forget how beautiful you are. How can that be? We live together. I see you every day."

Annie smiled. "I am going to remember to pay you back for that compliment."

She leaned over and hugged him.

"I need to go," she said.

He held her there. "Annie, I love you so much."

"Hey." She sat down at the edge of the bed. "Is everything okay?"

"Yes. I mean no. But we can talk later. It's fine," he said. "You need to go."

She looked at her husband, who looked bleary-eyed and rumpled. Brown hair ruffled. Eyes deep brown and worried.

"You are my number one concern, Mike, always," she said.

Eyes met eyes. Something was exchanged. Renewal. Commitment. Love. In one glance.

"I know," he said and smiled. "We will talk later."

"Good," she said. And it was about time.

What was it about the middle of the night? Some of their best moments as a couple were during talks in the middle of the night. Was it a sense of vulnerability? Or just the opposite? A sense of safety? And how many times had she wakened in the middle of the night just to check on her boys with a sense of pending horror? Feeling like something was wrong? What a relief it was to see them sleeping snug in their beds.

Vera was living every mother's worst nightmare.

* * *

Beatrice's living room door was open, and Annie walked in. She had expected to see chaos, but instead was surprised to find a team of officers quietly moving about their home. Beatrice, Sheila, DeeAnn, and Paige were sitting at the kitchen table. The smell of strong coffee permeated the house.

"Where is Vera?" Annie asked.

Beatrice looked up at her. In her weary eyes, Annie saw the eighty-three-year-old woman that she was. That was rare with Beatrice.

"Vera is with Eric, upstairs in her room," Beatrice answered. "We are trying to keep it calm and quiet. She passed out, then was hysterical. He has given her something to calm her."

"A sleeping pill. But she can't sleep forever," Sheila said.

Annie glanced around the table at the normally jovial bunch, and they almost looked like different people. The strain showed in the way they held their mouths, eyes, jaws. Every mother's worst nightmare.

"Where is Detective Bryant?"

"Out. He had a gut feeling or something," DeeAnn muttered.

"Did he question you?" Annie asked Beatrice. "Have they sent out an AMBER Alert? Is it on the news?"

"Calm down, Annie," Sheila said. "Yes, he questioned Beatrice." She reached her hand out and held Beatrice's hand.

The next thing Annie knew, Jon was handing her a cup of steaming hot coffee and leading her to a chair at the table.

"Adam thinks it was Kelsey," Jon said. "He and his team are looking for her. Roadblocks and so on. It is under control. Inasmuch as it can be," he said.

"What makes him think that? I mean, we know she is disturbed, but to take a child?" Annie asked.

Nobody replied. Paige looked at her and shrugged. They were wilting.

"What can we do?" Annie said after downing a few sips of coffee. "Can we help search?"

DeeAnn looked up at her sheepishly. "I asked the same question and was given the smack down." She pointed at Beatrice.

"You all need to stay out of it. Let the law do its job. Two counties and the state police are looking. The best we can do is be here for Vera when she wakes up."

Sheila caught Annie's eye and nodded.

Annie's cell phone blared. It was her editor. "Yes," she said into the phone.

"Annie, I hear there's been a kidnapping. I need you to get to two-eleven Ivy Lane."

"I'm already there," she said, looking at the circle of women around the table. Did she really want to be the reporter in the crowd?

"What? Good work."

"I am not covering this one, Steve. I'm too close to it."

"What do you mean?"

"I am very close to the family and am really upset." Her voice cracked. Oh no. Was she going to cry sitting there in front of everyone and with her editor on the other end of the line? She choked it back.

"I'm sorry, Annie. I can find someone else," he said.

"I wish you would," she said and meant it. She couldn't write about this situation with any kind of objectivity. But she could not help it when her brain made leaps in logic and strange connections as she thought about Elizabeth and the fact that Bryant knew right away who to look for. She had known that he was holding something back from her. Kelsey must have more of a record or a problem than what

Annie knew. In fact, maybe he knew something like this was bound to happen.

And where was Bill? Had anybody even called him? Or was he waiting on the other end of Kelsey's path to take his baby away from her mother?

Chapter 64

Beatrice didn't want to mention the tightening in her chest. She was certain it was stress. Nothing to worry about. Of course she was stressed. Someone had taken Elizabeth out of her bed—in *her* home—in the middle of the night. Evidently, the intruder had used a ladder, one of the ladders that belonged to the Virginia Department of Historic Resources. Had just placed the ladder right under the window of Elizabeth's bedroom.

How did they know where to place it?

And on the same night that Vera woke Beatrice up out of a sound sleep with a pie slicer in her hand with blood all over herself.

So, hell yes, she was stressed. She took another deep breath. The tightening didn't get any worse.

It did not get any better, either.

DeeAnn had decided to bake some biscuits and was thrashing around in her kitchen.

Beatrice remembered the gravy in the refrigerator. With a houseful like this, she should be feeding them all. But she was afraid to move. If she moved, she was afraid what would happen. Something would change. They would get news. Bad news. No. She could not think about that.

She wouldn't move.

Every so often she glanced at the officers quietly moving through her home and remembered when she used to know every member of the three-person police squad in her town. She knew their families, as well. Oh, that was too many years ago to count.

And her baby was lying upstairs, half out of it from sleeping pills by this point.

And her granddaughter had been stolen.

Beatrice ran her hand along the surface of the table. It was hard, cold, real. She wasn't dreaming, as much as she wished it. This was real.

The scent of the biscuits. The people around her. Yes, it was all real. Too real for her. Elizabeth was gone.

Her telephone rang, sending her heart racing, and Annie picked it up. Annie seemed to be the appointed phone person in the crowd. If it wasn't her cell phone, it was another phone she was talking into.

Beatrice tried to read her expression and murmured something under her breath. "What was she saying?" Beatrice asked. "Who is she talking to?"

Sheila held up a finger.

"That was Detective Bryant," Annie said. "They found Elizabeth."

"And?" Beatrice said, unable to read Annie's expression. Was she relieved? Gathering strength to deliver bad news?

"Elizabeth is fine. They have taken her to the hospital to check her over. It's standard procedure."

Squeals of relief and sighs all around.

Beatrice cleared her throat. "Who did this? Was it Kelsey?"

"The police have Kelsey at the station," Annie said.

"Well, that is a miracle. The fastest police work I've ever seen. Especially around here," DeeAnn said.

"There is something else," Annie said.

They all looked at her.

"They have a warrant out for Bill."

"Surely not," Beatrice said." Surely Bill didn't have anything to do with this."

Paige spoke up. "It happens a lot. I was just reading about someone who grew up thinking their mother had died. Years later, they found out their father had just taken them to raise. Can you imagine?"

"Bill?" DeeAnn said.

Beatrice tried to process that, but it didn't sit right with her. Bill had done some surprising and odd things the past few years. But she wasn't sure she could see him actually trying to hurt Vera like that. Or Elizabeth. But then again, she could be wrong. It happened sometimes.

Jon's hand went to her shoulder. His hands. She loved them. She loved him. Thank the universe for this man who took care of everything when she sat there, barely able to breathe, as the intense emotions slammed into her. He made the coffee, answered the door, offered the chairs. Now he showed people out. And then her to her own bed, where she finally closed her eyes and rested.

Hours later, when she awoke, it was to the sound of a loud and happy three-year-old running through the house. The next thing she knew, Lizzie was in her bed.

"Get up, Granny!"

Beatrice pulled her down to her and wrapped her in her arms. A deep peace overcame her. It would be all right now. Now that Lizzie was home.

Vera sat on the quilt-covered bed with her mother and daughter. She was a little out of breath. "I can't keep up with you, Elizabeth. Are you okay, Mama?"

"Land sakes, can't an old woman take a nap?"

"Mama, you've been sleeping all day!"

"Look at you, Lizzie," Beatrice said. "I missed you."

"I missed you, too. Kelsey had candy."

Beatrice looked up at Vera, who grimaced.

"Really? Well, I have cookies," Beatrice said. "How about that?"

Elizabeth squealed. "Yea!"

"Supper first," Vera said. "How about spaghetti?"

Elizabeth turned and fell into her mother's arms. "I love you, Mama."

"I love you, too, girl."

Vera blinked away a tear—but Beatrice saw it. And she was blinking back a few of her own.

Chapter 65

Vera hated to leave Lizzie the next day. But the psychologists said that they needed to keep to Lizzie's routines. She would still have some fearful memories. But they were trying to let her believe that it was an outing, that Kelsey did not mean to take her away from her mother. Evidently, Bryant had caught her pretty quickly, and Elizabeth had seen him so often that she felt completely comfortable with him.

Still, Vera was shaken. So shaken that they had to cancel her hypnosis session, which was scheduled for today. They'd do it on Thursday now.

But she wanted to clean her studio, because in a few days she would start her summer schedule, which was jam-packed. And she needed to take care of the registrations and finances today. People hated it when they wrote checks that weren't cashed right away. She filled out all the paperwork and left the studio to walk toward the bank.

On the way, she passed the fountain her mother liked to sit at sometimes, but she wasn't there. A group of very pregnant women was hanging around, all dressed in the same style. Hadn't she seen them at the festival? She figured they were from out of town, but maybe not. Surely they wouldn't still be there if they had just been visiting a local family. There was something odd about them.

Vera walked into the cool air of the bank and took care of her business quickly, turned, and walked out. The group of women was heading into DeeAnn's Bakery. Should she? Oh, what could it hurt to follow them in there? She had plenty of time.

DeeAnn was nowhere to be found at first. Her intern helped the group of pregnant women, got them drinks and an assorted variety of baked goods. Soon enough DeeAnn came out to bring more scones to the display case.

"Hey, Vera," DeeAnn said. "You want one?"

Vera nodded. "Blueberry."

"Coffee?"

"Sure. Join me?"

"I can't now. I've got muffins in the oven," she said.

"I can take care of that," her intern said.

She and Vera sat close to the group of denim skirt– and jumper-wearing pregnant women.

"Do you know them?" DeeAnn asked.

Vera nodded in the affirmative.

"Who are they?"

Vera shrugged.

"Wonder what the professor would think of us eating sugary treats," one young woman said.

They laughed.

"Don't want his babies having sugar," another one of the young women said. "So stupid."

DeeAnn's eyes widened.

Vera sat back in her chair and took a bite of her scone. Who were they talking about? What were they talking about? Was their father a professor? Were they sisters? Surely not. There were five of them, and they all looked to be between, say, eighteen and twenty-two. Very close in age. Though it was getting harder for Vera to tell young women's ages just by looking at them.

The door flung open and another young woman walked through and the others greeted her. When she turned to look in the display case, Vera saw her face. She looked vaguely familiar.

"Miss Vera?" the young woman said.

Vera smiled. She was used to this. Girls remembering her. She had to search her memories to figure it out. "Yes?" Vera looked up at her.

"It's me, Chelsea Miller," she said. "I took dance classes with you."

"Oh, Chelsea!" Vera said, standing up and hugging a very pregnant former student. "I thought you were at college?"

"I am," she said. "I'm studying at the University of Virginia. I'll take some time off when the baby gets here."

"Yes," Vera said. "I imagine you will."

"Oh, not to take care of it," she said.

"No?"

DeeAnn was bursting. Vera didn't dare look further at her. Her face was beet red.

"I'm giving it up for adoption."

"Oh," Vera said, taken aback by the way she spoke of her baby as an it.

"Well, that's a smart choice," DeeAnn said finally. "You're too young to be saddled with a baby."

The table next to theirs quieted.

"And there's so many people who can provide a good home, who really want a baby," DeeAnn said.

"Yes," Chelsea said. "That's just what John said."

"John? The baby's father?" Vera asked.

"Chelsea!" One of the young women was now at her side, pulling her away.

"I'm sorry," she said, smiling. "It was nice seeing you."

Chelsea sat down at the table next to them. Vera was perplexed. They appeared to be a group of pregnant women who were in some kind of club. Were they all giving their babies up for adoption? Were they a support group? Was that it?

Vera felt the hair on the back of her neck prick at her. The oddest sensation. A cloud of danger and suspicion fell over her. Why? They just appeared to be harmless pregnant women. She should mind her own business. Why did she care? Maybe it was all the recent discussion about Alicorn and designer babies poking at her.

"After I get that report done for Reilly, I'm done for the summer," one of them said.

Reilly? How many University of Virginia professors were named Reilly?

DeeAnn looked at her in the eyes. "I know what you're thinking. Let's find out."

Chapter 66

Vera turned around.

"So, Chelsea, what are you studying?" Vera asked.

"Marketing," Chelsea answered.

"Are you all in the same major?" Vera asked.

"No," one of the young women said. "I'm an art major."

"Art?" DeeAnn said. "Too bad Sheila's not here. She was an art major. So talented. She'd love to meet you girls."

Just then one of DeeAnn's workers came up and asked her to sign a purchase order.

"I know Sheila," Chelsea said. "She's the scrapbook lady, right?"

Vera nodded. "Yes, but now she's looking into designing her own line of scrapbooks."

"Aww, now, that's cool!" Chelsea said.

She was very pregnant, yet she still sounded like she was twelve. Vera found it disturbing. Chelsea could not be more than nineteen. Where were Chelsea's parents these days? She'd not seen them in town recently.

"So, how did you all meet?" Vera said after taking a sip of her coffee.

"Through a mutual friend," said a young woman who

appeared to be the oldest of the group. She was drinking bottled water and had just taken a bite of a scone.

"Would you like some banana bread? It's whole grain. No sugar. Really good for you," DeeAnn said, rising from her chair and going over to the case.

"Thanks," said one of the young women. "So kind of you." She wore her hair in a ponytail. The others had their long hair pulled back, as well.

DeeAnn handed them each a thick golden slice. "No trouble at all," she said, smiling. "So how did this happen?" DeeAnn gestured to their bellies.

They tittered.

"I mean, I know how it happened. What I want to know is, I mean, you are *all* pregnant. All look about the same size. You understand how curious it seems," DeeAnn said.

They all just sort of looked at her, quieted.

"Well, I don't know how it happened," Chelsea said, her face pink. "All I know is I can't wait for it to be over."

"I hear ya," another of them said. "I hate being pregnant so much that I'm sure I'll never have sex again." She laughed.

"How will your boyfriend feel about that?" DeeAnn joked.

"I don't have a boyfriend," the young woman snipped.

"Oh," DeeAnn said. "No boyfriend?"

"I loved being pregnant," Vera said. "It felt like such a miracle to me. Of course, I was much older than you girls. I was single, too."

They quieted again and looked at her.

"I loved it when the baby kicked me or I could feel her turning, or when she had hiccups. . . . It was such an honor for me. I don't know how else to explain it," Vera said in a hushed tone.

"Did you keep your baby?" one of them asked.

"Well, yes, of course I did," Vera replied. "But I'm a grown woman, have a business, and can support a child. If I'd been younger, I don't know what I'd have done."

But that wasn't quite the truth, Vera knew. She'd had an abortion years ago, way before she was ready to have a child. But she wasn't going to tell these women that.

"Are you all putting your babies up for adoption or just Chelsea?" Vera asked.

"All of us," Chelsea said. "They are paying us well for our babies. We're students and need the money."

"Who is paying you?" Vera asked.

She shrugged. "Some adoption agency one of our teachers knows about."

"Alicorn?" Vera asked.

"No, that's not it," the oldest one answered. "Our checks didn't come from there."

"Where did they come from?" DeeAnn asked.

"Look, I don't know why you're so curious about this, ladies," the young woman said. "It's all perfectly legal. We've signed contracts. We're working with a broker. We don't need to know the name of the agency. We get our money, and they get their baby. Fair and square."

"Whatever," Vera said. "It's no big deal to me. It's totally your decision, of course. Very personal."

The women murmured in agreement.

"I hope you understand, of course, that it's likely not going to be as easy as you think to give up your babies. Just prepare yourself for the hormonal onslaught," Vera said, waving, trying to make light of it, but hopeful that one of them heard her. "Who is the teacher that is helping you out?"

"Dr. Reilly," Chelsea said. "He's a business professor."

Chapter 67

Annie was disappointed to learn that the hypnosis session had been canceled, but she could certainly understand that Vera needed a few days to gather her strength. So she and Bryant had a plan.

They invited John and Leola Reilly and Bill to the hypnosis session. The Greenbergs were also staying in town one more week, so they could participate, but Vera wouldn't be told about it. The doctors planned on taking them to another location and then bringing them in once they started the hypnosis.

Bryant theorized that if that they didn't kill Emily McGlashen, these folks knew more than what they were saying, and could therefore lead them to her killer. He thought if they saw Vera's emotional walk through the crime, each one of them would be more ready to talk. A bevy of plainclothed police officers would observe their behavior.

"There are just way too many strange coincidences. They were all involved in this Alicorn place? C'mon," he had said to her on the phone earlier that day. "And I don't care how much you want a baby. How many thousands can you spend on it? I can't understand that."

He could not understand, but Annie could. She and Mike had gotten themselves into a mountain of debt with their IVF treatments to get pregnant. She, so successful at everything she did, could not succeed in having a baby. It felt as if her body had betrayed her. Over and over again.

They had just decided to stop treatments and seek adoption opportunities when she found that she was pregnant. Ordered to complete bed rest for the first six weeks because she had miscarried so many times, she did nothing but read about parenting and babies. Could she allow her hopes to fly, to soar? Would she have the privilege of being a parent?

A knock on her front door interrupted her thoughts.

DeeAnn, Vera, and Sheila walked into the house. Sheila handed her a coffee.

"We have news for you," she said. "You'll need to sit down for this."

"Okay," Annie said, taking a sip of the coffee as she sat down.

"You know that group of women we keep seeing around?" Vera said.

"The pregnant women." DeeAnn interrupted.

"Oh yeah. The ones at the festival?" Annie said.

"I ran into them today and followed them into DeeAnn's—"

"And they were talking about a professor and—" DeeAnn said.

"One of them was my student. She recognized me and talked to me. Said she was putting her baby up for adoption," Vera said.

"Well, I know that family very well," Sheila said. "I know that they could not afford to send her to college. I thought maybe she was on a scholarship. So when DeeAnn and Vera came to me, I called her mother."

"And her mother has not heard from her in months," DeeAnn said.

"Because of the pregnancy?" Annie asked.

"Yes, not just that, but she'd gotten mixed up with a professor there. You'll never guess who," Sheila said.

"Well, since we all know only one professor, I'd guess that it would be Reilly," Annie said. "But what's the big deal about that? Professors and their students have been messing around for ages. C'mon."

But wait. He was on her list. And he was a board member at Alicorn.

"But here's the thing," Sheila said. "Her mother said she was paid very well to have this baby. Her mother did not approve of this at all. She said there were other young women who were students, her friends, that were doing the same kind of thing."

"Sort of like surrogacy?" Annie said. Tricky business.

Sheila nodded. "All of them being paid thousands."

"Thousands? You must be mistaken," Annie said. "For babies?"

"For several babies," Sheila said. "All belonging to John Reilly."

"These girls are in it for several years, evidently," Vera said. "Doesn't it just break your heart? The girls also told us that Reilly was their broker. Their go-between to the agency. They didn't even know the name of the place."

Annie mentally sorted through everything she knew, everything she was just told. But it still didn't add up to murder. Unless . . .

"Vera, you said that this young woman used to be a student of yours. Did she know Emily? Could she have been one of her students?"

"I don't know," Vera said. "Come to think of it, she did stop dancing with me about the time Emily came to town.

I thought it was because she had graduated from high school and had just, you know, moved on. "

Annie picked up her cell phone and dialed Detective Bryant.

"Adam, do you have the list of Emily McGlashen's students?"

"Why?"

"I think we may have stumbled on a lead for you. Bring your list and come to my house."

"Now?"

"As soon as you can," she said.

Annie turned to face her friends.

"Did you have to get him involved?" Sheila said.

"Well, yes," Annie said. "Reilly was on the list of donors at Alicorn. And he's a board member there."

"You saw a list?" Sheila asked.

"Yes, but the only names I recognized were Reilly, Vandergrift, and Bill."

"Bill Ledford?" Vera said.

Annie's heart sank. She had not planned to tell Vera.

"You mean my ex-husband is donating sperm to a sperm bank?"

Annie nodded.

"I just don't know what to think of that . . . ," Vera said, becoming paler by the minute.

"Obviously, he wants another baby at some point," DeeAnn said.

"I can't imagine," Vera said.

"Some men are funny about wanting to leave a son behind," DeeAnn said. "You know sometimes I wonder about them. Men, I mean."

"Don't try to change the subject, DeeAnn," Vera said. "Bill and I, we tried for years . . . and all along he was do-nating sperm?"

"It's probably recent," Annie said.

"Yes, but why wouldn't he just impregnate Kelsey the old-fashioned way?"

"Maybe she can't get pregnant."

"Well, thank God for small favors," Sheila said. "That woman should not be a mother."

"And you have to wonder about Bill," DeeAnn said.

"Oh, I'm one step ahead of you on that," Vera said. "The police questioned him about Kelsey taking Elizabeth. He claimed he knew nothing about it."

"Do you believe him?" Annie asked after the room was silent a few moments.

"I don't believe anything he says anymore. I feel like I don't even know the man," Vera said.

Chapter 68

"Detective Bryant has taken John Reilly in for questioning about Emily McGlashen's murder," Vera told Beatrice when she walked up the stairs to the front porch.

"Well, now, isn't that something?" Beatrice said.

Vera sat in the wicker chair next to her mother.

"Do you think he did it?" Beatrice said.

"I don't know why not," Vera said. "He's impregnating young women and paying them to have his baby."

"What? Have you gone off your rocker, girl?"

"No, I wish I had. I don't get it. Evidently, he's helping several young women get through school by paying him to carry his babies."

"Now, that sounds like something straight out of a B movie or a bad, bad science fiction novel."

"Don't I know it," Vera said and sank into her chair.

"Just because he's done that doesn't mean he killed Emily," Beatrice pointed out.

"I know. Oh, Mama, I've got such a headache trying to figure it all out. I'll let Detective Bryant do it," she said and sighed.

"Good idea," Beatrice said. "Look at that hummingbird."

She pointed out a bright hummingbird buzzing around her feeder. "I think he was here last year. Those male birds are the lookers, you know."

"Pretty," Vera said.

"Where would John Reilly get the money to pay women to have his children?" Beatrice said after a few moments.

"That seems to be the million-dollar question," Vera said. "Nobody knows. I suppose they will find out."

"Maybe this will clear you," Beatrice said.

Vera harrumphed. "I hope it's not too much to hope for."

A quiet calm overcame them then as they both sat and watched the hummingbirds. Beatrice's garden bloomed with Virginia bluebells, bleeding hearts, and bright red tulips.

When Beatrice went to bed that night, she was happy. They had another suspect. Her daughter would be allowed to live her life in peace.

They all went to bed that night with a measure of relaxation that they had not felt in a long time.

But a loud gunshot in the middle of the night tore into that bliss Beatrice had been feeling.

What was that? Who was that?

She grabbed her robe, met Vera and Jon in the hallway, peeked in on Elizabeth.

She was there.

Another shot sounded.

Was someone shooting on the street in front of her house?

"Call the police," Beatrice said to Jon and reached for her pistol in the downstairs drawer.

"Mama, put that thing away," Vera said.

"Unhand me, girl," Beatrice said as a woman's piercing

scream invaded their neighborhood. A great commotion of house doors opening and people yelling ensued.

By the time Vera and Beatrice got to their front doorstep, the neighborhood was well lit. As they walked out along Beatrice's sidewalk, Beatrice found herself blinking. Her heart pounded furiously. *Old heart of mine, don't fail me now,* she thought and blinked again. Was she really seeing what she thought she was seeing?

Leola Reilly stood in the middle of Ivy Lane with a smoking shotgun in her hand, her husband splayed on the street in front of her. Vera wanted to go to him. Beatrice stopped her.

"Stay back. The woman is crazy, and she has a shotgun," she whispered.

"You killed her!" Leola screamed at him. "You killed the love of my life!"

She looked like a madwoman. Her face was red and contorted, and she was flinging the shotgun around as if it were a baton.

"Now, Leola," he said, holding his shoulder, obviously injured, bright red patches of blood soaked through his pajamas.

"Why? Why? Just because she was onto you and your little seedy game?" She looked up, as if she had just realized she had an audience. "Yeah, that's right. He killed Emily. Why? Because she found out that he was taking money from Alicorn to fund his own little baby operation. Bastard!"

She lifted her shotgun.

"Leola!" Vera shouted. "Don't! He's not worth it."

"What?" she said and looked up at Vera.

"Leola, c'mon. Put the gun down. He's not worth going to prison for," Vera said, her voice shaking.

"What else is there for me? He killed her. My Emily!" she groaned.

"Yes, but your children. Your children need you," Vera said, moving toward her slowly. Beatrice held her back. "The police will send him off to prison. They are going to need their mama."

"That's right," came a male voice from somewhere near Vera. Soon he was in front of her. It was Detective Bryant. Where was his gun?

"I ought to shoot your ass, too," she flung at Detective Bryant.

"Maybe," he said. "But Vera is right. We have enough evidence to arrest him. Are you going to leave your children without parents?"

"He'd been funneling money from the foundation for years, Leola," Bryant went on. "He brought Emily into his scheme by promising her an all-Irish baby."

Leola sobbed, but she didn't lower her gun.

"The only problem was the lab could not accept her eggs. They were full of genetic mutations," Bryant continued. "The adoption agency she came from had lied. She was not one hundred percent Irish. She was not one hundred percent healthy. And she wanted out of his scheme. She was trying to do right by those girls. She tried to warn them."

An eerie stillness came over the scene. The tableau was dark and sordid, even as the white picket fences stood in watch. Porch lights and flashlights provided only spots of light here and there. Beatrice's neighborhood stood waiting, watching the drama unfolding before them. Leola held up the gun and pointed it at her husband.

Beatrice noticed the onlookers—the Chamovitzs, DeeAnn and her family, and Sheila and her husband. The whole neighborhood was witnessing the spectacle.

Leola looked like a crazed woman. Her eyes were lit by a fiery passion. Her husband whimpered like a wounded animal. She took a deep breath, lowered the gun, but lifted her leg and kicked him.

"Okay, Bryant," she said and handed him the shotgun. "We'll play it your way."

Vera looked over at Beatrice, who was watching her. Was that her daughter? The woman who helped talk down a crazed woman holding a shotgun to her husband? Beatrice swallowed hard. She didn't think she'd ever been more proud in her life.

Chapter 69

The Cumberland Creek scrapbookers gathered around Sheila's basement cropping table as Paige read from the newspaper.:

"When John Reilly found out his wife was having an affair with Emily McGlashen, he became livid enough to strangle her. According to pieces of interviews and forensic evidence, along with an account by an eyewitness, the scene unfolded like this.

"Emily had just finished the Saint Patrick's Day parade and show. She broke a shoelace and went back to the studio to get new laces. Distracted by the laces and her task before her, Emily didn't realize that John Reilly was waiting there for her. She hadn't bothered turning on the studio lights, just her desk lamp. She often placed one lace around her neck while she was working on the other one.

"All of a sudden, he lunged at her, pushed her to the floor. She screamed, but he placed one of his large hands over her mouth. She fought back, but he was too heavy and too strong. This is when an eyewitness entered the room, saw what was happening, panicked, dropped her purse, and ran out of the room. But she didn't remember the incident at all, because she was so traumatized by it."

"Oh, dear," Sheila said. "How awful for you." She placed her hand on Vera's shoulder.

Vera nodded. "Go on," she said to Paige.

"'We were following the money trail,' Detective Adam Bryant said. 'We knew Emily McGlashen was sending money to Alicorn. But we didn't know about the embezzlement, of course. Nobody did, except her, evidently. She had been investigating it for a while and had just sent an e-mail to one other board member about her suspicions.'

"'John W. Reilly had been embezzling money for five years,' a spokesperson for the company said. 'We are still investigating, but at this point it looks like that figure is somewhere in the millions.'

"A professor at the University of Virginia, Reilly was in the perfect position to make contact with young, struggling, but healthy women. He wanted babies, lots of them, so that he could adopt them out through Alicorn. 'He looked at us as an investment,' Chelsea Miller, of Cumberland Creek, said. 'But I didn't care. I just needed to pay for school—'"

"Doesn't that beat all?" DeeAnn interrupted. "He found girls who would have babies for college tuition. Now, that's just sad."

"I agree," Vera said. "But as sad as that is, let's not forget that Emily died over this."

"And what a horrible way to die," Annie said.

"I didn't like her when she was alive," Sheila said. "But now that we know . . . she was standing up for Chelsea and the other girls. She was trying to do the right thing for Alicorn, too. Just trying to do the right thing."

"With all that going on, no wonder she was not a pleasant person," Vera said.

"Indeed," Annie said, pouring wine in each woman's glass.

"I still don't really understand how he did it," Vera said.

"Well, he was a respected business professor, and he was

one of those people the agency thought had nearly perfect heritage. When he volunteered as a fund-raiser, he was very successful. And of course, they trusted him. At some point their records and bank accounts were completely open to him," Annie explained.

"And he couldn't resist," DeeAnn said.

"But that wasn't enough," Paige said.

"No," Sheila said. "He saw another way to make money from them through this surrogacy plan of his. To me, that's one of the sickest aspects of all it."

"I'll never completely understand his motivations," Paige said. "Just money?"

"I've been thinking about this," Annie said. "I don't think it's just about money. I think it's also about illusions of grandeur. It suits his personality type, you know? He's definitely under psych evaluation. Those results should be interesting."

"Well, he helped himself to my hind end while standing in my mother's kitchen," Vera pointed out.

"We know that," Sheila said, rolling her eyes.

Annie laughed. "You know that is really immature. I can see a high school boy doing that. But a grown man?"

Just then a knock came at the door.

"Must be Leola, Rachel, and Donald," Vera said. Vera and Leola had patched things up. Leola had apologized for nearly attacking her at the park. After considering the matter more closely and talking with Kelsey, Leola had come to her senses and hoped Kelsey would get the help she needed. Leola had her own problems, now that she was facing charges because of shooting her husband.

When she entered the room, they were all taken aback by how much weight Leola had lost. And had she slept at all?

"So glad you could make it," Sheila said and hugged them.

"Thanks so much for doing this. I know Emily wasn't

well liked. She was different. But I loved her," Leola said, looking at Rachel and smiling.

"And she loved you," Rachel said, beaming. Donald stood on the other side of her, smiling.

"Are you okay?" Annie asked Leola.

"I'm as okay as I can be," she replied. "Funny, a few months ago, I never would have wanted to tell my children that I'm gay. But now that they know, it's such a huge relief. I really think that I wasn't giving them enough credit. I know Emily was planning on telling you, Rachel, soon."

Rachel smiled and pulled out a DVD from her bag, and Sheila slid it into her computer as Annie poured wine and handed each person a glass.

"Of course, they have so much to deal with because of their dad that me and my story are nothing right now," Leola said.

Sheila hit PLAY, and the strains of an Irish fiddle erupted.

"To Emily McGlashen," Vera said, lifting her glass.

"To Emily," they chimed.

They watched the screen as Emily leapt across the stage. Her feet and legs moved to the rhythm with uncanny precision. Her green skirt moved against her body in its own cadence. Her body was gorgeous, lean, strong, graceful as she leapt and twirled.

A hush fell over the scrapbooking room. Leola sighed. Rachel's arm went around her.

"God," Vera said, "she was a beautiful dancer."

Leola nodded as a tear slipped down her face. Rachel sobbed out loud.

Later, as Annie walked home, she remembered that there was one more thing they had left to do in regard to Emily McGlashen. Beatrice was planning to have the Greenbergs to her home before they left town. Annie smiled. That Beatrice was becoming an old softy.

Chapter 70

Annie was remembering when she saw Bryant pull aside another cop after the incident in the street, it made her skin prick. He'd been less than honest with her, which she had half expected. So she reverted to her old reporter's way and eavesdropped. Well, as best as she could. It was one of the new police officers, and she was a woman. Interesting for Cumberland Creek.

Murmur. Murmur. "Investigation . . ."

Annie stepped out from behind the rhododendron bush, caught Bryant's eye. The officer whispered something to the detective, and he nodded, then slipped away.

"Annie," he said, walking up to her. "We need to talk."

He took her by the arm and led her to a bench, where they both sat down.

"You need to promise me that you will remain calm."

"Okay," Annie said. What the heck was going on?

"I know that you and Cookie were good friends."

Cookie? What does she have to do with any of this?

Annie's eyes went to her fingers. The best of friends. Or so she had thought.

"Yes?" Annie said.

"We've found her," he said with a barely audible voice. "She is . . . not well but will be soon. We hope."

Stunned, Annie didn't know what to say. But her heart raced; her skin tingled. Cookie was alive! A tear stung in the corner of her eye.

"Can you tell me anything?" Annie said, swallowing hard, trying not to sob.

"I'm afraid not," he said.

"Okay," Annie said, with a wild mix of emotions whipping through her. Anger. Sadness. Relief.

Bryant shot a glance of guilt and shame toward her. He had known all along. She quickly looked away from him.

"Why didn't you tell me earlier?"

He looked away from her. "I just couldn't. I've been kind of a mess about it. Sorting it out myself. Sorting out . . . other things."

"I just want to smack you," she said.

He laughed. "I guess you're okay, then."

A few moments of silence.

"And then there is this. I know that Cookie loved you. She loved your friends and family, too." he said. "Don't ask. I just know."

It hurt to breathe. Something caught in her throat. Annie couldn't speak. She was afraid that she'd sob out loud, scream, or throw up.

Annie was seized by an impulse to go back to Cookie's little yellow house on the cul-de-sac. She had been there from time to time over the past year, while Cookie was missing. Nobody had rented or purchased it. It was still wide open for anybody to wander through. Though as far as she knew, nobody else had. *Only in Cumberland Creek.*

Later that day, Annie walked to Cookie's place to sort this out in her mind and in her heart.

Every so often when she walked through the door of

Cookie's home, she smelled something sweet, homey, like something had recently been baked. Once or twice she had found bits and pieces of things. Once it was an old photo. Another time, it was a small stone with a rune painted on it.

As she walked in later in the day, Cookie's place held only the odor of must and mildew. Closed spaces. She walked over to the window, the one that she was drawn to every time she entered Cookie's home. She cracked it open as she looked out toward the mountains and breathed in a little fresh air. She remembered when she and the others came in and found Cookie's scrapbook of shadows and how surprised they were at the sparseness of her home. The lack of clothing, furniture—well, everything.

Then she remembered being here with Bryant, which was the first time he had ever let down that cocky attitude of his and let her glimpse another part of him. That was when she really started to trust him. He had taken advantage of it. Thank God she never slept with him.

She heard someone at the door. *Adam? Again?*

When it opened, she was surprised to find her own husband standing there.

"Hey," he said. "I was dropping Ben off to play down the street, and I saw your car here. You okay?"

"Yeah," she said. "C'mon in."

"What are you doing here?" he said and kissed her.

"I've been thinking about Cookie. I just talked to Bryant, and he told me that Cookie has been found, that she's going to be okay."

"Oh, Annie," Mike said, pulling her close to him. "That's great news."

"But she is being whisked away to heal somewhere," she said. "It's all very secretive. I think he must have known it for a while."

He thought for a moment. "Yeah, you're probably right."

"Look at this view," she told him, pulling him to the window.

"Wow," he said. "What's this?"

He picked up a shiny object that was on the ledge. Why hadn't she seen that before? He held it up to the light. It shimmered. It was gold, a lovely Star of David.

Annie gasped. "Look at that."

He handed it to her. "You might as well take it. Nobody else around here would wear it."

She smiled and slipped it into her bag.

Mike pulled her closer to him. "You are one sexy Jewish woman."

He grinned as she laughed, and then he pulled her closer, kissed her.

Finally, he pulled away from her, his face lit with passion.

"I'm going to lock the door," he said hoarsely.

"What?" she said and grinned. "Why?"

He took his shirt off, spread it on the floor, and proceeded to show her why.

Chapter 71

Murder solved, her custody hearing pending, Vera breathed a sigh of relief as she looked into Eric's eyes. They were in a secluded spot at the park. He had spread a blanket and had brought a basket of cheeses, crackers, fruit, and wine.

He guided her chin to his mouth and kissed her, so tenderly that it almost broke her heart as other parts of her were coming alive, swirling almost as strongly as the river currents in the background.

He pulled away and looked at her. "You are a hell of a woman," he said, his eyes and voice both smoking with passion.

"Oh my," she said and pulled him toward her.

When would he invite her to his place? When would they finally make love?

They lay back on the blanket. Surely not here? Though Vera was afraid she'd not say no. Could she? Would she? Here at the park?

"Hey!" Vera heard a sort of familiar voice yell. "Get a room!"

Vera and Eric sat up. How embarrassing! But as the

person came closer, she could see that it was Bill, and she waved him off.

"Get lost, Bill," she said, standing, feeling wobbly at the knee.

Bill stood there, placing his hands on his hips. "I'm not going anywhere. Get off my w—"

Vera stood. "I'm not your wife!"

"Calm down, Vera," Eric said, now standing beside her, holding her arm.

She took a deep breath.

"What are you doing here, Bill?" Eric asked.

"Just out for a walk," he said, eyeing Eric. "Dr. Green." Eric nodded.

"I've got nothing to say to you, Bill," Vera said. "Not until you tell me why you donated your sperm to that place. And even then, I'm not sure I want you anywhere around me."

"Do we have to do this here?" he said, nodding toward Eric.

"I'm not hiding anything from Eric. We have no secrets."

Bill kicked around the dirt a little and looked up at her.

"I donated years ago, before I met Emily or Kelsey or any of them. Back when we were having problems. I just thought that I wanted a child of my own someday and—"

"It didn't look like I could give you one," she said, her voice breaking.

Bill looked away from her. Eric reached for her hand.

"You said . . . you said it didn't matter. All those years. You said it didn't matter."

Bill shrugged. "I'm sorry, Vera. I really did want a baby."

Vera's hand went to her chest. "So did I," she managed to say.

He walked toward her and reached for her. She sank closer to Eric and shook her head.

"When Alicorn contacted me and said Emily was interested in my sperm . . . because of my heritage—"

"You allowed it?" Vera almost shouted. "You would have allowed her to have your baby? A half sister to Elizabeth? The woman who almost destroyed me? Oh, God."

Vera's mind sifted through the years of tenderness, the years of lies, the years of stagnation. The memories were swirling through her. He had betrayed her for the last time. Never again.

"Leave, Bill," she said. "I really never want to see you again."

"Vera, c'mon," he said.

Eric spoke up. "Look, I've been trying to stay out of this, but the lady asked you to leave."

Bill snorted and turned to go.

Vera fell into Eric's arms.

"How did you get messed up with that jerk?" Eric said.

"It's a long story," she said. "I'm ready to put it behind me."

"Hey," he said, gathering the blanket and basket. "Let's get out of here."

"Where do you want to go?" she said.

"I think it's time I brought you home."

"Home?"

"Yeah, my place. C'mon," he said, reaching for her hand and dragging her along.

"Shouldn't we talk about this?" Vera said after buckling her seat belt.

"I'm through talking, Vera. I love you, and I want you in my bed. Have a problem with that?"

"No. I don't have a problem with any of it," she breathed.

She was a jumble of emotion. Bill had just confessed, basically, that their whole life together had been a lie. But, deep down, she had known it all along, hadn't she? It hurt, but at the same time it was freeing. She felt stronger than ever. She was a mother, a dancer, a daughter, and soon to be a lover.

When Eric led her up the stairs to his room, she swore she levitated. And when she looked back on it, she was still certain her feet had not touched the floor.

Turned out that some men were worth trusting and taking a chance on.

Chapter 72

The Saturday night crop had much to discuss and much to work on. Vera had decided to let bygones be bygones and make a scrapbook for Emily's parents and one for Leola. So with all the pictures, papers, clippings, awards, and so on they had gathered, the scrappers began to piece Emily McGlashen's life together.

"I don't know why, but I'm thinking of Maggie Rae as we do this," Sheila said.

"I am too," Vera said.

"We are piecing her life together, just like we did Maggie Rae's," Annie said, then bit into a chocolate cupcake.

"One major difference," DeeAnn said. "We already know who killed Emily. With Maggie Rae, we had no idea when we first started on those books."

"Yeah," Sheila said. "We had no idea about a lot of things then."

"Tell me about it," Annie said. "Look at that beautiful photo of Emily."

She was maybe thirteen, looking sweet and innocent in a school photo.

"I never really thought of her as pretty," Paige said. "But

I think it was her personality I was seeing. But she does look pretty here. So young and pretty."

"Speaking of young and pretty," Sheila said, opening her laptop, "what in the world is going to happen to those young women who are having babies?"

"They will be given the option of adoption. Legitimate adoption, that is, by Alicorn," Annie replied. "The last I talked to them, some of them seemed to be changing their minds and wanting to keep their babies."

"But what about their educations?" DeeAnn asked.

"I think that they are a little shell-shocked. I'm not sure they can handle school right now. They are going to need some time," Annie replied. "Hopefully, time with their families."

"This is sweet. A note from one of her former students," DeeAnn said. "Wow. You know, it's amazing how many faces this Emily McGlashen wore. We knew her as a bitch. But she was 'the world's best dance teacher,' according to this girl. And Leola loved her. What did she see in her that I never saw?"

DeeAnn's words hung in the air.

Annie heard paper being sliced by the cutter, pages being turned and slicked over, and pens and little boxes being dropped back on the table.

But Annie knew the feeling DeeAnn was conveying. She'd often wondered how well she knew anybody around this table. Hell, not even just around this table, but people she'd worked with, neighbors, kids she grew up with, and yes, even herself. A few years ago, if someone had told her she'd be tempted in her marriage by a cop, she'd have told them they were crazy. She was solid in her marriage and had always been. Until recently.

She took a deep breath and a swig of beer. Maybe her brother was right. Maybe she drank too much.

She pasted some ribbon to the edge of the page she was working on. Ah yes, she was back to feeling solid in her marriage, and that was a good feeling, one that she hoped lasted.

"Well, we're almost done with this one," DeeAnn said. "Ohmigoodness, who made these little cheese fritters? They are divine."

"I did," Paige said. "You think you're the only baker in the crowd?"

"Humph," DeeAnn said.

"We're moving right along on our book, too," Vera said.

"Soon this will all be over," Sheila said. "And we can all get on with our lives."

"What?" Annie said, smiling. "Do you mean this isn't our lives?"

Chapter 73

The next day, Beatrice sat on her front porch, watching the hummingbirds. Some things never changed. The birds. The mountains. They would always be here. People? That was another matter.

She leafed through the past several days in her mind. Her granddaughter was back. Safe and sound. Better than ever. A murderer was off the streets. Bill was out of their lives. Someday, he might be allowed back in Elizabeth's life. Not for the foreseeable future.

Everybody was getting some closure—most particularly, the Greenberg couple. Finally. Soon they would be leaving Cumberland Creek. Beatrice hated to see them go. Oddly enough, she found that she had a lot in common with the aging hippie couple, especially Rachel. They were coming by today, as were the croppers with scrapbooks they had made for them.

Right as she thought this, Sheila, Paige, and DeeAnn came walking through her front gate and sat down next to her.

"Hey, ladies," Beatrice said. "If you want some tea, help yourselves."

A pitcher of iced tea, with glasses next to it, sat on the

wicker table. But they all just gathered on her porch, watching the hummingbirds.

Annie drove up in her car, with Rachel and Donald Greenberg inside.

"Well, what is this? Grand Central Station?" DeeAnn said.

"Come on in," Beatrice said. "Pull up a chair."

The Greenbergs looked happier, livelier than she'd seen them over the past several weeks. They seemed more at peace.

"I'm so glad you came," Beatrice said. "I have something for you."

"For us?" Donald said. "Really?"

His hair looked cleaner, Beatrice noted, and he was clean shaven. He wasn't too bad looking when he was cleaned up.

Paige stood up. "We've researched Emily's biological family history. It turns out that your daughter's lineage was indeed a part of this town and its history."

"Well, well, well." Rachel beamed. "She was right, after all."

"Yes, but she could not have imagined the depth of the story," Beatrice said. "This has been hidden for years. A story with many secrets and cover-ups." She handed them the memory book she found buried in her backyard. "The book was buried in my backyard, along with some of the things belonging to the McGlashen family. Most of them the state owns. I donated them. They really held no personal significance. But this, this book does. You should have it."

"Intriguing," Donald said, his head tilting, brows knitting.

"Thanks," Rachel managed to say through a huge smile and watery eyes. "You can't imagine what this means to me. To us. I know Emily was difficult. And it must seem strange to you, but I feel so close to her here. And now this. I feel her here with us now."

They all grew quiet.

"One of the items in the book was a lock of red hair. I asked the guys from the Virginia Department of Historic Resources to compare the DNA of the hair to the DNA of the bones they found in my yard. Turns out it was a match. Same family, at least. Maybe even the same person. So this is truly the McGlashen homestead," Beatrice said and then hugged Rachel.

"It's remarkable," she said.

"We have something for you, too. You can't leave without this." Sheila held up a bag. "But I know that Vera wanted to be here for this," Sheila said. "Where is she?"

"She's napping," Beatrice said. "Why don't you go and wake her?"

Sheila came back momentarily. "Which room is she in?"

"Hers. Why?"

"Her room is a mess. Scattered boxes, pictures, all kinds of junk. But she's not in there."

Beatrice stood. "Vera!"

She moved through her house, searching. Where could she be?

"Oh, bother!" she said as she came back to the porch. "I don't know where she's gone. Her room is a mess, and that's so unlike her."

"Was she okay?" Annie asked.

Beatrice shrugged. "She's been strange. The whole thing with Bill . . ."

"Bill?" Sheila said. "Weren't her wedding albums in that gold box?"

"I think so," Beatrice said.

"Well, it's empty," Sheila said.

"Are you sure?" Beatrice said, leading them into Vera's room.

She reached for the shiny gold box. It was empty except for a pair of scissors and some cut paper.

"That's not just any old paper," Sheila said. "That's the paper out of her wedding album. I remember that color."

"Odd," DeeAnn said. "So Vera is gone with her photos?"

"Where would she be?" Annie said.

Beatrice wondered. Where would Vera go with her photos? Back to Bill? No. Any person she would go to was right here at this very moment. Well, everybody but Eric. It seemed to Beatrice that they'd recently gotten much closer.

Just then her phone rang. Jon picked it up, and she vaguely heard him murmuring. "No, we will handle it. Thank you."

"Beatrice, that was Adam Bryant," Jon said. "Vera is at the park."

"At the park? Is she okay?" Beatrice's voice lifted a decibel or two, betraying her clam face. She was worried about Vera because of the sleepwalking, even though they'd gotten to the bottom of it. Who knew how witnessing that murder would bubble up in Vera again?

"She seems to be fine, Adam said, but he received a call about her and thought it best if you go and collect her."

"I'll take you," Annie said, pulling her keys out of the pocket of her blue jeans.

The lot of them tried to pile in Annie's car; others took off on foot, even the Greenbergs, carrying their prized book. Once Annie reached the edge of the park, Beatrice ran out of the car before Annie could put it in park. Beatrice's legs were strong and sturdy from walking in the mountains for many years. She could be quick on her feet, too. But she felt as if she were moving too slowly. What on earth was her daughter up to now? And the police had called? What could it be? Her old heart pounded in her chest as she rounded the corner to the park.

She scanned the area and saw a small crowd gathered by the river. That must be where Vera was. Beatrice walked over to the riverbank.

There Beatrice found Vera and stood in amazement. Her forty-three-year-old daughter was knee-deep in the river, surrounded by floating photos and boxes. She was a grown woman, yet Beatrice swore she looked like she was still twelve, standing there, praying to her mountain. The years seemed to have been stripped away from her.

Vera turned and looked at Beatrice. "I'm afraid I've made a mess here, Mama." She watched as the river carried away her wedding photos.

"That's all right, girl. The river's going to take care of it," Beatrice said quietly. "Let me help you out of there."

By the time Vera made her way out of the rocky, shallow river, Sheila, Paige, Annie, and DeeAnn were coming up behind Beatrice. They were all out of breath and sweaty.

"Oh, girl, what are you doing now?" Sheila said, shaking her head full of wiry hair.

"It's done, I'd say," Beatrice said, taking a deep breath.

Sheila stood and took it in, the photos drifting, swirling in the currents. "Finally," she said, then wrapped her arms around Vera.

Glossary of Basic Scrapbooking Terms

Acid-Free: Acid is a chemical found in paper that will disintegrate the paper over time. It will ruin photos. It's very important that all papers, pens, and other supplies say "acid-free," or eventually the acid may ruin cherished photos and layouts.

Adhesive: Any kind of glue or tape can be considered an adhesive. In scrapbooking, there are several kinds of adhesives: tape runners, glue sticks, and glue dots.

Brad: This is similar to a typical split pin, but it is found in many different sizes, shapes, and colors. It is very commonly used for embellishments.

Challenge: Within the scrapbooking community, "challenges" are issued in groups as a way to instill motivation.

Crop: Technically, "to crop" means "to cut down a photo." However, a "crop" is also when a circle of scrapbookers gets together and scrapbook. A crop can be anything from a group of friends getting together to a more official gathering where scrapbook materials are for sale, games are played, and challenges are issued, and so on. Online crops are a good alternative for people who don't have a local scrapbook community.

Die-Cut: This is a shape or letter cut from paper or cardstock, usually by machine or by using a template.

Embellishment: An embellishment is an item, other than words or photos, that enhances a scrapbook page. Typical embellishments are ribbons, fabric, and stickers.

Eyelet: These small metal circles, similar to the metal rings found on shoes for threading laces, are used in the scrapbook context as a decoration and can hold elements on a page.

Journaling: This is the term for writing on scrapbook pages. It includes everything from titles to full pages of thoughts, feelings, and memories about the photos displayed.

Matting: Photos in scrapbooks are framed with a mat. Scrapbookers mat with coordinating papers on layouts, often using colors found in the photos.

Page Protector: These are clear, acid-free covers that are used to protect finished pages.

Permanent: Adhesives that will stay are deemed permanent.

Photo Corner: A photo is held to a page by slipping the corners of the photo into photo corners. They usually stick on one side.

Post-Bound Album: This term refers to an album that uses metal posts to hold the binding together. These albums can be extended with more posts to make them thicker. Usually page protectors are already included on the album pages.

Punch: This is a tool used to "punch" decorative shapes in paper or cardstock.

Punchie: The paper shapes that result from using a paper punch tool are known as punchies. These can be used on a page for a decorative effect.

Repositionable Adhesive: Magically, this adhesive does not create a permanent bond until dry, so you can move an element dabbed with the adhesive around on the page until you find just the perfect spot.

Scraplift: When a scrapbooker copies someone's page layout or design, she has scraplifted.

Scrapper's Block: This is a creativity block.

Strap-Hinge Album: An album can utilize straps to allow the pages to lie completely flat when the album is open. To add pages to this album, the straps are unhinged.

Template: A template is a guide for cutting shapes, drawing, or writing on a page. Templates are usually made of plastic or cardboard.

Trimmer: A trimmer is a tool used for straight-cutting photos.

Vellum: Vellum is a thicker, semitransparent paper with a smooth finish.

Scrapbook Essentials
for the Beginner

Getting Started with Scrapbooking

When you first start to scrapbook, the amount of products and choices available can be overwhelming. It's best to keep it simple until you develop your own style and see exactly what you need. Basically, this hobby can be as complicated or as simple as you want. Here is all you really need:

1. Photos
2. Archival scrapbooks and acid-free paper
3. Adhesive
4. Scissors
5. Sheet protectors

Advice on Cropping

Basically, two kinds of crops exist. An "official" crop is when a scrapbook seller is involved. At an official crop, participants sample and purchase products, along with participating in contests and giveaways. The second kind of crop is an informal gathering of friends on at least a semi-regular basis to share, scrapbook, eat, and gossip, just like the Cumberland Creek croppers.

1. In both cases, food and drinks are usually served. Finger food is most appropriate. The

usual drinks are nonalcoholic, but sometimes wine is served. But there should be plenty of space for snacking around the scrapbooking area. If something spills, you don't want your cherished photos to get ruined.

2. If you have an official crop, it's imperative that your scrapbook seller doesn't come on too strong. Scrapbook materials sell themselves. Scrapbookers know what they want and need.

3. Be prepared to share. If you have a die-cut machine, for example, bring it along, show others how to use it, and so on. Crops are about generosity of the spirit. This generosity can entail something as small as paper that you purchased and decided not to use. Someone will find a use for it.

4. Make sure the scrapbooking area has a lot of surface space, such as long tables, where scrapbookers can spread out. (Some even use the floor.)

5. Be open to both giving scrapbooking advice and receiving it. You can always ignore advice if it's bad.

6. Get organized before you crop. You don't need fancy boxes and organizing systems. Place the photos you want to crop with in an envelope, and you are ready to go.

7. Go with realistic expectations. You probably won't get a whole scrapbook done during the crop. Focus on several pages.

8. Always ask about what you can bring, such as food, drinks, cups, plates, and so on.

9. If you're the host, have plenty of garbage bags around the scrapbooking area. Ideally, have one small bag for each person. That way scrapbookers can throw away unusable scraps as they go along, which makes cleanup much easier.

10. If you're the host, make certain the scrapbooking area has plenty of good lighting, as well as an adequate number of electricity outlets.

Frugal Scrapbooking Tips

1. Spend your money where it counts. The scrapbook itself is the carrier of all your memories and creativity. Splurge here.

2. You can find perfectly fine scrapbooking paper in discount stores, along with stickers, pens, and sometimes glue. If it's labeled "archival," it's safe.

3. You can cut your own paper and make matting, borders, journal boxes, and so on. You don't need fancy templates, though they make it easier.

4. Check on some online auction sites, like eBay, for scrapbooking materials and tools.

5. Reuse and recycle as much as you can. Keep a box of paper scraps, for example, that you might be able to use for a border, mat, or journal box. Commit to not buying anything else until what you've already purchased has been used.

6. Wait for special coupons. Some national crafts stores run excellent coupons—sometimes 40 percent off. Wait for these coupons, and then go and buy something on your wish list that you could not otherwise afford.

7. If you have Internet access, you have a wealth of information available to you for free. You can find free clip art, ideas for titles for your pages, or even poems, fonts, and so on.

Digital and Hybrid Scrapbooking

Digital scrapbooking involves using your computer and a photo-editing program to create part or all of your scrapbook page. Hybrid scrapbooking is a combination of digital scrapbooking and traditional paper scrapbooking. For example, you might print off some online scrapbooking elements, cut them out, and then use them on your traditional paper scrapbook page.

Digital scrapbooking allows you to do the following:

1. Print an element out on photo paper to put in a scrapbook album. Remember a scrapbook page can be 8½ x 11 inches or smaller, so you can print from your home printer.

2. Send files to a print shop for printing, a good option for bigger pages.

3. Upload an image of a page to an online photo gallery for sharing with others. (I highly recommend Smilebox, both for this purpose and as a way of getting used to the idea of digital scrapbooking.)

4. E-mail a copy of a page to family and friends.

5. Burn a copy of a page to a DVD for safekeeping or use a USB flash drive for this purpose.

Great Ways to Learn Digital Scrapbooking

A really good way to transition from conventional paper scrapbooking to digital scrapbooking is to explore these Web sites:

1. Smilebox (www.smilebox.com) is a very user-friendly Web site that allows you to choose a scrapbook design, personalize it with your own photos, embellishments, and journaling, and then share your scrapbook via e-mail, social networks, burned DVDS, and print.

2. Digital Scrapbooking HQ (www.digitalscrap-bookinghq.com) offers a blog with great tips on digital scrapbooking, as well as tutorials and sometimes freebies.

3. Sweet Shoppe Designs (www.sweetshoppe-designs.com) is not only an online shop that sells digital scrapbooking supplies, but it is also a repository of good information and a source of plenty of freebies. My advice is to rely on freebies as much as you can until you see if you like digital scrapbooking. There are many digital scrapbooking freebies on the Web.

Digital Scrapbooking Apps

There are two different ways you can approach digital scrapbooking: using apps for your devices and/or apps for your computer.

For your devices (apps I've used on my iPad):

1. Coolibah. This app is free and easy to follow, and I highly recommend it. But here's the rub: you can use only the kits they have in their gallery. They have plenty to choose from, but if you want more or a different kind of design, you must look elsewhere.

2. Martha Stewart CraftStudio. This app is designed so well. For instance, it has little digital drawers to hold all the materials, including paper, and you

open them with just a touch. It offers glitter, stamps, pens, and glue. It's great fun to play with. This app is best for greeting cards and mini scrapbooks.

For the computer:

1. Photoshop/Photoshop Elements (PE). PE is a less complex version of Photoshop, and while I can see that it is user-friendly, it's just a bit too complicated for me to learn with the hectic life I lead. But I'd like to learn more.

2. MyMemories Suite. This is what I like using the most. You can jump right in there and scrapbook with simplicity. MyMemories Suite allows you to do more complex techniques, like layering and shadowing, which I have yet to get into. They offer you paper, elements, types, and more, but you can also import your own.

Turn the page for an excerpt from
the first Cumberland Creek mystery

SCRAPBOOK OF SECRETS!

On sale now!

Chapter 1

For Vera, all of the day's madness began when she saw the knife handle poking out of her mother's neck. Her mother didn't seem to know it. In fact, she was surprised that the blade was inside her. "How did that happen?" she demanded to know from her daughter.

Vera just looked at her calmly. "Well, now, Mother, we need to call someone, an ambulance . . . a doctor. . . . I don't know. Should we pull it out, or what?"

If Vera only had a nickel for every time her mother gave her that look. A look of unbelieving pity, as if to say, *Sometimes I can't believe the stupidity of my grown daughter.* Having a brilliant mother was not easy—ever—especially not as an adult. As a child, Vera assumed all grown-ups were as smart as her mother, and it was easy to acquiesce to her in all of her grown-up, brilliant, scientific knowledge. At the age of eighty, Beatrice showed no signs of slowness in her mind or any forgetfulness. Nothing. Vera almost looked forward to the day she could help her mother remember something or even tell her something that she didn't know.

As she sat in the X-ray waiting area, looking out the window over a construction site, with a huge dilapidated barn in the distance, she marveled once again at her mother's strength and tenacity. Evidently, she was stabbed during her travels through the town this Saturday morning. She didn't feel a thing—and with three grocery bags in her hands, Beatrice walked four blocks home, the same path she'd traveled for fifty years. "Four different grocery stores have been there and have gone out of business," Beatrice would say. "Yet, I'm still here, walking the same street, the same path. I refuse to die."

Beatrice would not allow her daughter—or anyone—to pick up groceries for her or take her shopping. She said that as long as she could keep getting herself to the grocery store, she knew she was fine. Food is life. "It's the ancient food-foraging impulse in me. I feel it even stronger, the older I get. I want to take care of myself."

How could a woman who still fended for herself every day—cooking, gardening, canning, cleaning, and writing—not feel a knife jab into her neck?

"Vera?" said a man in medical garb who stood in front of her.

"Yes," she said, standing up.

"I'm Dr. Hansen. We've just X-rayed your mom and looked over the film," he said, smiling, revealing two deep dimples and a beautiful set of teeth. He held the film in his hands. "Would you like to see them?"

She followed him over to the wall, where he clicked on a light and clipped on the X-ray to it.

"As you can see, the knife is pretty deep." He pointed to the blade. His nails and hands were the cleanest Vera had ever seen on a man. An overall well-manicured appearance.

"Y-yes," she stammered. That was a knife in her mother's neck. A knife. Long and sharp. Menacing.

"Here's the thing, rather than give you a bunch of medical mumbo jumbo, I'm just going to put this in lay terms."

She despised his patronizing tone. He wasn't even born yet when her father was practicing medicine out of their home. She knew about the human body. She was a dancer; her father was a physician. Her mother might be old, but she was no slouch.

"The reason your mom didn't feel this is because it's lodged in an area where there are few nerve endings, which is a blessing because she is not really in any pain," he said, taking a breath. "You just don't see this every day."

"No," Vera said.

"We can pull it out, using local anesthesia, with great risk for potential blood loss and so on. If she flinches or moves while we're removing it, the damage could be severe. We can also operate to remove it, put her under, which I think is the safest thing."

Vera looked at him for some guidance or answer. *Damn it, Bill is out of town.* "Have you talked to her about it?"

"Well, yes. . . ."

"And?"

"She doesn't want surgery. She wants us to pull it out."

"So what's the problem? It's her body. I can't make decisions like that for her."

"Your mom is eighty years old and we're not sure she's thinking clearly. And the danger—"

"Doctor," Vera said, trying not to roar. She felt an odd tightening in her guts. She stood up straighter. "My mother's mind is perfectly fine. It's her neck that seems to be the problem right now, and the fact that a knife is sticking out of it."

He looked away. "Vera, I know this might be hard for you. A lot of times we don't see the truth when it comes to our aging parents."

"What exactly are you talking about? I am very close

with my mom and would know if something was wrong. I don't understand."

"Well, she's been talking to herself, for one thing."

Vera laughed. "No, she's not. She's talking to my dad. He died about twenty years ago. She talks to him all the time."

He looked at her as if she had lost *her* mind. "Do *you* think that's normal?"

"For her, it is."

Vera's mind wandered as the doctor was called away. He said he'd be back. She looked at the crisp blue hospital walls, with beautiful landscape paintings, all strategically placed. One was above the leather sofa so you could lie or sit in style to await the news about your loved ones and gaze into the peaceful garden gazebo landscape; one was above the chair; the hallways were lined with them. Vera saw herself walking down the hall and looking at the same prints twenty years ago. Tranquil settings of barns and flowers did not help the pain. She was only twenty-one then, and she thought she'd soon be back in New York City. As soon as her father healed, got home, and was on the road to being himself, she'd hop on the train to continue her dancing career. She had no idea she'd never see her father again—nor would she ever dance professionally again.

The last time Vera was here was with her father. The hospital had just opened, and he was impressed with the technology and the vibrant pulse of new medicine. The research arm intrigued him. Some older doctors were jaded and looked at the new hospital with suspicion, but not her father. Ironic that he died here, under the new establishment's care.

She sighed a deep and heavy sigh.

"Vera!" It was Sheila running up the hall, wiry brown

hair needing combing. She was dressed in a mismatched sweat suit. "Oh, girl! What on earth is going on? I've been hearing rumors. Is your mama okay? Lord!"

For the first time that day, Vera smiled. "Sit down, Sheila. You're a mess."

Sheila took a quick look at herself and laughed. "You know, I just threw anything on. Is your mother—"

"She's fine," said Vera. "She's trying to tell the doctors what to do."

"Really?" Sheila sat up a little straighter, looking very serious. "I can hardly believe *that*," she said, and a laugh escaped. Then she grabbed her belly and howled in a fit of laughter.

Vera felt tears coming to her eyes through her own chortles. "You haven't heard the best part," she managed to say, trying to calm herself down as a nurse passed by, glancing at them. "Mama was stabbed and she never felt a thing."

"What?" Sheila stopped laughing for a minute. "Are you serious?" Her face reddened and laugher escaped. "Oh, girl, only Beatrice. Only Beatrice."

Vera's mother had just been stabbed, and she and her best friend were laughing about it, like schoolgirls unable to control their nervous giggles. A part of Vera felt like she was betraying her mother. However, she knew if Beatrice had been in this room, she'd be laughing, too.

When the women calmed down, Sheila brought up Maggie Rae, which was the other startling news of the day. "Did you hear the news?"

Vera sighed. "Yes, I heard about it. I saw the ambulances and police at her house and went over to see what was happening. You know, I blame myself. I knew something was wrong. I just didn't know what to do about it, or maybe I just tried to talk myself out of it."

Vera thought about the tiny young mother, always with her children clinging to her, and with a baby on her hip—or in a stroller. She was pretty in a simple way—never made-up, always pulled her long black hair into a ponytail and wore glasses most of the time. Though once or twice, Vera had seen her wearing contacts, which really opened up her face. Even though Maggie Rae rarely made eye contact, she always held herself erect and moved with a graceful confidence and sway in her hips.

"Now, Vera," said Sheila, "you hardly knew that woman. Who really knew her? She kept to herself."

"She brought Grace in for dance lessons once a week," Vera told her. "I know her as well as any of the rest of them. Except she was awfully quiet. And so small. Like a bird. Every time I saw her, it looked like she had gotten even thinner."

"Hmm-hmm, I know. It's odd. She was one of my best customers, but she never came to a crop," said Sheila, who sold scrapbooking supplies for a living. "I invited her. She never came, so I just . . . stopped. You know, you can only push so far. "

They sat in their own silence, with the hospital noise all around them, each knowing her own sadness and her own triumphs and joys, but neither knowing what it was like to be pushed quite that far. To be pushed far enough to put a gun to one's heart while the children were peacefully sleeping upstairs. What kind of darkness led Maggie Rae Dasher to that moment? And what do people ever really know about the neighbors and townsfolk who live among them?

"Did she leave a note or anything?" Vera wondered out loud.

Sheila shrugged.

A nurse dressed all in blue passed them; a mother carrying a baby in a carrier and holding the hand of a toddler limped along; someone was coughing and another person laughed. A man in a wheelchair wheeled by them, while another gentleman hobbled with a cane. Phones were ringing. Announcements were being made, doctors were paged.

"Damn," said Sheila. "This place sucks."

"Wonder where the doctor is?" Vera looked around. "I'm going over to that desk to see what's going on. I should at least be able to see Mama."

As Vera walked around the nurses' station to try to find some help, she thought she could hear her mother's voice.

"What?" the voice said. "Listen, you twit, you'll do it because I said you will. Stop treating me like I am five. I am eighty, of sound mind and body, except for this friggin' knife hanging out of my neck. And oh, by the way, I am a doctor of physics myself. So don't tell me—"

"Mama," Vera interrupted as she walked into the room. Sitting up in bed, her mother looked so small, which belied the sound of her voice and the redness of her face. "Calm down, sweetie."

She folded her arms over her chest. "Son of a bitch!" She cocked her head and looked behind Vera. "What's the scrapbook queen doing here? Am I dying or something?"

"Hey," Sheila said. "You've got a knife sticking out of the back of your neck. Don't get too cocky, old woman."

"Huh!" Beatrice said, and smiled. "Glad to see you, too. Now, Vera, what are we going to do about this mess?"

"I told the doctor that it's your body. You do what you want, Mama."

"Yes, but," she said, after taking a sip of water, leaning forward on the pillows that were propping her in an awkward position, which forced her to sit up so the knife would not hit the bed, "what do you think? What would you do?"

Vera could hardly believe what she was hearing. Her mother was asking for her advice. She couldn't remember if that had happened before. "Honestly, if it were me, I'd want to be put out. I'd be afraid of moving, you know?"

"I don't know about being operated on at my age. . . . You know they killed your daddy. What if they kill me, too? I can't leave yet. I've got too much work to do, and then there's you. I can't leave you without a parent," she said quietly.

Vera knew that's what it would come to—this is where he died, not for his heart problems, but from a staph infection.

"Just do what she asks," Vera said to the young doctor, who was still hovering. "She won't move."